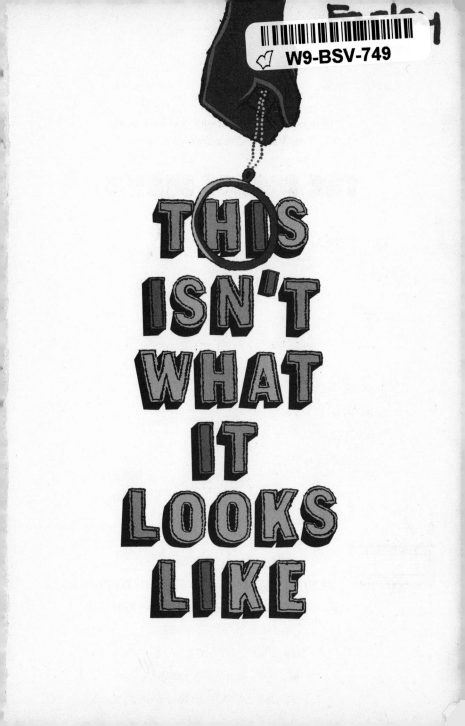

THIS ISN'T WHAT IT LOOKS LIKE

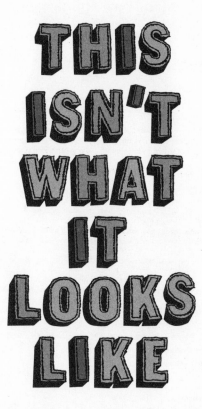

THIS ISN'T WHAT IT LOOKS LIKE

pseudonymous bosch

Illustrations by Gilbert Ford

LITTLE, BROWN AND COMPANY

New York Boston

Little, Brown and Company

Hachette Book Group
237 Park Avenue, New York, NY 10017
Visit our website at www.lb-kids.com

Little, Brown and Company is a division of Hachette Book Group, Inc.
The Little, Brown name and logo are trademarks of Hachette Book Group, Inc.

The publisher is not responsible for websites (or their content) that are not owned by the publisher.

First Paperback Edition: September 2011
First published in hardcover in September 2010 by Little, Brown and Company

The characters and events portrayed in this book are fictitious. Any similarity to real persons, living or dead, is coincidental and not intended by the author. Then again, he never intended to write this book in the first place.

Library of Congress Cataloging-in-Publication Data

Bosch, Pseudonymous.
    This isn't what it looks like / Pseudonymous Bosch ; illustrations by Gilbert Ford. —1st ed.
        p. cm. —(Secret series ; bk. 4)
    Sequel to: This book is not good for you
    Summary: Cass finds herself alone and disoriented in a dream-like world, while back at home she is in the hospital in a coma with Max-Ernest desperately searching for a way to awaken her.
    ISBN 978-0-316-07625-8 (hc) / 978-0-316-07624-1 (pb)
    [1. Time travel—Fiction.   2. Adventure and adventurers—Fiction.   3. Magic—Fiction.
4. Immortality—Fiction.   5. Chocolate—Fiction.]   I. Ford, Gilbert, ill.   II. Title.   III. Title: This is not what it looks like.
    PZ7. B6484992Thi 2010
    [Fic]—dc22
                                                                                                    2010010519

10 9 8 7 6 5 4 3

RRD-H

Printed in the United States of America

FOR

Sofia Carolina (so nice, they named her twice); Izzy and Jack; Elijah; Isabella; Kate P. and Emma (even if she's too old) but not May again (wouldn't be fair); Kate G. and Sam; Ella and Margaux; Lily with a *Y*, Gideon, and Rufus; but not Lilli with an *I* or Lucas or Madeleine (see Book Two); and not India and Natalia, either (well, maybe we'll leave that open for discussion); also for Ava and Sylvie; Lucy and Levi; Dulce and Olivia; Tyler x 2; Iris; Stash; Lorenza; the local cousins: Lev, Dante, and Molly; the northern cousins: Naomi, Eli, and Jacob; the mysterious cousin, Sophia; and finally for Nabu and Kiwi Skunk and my "Most Annoying Fan Ever" and my Secret Agent in Kentucky and all my Secret Agents everywhere

WARNINGS, DISCLAIMERS, FINE PRINT & ETC.

Do not read this book standing up. You may fall down from shock. • Do not read this book sitting down. A quick escape may be necessary. • Operating a moving vehicle or any kind of heavy machinery while reading this book is forbidden. It might distract you from the plot. • Prolonged exposure to this book may cause dizziness and, in extreme cases, paranoid delusions or even psychosis. If that is your idea of fun, by all means keep reading. If it's not, then this isn't your kind of book. • Use of this book for other than the intended purpose is not advised. While it may seem like an ideal projectile, the makers of this book cannot guarantee your safety if you throw it at someone. There is always the possibility that that person will throw it back. • You should not read this book if the cover has been tampered with or removed. If you suspect that your book has been deliberately altered by your enemies, you should report it to the makers of this book. However, they will probably think you are crazy. Under no circumstances should you consult a doctor. He will definitely think you are crazy. • The contents of this book may appear to have shifted over time. Do not be alarmed. This is a natural occurrence that affects all books and does not necessarily mean that your book has rewritten itself. Then again, it might have. • Remember, nothing in this book is what it looks like.

PSEUDO-MANIFESTO*

1. Truth is only stranger than fiction if you're a stranger to the truth. Which means you're either a liar or you're fictional.

2. A realistic story is a story lacking in imagination. (What does *realistic* mean, anyway? Would you say something is true-istic?)

3. I've never met a joke so bad I didn't like it. Then again, I've never met a joke.

4. When in doubt, you can't be wrong.

5. Whether it's chocolate or socks, the rule is the same: the darker the better.

---

*A *MANIFESTO* IS NOT A FIESTA FOR A MAN. IN FACT, IT IS NOT A FIESTA OF ANY KIND. IT IS NOT EVEN A *FIESTO*. RATHER, IT IS A STATEMENT OF PRINCIPLES. USUALLY POLITICAL OR ARTISTIC PRINCIPLES. BUT YOU COULD WRITE A MANIFESTO ABOUT ANYTHING. FOR INSTANCE, CHOCOLATE OR CHEESE. A *PSEUDO-MANIFESTO* IS EITHER A FAKE MANIFESTO OR A MANI-

6. There is more to life than chocolate. There is, for example, cheese.

7. If a waiter accidentally serves you a burger with mayonnaise, it's not enough for him to scrape it off. He must order you a new burger.

8. It's pronounced *sue DON im us*.

9. Secret? What Secret?

10. I know you are, but what am I?

FESTO WRITTEN BY PSEUDONYMOUS BOSCH. SO PERHAPS I SHOULD HAVE CALLED IT A *PSEUDO*-PSEUDO-MANIFESTO. BEFORE READING FURTHER, WHY NOT WRITE YOUR OWN MANIFESTO? THEN YOU CAN SEE HOW MANY WAYS MY BOOK FAILS TO MEASURE UP TO YOUR IDEAS ABOUT THE WAY THINGS SHOULD BE. JUST DON'T TELL ME ABOUT IT.

*As you will discover, I have numbered this and several other chapters negatively, so to speak. Alas, I cannot tell you why without giving away too much. But if you have

(CONT.)

ow shall I put this? I must choose my words carefully.

(I know how you are. Always ready to jump on my mistakes.)

Somewhere, at some time, a girl walked down a road.

I say *somewhere* not because the where is secret, although it is.

I say *some time* not because the when is secret, although it is.

And I say *a girl* not because her name is secret, although it is.

No, I use these words because the girl herself did not know where she was.

Or when.

Or who.

She had woken standing up. With her eyes open.

It was a very strange sensation. Like materializing out of nowhere.

Her fingers and toes tingled. The tips of her ears burned (whether from heat or cold she wouldn't have been able to say).

Sunspots lingered in her eyes, blurring her vision. But when she looked up she saw there was no sun. The sky was cloudy.

STUDIED INTEGERS, YOU MAY WELL BE ABLE TO GUESS. YOU KNOW, FOR EXAMPLE, THAT A NEGATIVE NUMBER IS A NUMBER WHOSE VALUE IS LESS THAN ZERO, AND THAT THE "HIGHER" THE NEGATIVE NUMBER IS, THE LOWER ITS VALUE. THUS, WHEN YOU ORDER TWO NEGATIVE NUMBERS IN

Had she fainted? Did she have a concussio
(She knew that confusion and blurred vision w
symptoms of concussion, but she couldn't remember
how she knew it.) She touched her head, but she
found no injury.

Gradually, the sunspots disappeared and her
vision cleared. She looked around.

She had no idea where she was.

She seemed to be in the countryside, but of what
country wasn't immediately apparent. There were
fields to either side of her, but they were dry and
empty. Trees dotted the landscape but in no obvious
pattern. There were no signs of life.

Be systematic, she told herself. If you retrace
your steps, you'll figure out where you are.

But she couldn't remember a thing that had
happened before she was where she was. It was as if
she had been born a moment ago.

Who am I...?

The realization that she didn't know her own
name came over her belatedly, like a chill you don't
notice until you see your breath clouding in the air.

She felt uneasy but not exactly frightened. Real
amnesia, she knew (although she couldn't remember how she knew it), was exceedingly rare. Most
likely, her memory would return in a moment.

SEQUENCE, THE HIGHER OF THE TWO ALWAYS COMES *BEFORE* (HINT, HINT)
THE LOWER. NEGATIVE TEN COMES BEFORE NEGATIVE NINE, AND SO ON,
UNTIL YOU GET TO ZERO AND THINGS TURN NORMAL—MORE OR LESS.

She decided the best thing was to walk.

The walking was not easy. There were no signs or streetlights to guide the way. The road was not paved, and it was riddled with rocks and tree roots and mud holes.

She stumbled more than once, but she trudged forward. What else was there to do?

An hour passed. Or maybe two. Or was it less?

She didn't see anyone else. Until she did.

Ahead of her, just a few feet off the road, a little boy was climbing a big tree. Like a cat, he made his way on all fours out onto a long branch. Like a cat, he got stuck.

"Father...Father!"

His cries grew louder, but nobody came.

I wonder if he'll recognize me, the girl thought. He could be my little brother for all I know.

"Don't worry, I'll get you down!" she shouted.

If the boy heard her, he showed no sign. "Father!" he kept yelling.

An old hemp rope lay beneath the tree. The remains of a swing. The girl picked it up, then automatically started to climb the old and twisting tree trunk. As if it were the natural thing to do. As if she had rescued many other children before.

Remember the Three-Point Rule, she told herself. But she couldn't remember how she knew the rule.*

"You shouldn't climb up trees if you're too scared to climb down," she said when she came close to the boy.

He ignored her, continuing to yell for his father. It certainly didn't seem as though he recognized her.

"Are you deaf? I'm trying to help...."

The boy's shirt—little more than a rag—had caught on a branch. As soon as the girl started to untangle him, the boy jumped in fright—and almost fell out of the tree.

She gripped him tight. "Careful—"

He screamed, "Goat! Goat!"

At least that's what it sounded like.

"Calm down—you're OK."

She gave him a pat of reassurance, but his cries only grew louder and more hysterical.

"I'll get you down, no problem."

Expertly, she tied the rope to the tree. A *Buntline Hitch Knot*, she remembered the knot was called. But she didn't remember how she knew the name.

She tugged on the boy's shirt collar. He clung to the tree branch, refusing to move.

"Goat! Goat!"

"Is there a goat down there? Is that what's

*ALWAYS CONNECT TO WHAT YOU'RE CLIMBING WITH AT LEAST TWO FEET AND ONE HAND OR TWO HANDS AND ONE FOOT. YOU MIGHT REMEMBER THIS HELPFUL RULE FROM A HIGHLY EDUCATIONAL AND FRANKLY RATHER BRILLIANT BOOK CALLED *IF YOU'RE READING THIS, IT'S TOO LATE*.

scaring you? Don't worry, it won't hurt you. Goats don't eat people. Tin cans, tennis balls, maybe—but not little boys. Not usually, anyways." She smiled to show she was joking, but he didn't smile back.

Eventually, she coaxed him down by gently placing his hands on the rope—then forcibly pushing him off the branch.

"Pretend it's a fire pole!" she called after him.

He slid down the rope, a look of terror on his face.

As soon as his feet hit the ground, the boy bolted.

"You're welcome," said the girl under her breath.

In the distance, a man—presumably the boy's father—waited. He wore a plumed hat, dark vest, and big, billowing sleeves. He looked like a musketeer.

He must be an actor, thought the girl. Maybe there is a theater nearby.

The boy was still crying about the goat as he jumped into his father's arms.

The girl waved. But the man didn't acknowledge her.

Gee, people are really friendly around here, thought the girl.

Shaking her head, she returned to the road — and stepped right into a puddle.

She grunted in annoyance.

As she shook water off her foot, she looked curiously at the puddle. The muddy water reflected blue sky and silver clouds and a flock of birds passing by.

But there was one reflection she could not see: her own.

Not *goat*, she thought.

Ghost.

ax-Ernest arrived at the hospital at exactly 7:59 p.m.

A nurse waved cheerily from behind the front desk. "Hi, Max-Ernest! Just in time, as usual."

Visiting hours ended at eight. If he got there any later, he wouldn't be let in since he wasn't part of the patient's family. At least not the way the hospital defined it.

Max-Ernest waved back halfheartedly.

"C'mon, honey—let's see you turn that frown upside down. Don't forget—"

The nurse pointed over her shoulder to a poster of a puppy wearing a red clown nose. **LAUGHTER IS THE BEST MEDICINE!**

Max-Ernest gritted his teeth and forced himself to smile.

That doesn't make any sense, he almost said. How can laughter always be the *best* medicine? What if there's a medicine that would save your life—like penicillin? Wouldn't that be the best? And what if you have a broken rib? Or lung cancer? Or asthma? Laughter would make it worse, not better. And *whose* laughter are we talking about, anyway? Your own or somebody else's? What if somebody is laughing *at* you instead of *with* you—is it still medicine then?* How 'bout that? Oh, and by the way, dogs don't laugh. Some scientists think that gorillas and chimpanzees laugh. But not dogs. Not even puppies with clown noses...!

But, and this will surprise you if you know anything about him, Max-Ernest didn't say a word. He just kept gritting his teeth and headed for the third elevator on the right.

The one marked **PICU**.

Every time Max-Ernest saw those four letters, he made up new meanings for them... *Primates Invade Curious Universe... Penguins, Icelandic, Carry Umbrellas... Pick Icky Cuticle Up... Purple Insect Crawls Underground... Principals In Colorful Underwear... People I Can't Understand...* and so on. But the word-

---

*THIS WAS A DISTINCTION THAT MAX-ERNEST—WHO'D ALWAYS WANTED TO BE LAUGHED *WITH*, BUT WHO WAS FAR MORE OFTEN LAUGHED *AT*— WAS ONLY TOO AWARE OF.

play was simply an old habit, a mental tic, rather than a way of amusing himself. Not even the thought of principals in colorful underwear could make him laugh now, whether laughter was the best medicine or not.

He knew too well what the letters stood for.

PICU: Pediatric Intensive Care Unit.

Perhaps the least funny place on the planet.

Max-Ernest had a lot of experience with hospitals.

His childhood had been one long battery of medical tests. Skin tests. Bone tests. Eye tests. Hearing tests. DNA tests. IQ tests. (Too much ability, they said, is a disability.) Rorschach tests. Psychological evaluations. Neurological evaluations. Cardiological evaluations. X-rays and CAT scans. They'd tested all his reflexes and tested him for all the complexes. They'd watched him eat and listened to him sleep. They'd measured his dexterity and quantified his creativity. He'd given blood samples and urine samples and even once (though he'd like to forget it) a *stool* sample.*

That Max-Ernest had a condition, everybody was certain; but what the condition was, nobody knew. The only thing the experts agreed on was that the main symptom was his ceaseless talking. Of course, it didn't take an expert to tell you that.

---

*IF YOU DON'T KNOW WHAT A STOOL SAMPLE IS, PLEASE ASK SOMEBODY ELSE. I'D RATHER NOT HAVE TO EXPLAIN IT MYSELF — IT'S TOO DISTASTEFUL A SUBJECT.

A funny thing had happened recently, however. Funny *weird*, that is. Not *funny* funny.*

Max-Ernest, the talker, had stopped talking. Not entirely. But almost. Most of the words he uttered now were single syllables — like *yes* or *no* — and they came out in little grunts, hardly recognizable as language.

It wasn't so much that he *couldn't* talk. There were still plenty of words in his head, and he could still push air out of his lungs and move his lips and tongue. It was just that talking had become a tremendous effort. Even more of an effort than it used to be for him *not* to talk. Words used to come out of his mouth in a nonstop torrent; shutting them off was like trying to dam a river. Now, suddenly, the river had switched direction, and talking was like trying to swim upstream when it was all he could do to swim in place.

This new condition, this unwilled silence, had fallen over him ten days ago. The day Cass had gone into the hospital. The day she had fallen into a coma.

"Not a coma like you're thinking," the doctor had hastily explained when she saw Cass's mother react to the news, almost falling into a coma herself. "Not a coma like you see in the movies. Cass's brain

---

*ANOTHER DISTINCTION THAT MAX-ERNEST, WHO'D ALWAYS LONGED TO BE *FUNNY* FUNNY BUT WHO WAS MOST OFTEN FUNNY *WEIRD*, KNEW ONLY TOO WELL.

is very active. And she seems to be going in and out of REM cycles. She's simply...asleep. In all likelihood, she'll wake up very soon."

Still, Max-Ernest knew, a coma was a coma. Even if it wasn't a *coma* coma. Even if you called it sleep. After all, sleep was *not* not a coma. Max-Ernest had looked up the word in a dictionary: *coma* meant "deep sleep" in Greek.

His silence was very frustrating for the people around him. Especially for Cass's mother and for the doctors and nurses who were trying to figure out what had happened to Cass. Max-Ernest admitted he'd been with Cass when *it* had happened, but whenever anybody asked him just what exactly *it* was, he would shrug or look off into the distance.

Without her coming right out and saying so, it was clear Cass's mom thought he was hiding something. "Why is it Cass is always with you whenever—?" she started to ask at one point, but she didn't finish her question. "Are you sure you didn't—?" she started to ask another time, but she didn't finish that question, either.

She hadn't wanted to allow Max-Ernest in the hospital room, but Cass's grandfathers had intervened and reminded her that Max-Ernest was Cass's best friend.

"Cass would want him here—you know that," said Grandpa Larry. "And the poor boy feels bad enough as it is—look at him."

"Besides," said Grandpa Wayne, "maybe the sound of his voice will wake her up."

If only it were that simple! thought Max-Ernest. Then he would force himself to start talking again, no matter how hard it was. If he thought it would help, he would never stop talking. Not even to eat or sleep. Not even to breathe. He would take his old condition back a thousand times over if it meant curing Cass's. He wanted his friend back more desperately than he'd ever wanted anything in his life.

Tonight, Cass's mother was leaving early. Everyone at the hospital agreed it was time for her to get some sleep.

When she passed Max-Ernest in the hallway, she grabbed his wrist. Her eyes were red with tiredness.

"Max-Ernest, please, when are you going to...?"

Then she let go, as if she didn't have the strength to ask the question. She walked away, shaking her head.

Max-Ernest opened his mouth for a second, then closed it without saying anything.

Cass's mother was right; he *was* hiding something. But even if he'd been at liberty to speak, even if he hadn't taken a sacred vow of secrecy, even if he'd risked all and told his story, nobody would have believed him. The truth was so incredible, so out-landish, so utterly bizarre, he would be branded as a liar, or delusional at best. So what was the point?

It was better not to say anything at all.

There was a vending machine next to Cass's room.

Max-Ernest fumblingly fed a dollar into it and selected the largest and plainest chocolate bar avail-able. He proceeded to eat the bar so fast, a passerby might have thought it was his first meal in weeks.

"Hmmgh..."

As he ate, he made a peculiar sound — part hum, part groan — that he made only when he was eating chocolate. A sound he couldn't control any more than his urge to eat chocolate in the first place.

"Hmmgh...hmmmgh...hmmmmgh..."

Hardly hesitating, Max-Ernest bought three more chocolate bars and wolfed them down in as many bites. Then he bought a fifth bar and put it in his pocket for later. He looked into the machine, considering a sixth bar, but the machine was alarm-ingly empty-looking. At this rate it would run out of chocolate bars in less than a day.

The thought filled him with a sense of panic. Ever since he'd discovered he wasn't allergic, Max-Ernest had been feasting on chocolate in quantities that would have astonished all but the most voracious chocolate eaters. Ten bars a day on average, if you had to count (and if you know Max-Ernest, you know he *always* had to count). What would he do, he worried now, if the hospital's chocolate supply was not replenished?

How could he continue to visit Cass without the rich, ripe, dark, deep, zippy, zesty, wicked, wonderful, delicious, delightful, delectable, and even electable (if he could vote), vibrant, vivacious, seductive, addictive, oh-so-very-attractive, nourishing, flourishing, rather ravishing, beautiful, buttery, sometimes bittersweet but never bitter, gorgeous and worth gorging on, berry-ish, cherry-ish, meaty yet fruity, elemental yet complex, mellow yet electric, soothing yet energiz-ing, earthy yet heavenly, melt-in-your-mouth pleasure of chocolate?*

He would have to plan ahead and carry choco-late with him — that was the answer to this particu-lar dilemma — but the thought did nothing to reassure him. Normally, Cass was the plan-ahead person. Whenever they went on a mission for their secret organization, the Terces Society, Max-Ernest could count on Cass to pack her famous "super chip" trail mix, which contained a portion of chocolate chips so generous that the trail mix invariably melted into a

---

*THOSE WEREN'T ACTUALLY THE WORDS IN MAX-ERNEST'S HEAD — I'M AFRAID I GOT A LITTLE CARRIED AWAY — BUT I CAN PROMISE YOU THEY GIVE A SENSE OF WHAT HE FELT.

big chocolaty clump. Alas, he had never tasted the trail mix because of his supposed allergies. It was something he'd been looking forward to. But now...? His panic was replaced by a wave of sadness.

Would his survivalist friend survive? Cass had spent her entire life preparing for disasters of one kind or another. Earthquakes. Hurricanes. Tornadoes. Not to mention the extinction-level events. Giant meteors. Global warming. Nuclear war. And here she was, done in by such a piddling thing? A mere trifle — indeed, a mere truffle. Had she trained all those years for toxic sludge only to succumb to toxic fudge?*

Yes, chocolate was the culprit.

Cass's doctors had not been particularly surprised to find traces of chocolate in Cass's stomach — she was a kid, after all — and had quickly dismissed it as a possible cause of her condition. Chocolate allergies were very rare, they said. And they hardly ever induced such severe reactions.

Max-Ernest could attest to that last point. His allergy, at any rate, had turned out to be a phantom. Nonetheless, he, and he alone, knew that it was a bite of chocolate that had brought on Cass's coma.

Not just any chocolate, of course. Not chocolate like he ate every night from the hospital vending machine. Not *chocolate* chocolate.

---

*AGAIN I MUST APOLOGIZE FOR PUTTING WORDS IN MAX-ERNEST'S HEAD — AND FOR WAXING POETICAL (RATHER THAN PHILOSOPHICAL) AT SUCH A SERIOUS TIME. IT'S JUST THAT CHOCOLATE MAKES ME WANT TO RHYME. (GET IT — *TIME, RHYME?* OH NEVER MIME.)

No, this was extra-chocolaty chocolate.

Extreme chocolate.

Extremely dark, that is. The darkest chocolate of all time.

Chocolate made with the legendary Tuning Fork—the magical (there was no other word to use, although it made Max-Ernest wince to think it) cooking instrument of the Aztecs.

Time Travel Chocolate, as Cass and Max-Ernest had come to think of it.

Chocolate that sent the eater back into her ancestral past. (Although whether or not Cass had in fact gone back into the past was debatable. After all, her body was still in the present. It was her mind that was gone.)

As the Secret Keeper, Cass held knowledge of the Secret—the very secret that the Terces Society was sworn to protect—buried in her ancestral memory.

The wicked master chef, Señor Hugo, had made the chocolate specifically for Cass so she would reveal the Secret to Hugo's colleagues, those cunning alchemists known as the Masters of the Midnight Sun. (The Masters believed the Secret was the key to immortality and they would stop at nothing to uncover it.)*

---

*I TELL THE STORY OF CASS AND SEÑOR HUGO IN MUCH GREATER DETAIL IN MY LAST BOOK, *THIS BOOK IS NOT GOOD FOR YOU*. BUT IF YOU HAVEN'T READ THAT BOOK, I'D ADVISE AGAINST IT. AS IT HAPPENS, THE TITLE IS SOMETHING OF AN UNDERSTATEMENT. I HAD ORIGINALLY AND MORE ACCURATELY CALLED IT *THIS BOOK IS ABSOLUTELY TERRIBLE FOR*

The first time Cass ate the chocolate, she'd been tricked into it and had only escaped giving away the Secret by the narrowest of margins. This last time, Cass had eaten the chocolate voluntarily—and against Max-Ernest's explicit advice, as he often reminded himself—in order to learn the Secret herself.

As far as they knew, only a specially pre-pared antidote—a mysterious milky-white substance whipped up with the Tuning Fork—could bring her back to present-day reality. Cass had left the Tuning Fork with Max-Ernest so he could administer the same antidote the second time around.

But it didn't work. She had eaten too much of the chocolate. Or he had made the antidote incor-rectly. Or he had waited too long to give it to her (only five minutes, though it seemed like five hours). Or...Max-Ernest could think of dozens of things that might have gone wrong.

Before he could try again, Cass's mother had unexpectedly arrived at Max-Ernest's house to pick up Cass. As soon as she saw Cass lying unconscious on the floor, she called an ambulance—and she'd barely left her daughter's side since. Max-Ernest never had another chance to be alone with Cass.

YOU, BUT MY PUBLISHERS WERE AFRAID THE TITLE WOULD SCARE READERS AWAY. THEY WANTED TO CALL IT *THIS BOOK IS GOOD FOR YOU*. I WAS ONLY ABLE TO SLIP IN THE *NOT* AT THE LAST MOMENT WHEN THEY WEREN'T LOOKING.

Tonight was different. Tonight, Max-Ernest was determined to give her the antidote once more.

Not for the first time since Cass's collapse, he wished their friend and fellow Terces member Yo-Yoji were there to help. But Yo-Yoji was back in Japan for two months with his family. Yo-Yoji had tried to persuade his parents to let him stay with Max-Ernest, but of course he wasn't able to tell them the real reason he didn't want to leave the country. Any mention of the Terces Society was strictly forbidden.

They'd e-mailed each other from time to time, encrypting their messages, naturally, with their usual keyword code. (Hint: keyword = first part of Yo-Yoji's band name.) But the e-mails had only made Max-Ernest feel more isolated. The last one from Yo-Yoji had been particularly discouraging:*

From: ohnoitsyoyo@xxxxx.com
Subject: fuji-bound
To: mdash@xxxxxxxxx.com

Euen, gust jnttfmc u hmow f wfjj ln obbjfmn bor a wh. Lakpfmc w tdn 'rnmts om Kt Bugf so eae iam bfmfsd tdat pojjutfom stuey bruk jast yr. You hmow tdn rujn—mo njnitromfi motdfmc fm maturn. (Mot nvnm kusfi!!! Aaarcd—

*IN CASE YOU DON'T REMEMBER THE FIRST WORD OF YO-YOJI'S BAND NAME (IT DOES APPEAR LATER IN THIS BOOK) OR IN CASE YOU'RE THE LAZY TYPE, THE DECODED E-MAIL IS INCLUDED IN THE APPENDIX. AS FOR HOW

Suihacn!) Wfjj idnih u out soom as F'k laih. Dopn Lass oh ly tdnm.

Stay cool, yo. Y-Y

\m/ (>.<) \m/

(Rock On!)

It was up to Max-Ernest to do the job alone.

For a moment, after he entered Cass's room, Max-Ernest just stared. At the tubes going in and out of her. At the jagged green line on the monitor measuring her heart rate.

Eyes closed, lips still, her face was so expressionless she could have been anyone. Only the big, pointy ears were indisputably Cass's. They twitched every once in a while as if to reassure Max-Ernest that, yes, in fact, this was his friend lying in front of him.

"Hi...Cass," he said. Speaking was such an effort that his voice came out in monosyllabic squeaks. "It's...me...I'm...here."

He exhaled, relieved that the talking part was over. Then he pulled an ancient two-pronged

---

TO DECODE A KEYWORD CODE GENERALLY, YOU'LL FIND INSTRUCTIONS AT THE END OF MY FIRST BOOK. AND IF YOU DON'T KNOW WHAT THAT BOOK IS CALLED, WELL, YOU'RE NOT ALONE.

instrument—the Tuning Fork—out of his jacket pocket, located a pitcher of water, and went to work.

Absorbed in his task, Max-Ernest didn't notice his friend's lips forming the word *ghost* again...

and again...
and again...
and again...
and again...

CHAPTER
-NINE

THE SEER

f I am a ghost, I must be dead.

The girl glanced down. To the rest of the world she might have been transparent, but to her own eyes her limbs looked solid. There was nothing she could see that indicated a death, whether recent or long ago. No sign of accident or bodily trauma. No evidence of decay or flesh-eating maggots. She looked nothing like the walking dead in a horror movie.

She tried holding her breath. Logically, a dead person should not need to breathe, but she soon found herself coughing for air.

She jumped up to see whether she would float or even fly—

"Ow."

Alas, the laws of gravity were in full effect.

(Actually, it didn't hurt very much. Her exclamation was an instinctive reaction to a slight twist of her left ankle as she landed.)

As for her surroundings, they looked lifelike enough, even if she didn't recognize where she was. If this was some kind of otherworldly limbo, it wasn't what you'd imagine. There were no spooky wisps of fog. No lost souls wandering the streets.

She certainly didn't *feel* dead. (Although how would you know what you would feel?) And yet she didn't feel fully alive, either. She felt very little at all, really — very little physically, very little emotionally. It was as if her invisibility insulated her from the world, separating her from all experience.

She kept walking. What else was there to do?

Finally, a town — well, a few houses and a horse — appeared on the horizon. She quickened her pace.

Her first thought was that she had entered one of those Renaissance faires where people dress up in velvet tunics and green tights, or sometimes just burlap sacks and Birkenstocks, and say "Hear ye, hear ye!" over and over. She couldn't remember the details, but she had a vague recollection of just such an event. (A school field trip, maybe? Did she go to school?) But here there were far fewer lords and ladies and far more peasants. Also, there were no funnel cakes or deep-fried Twinkies for sale, just muddy carrots and wilting cabbages. Mangy turkeys and scrawny chickens wandered loose, running in and out of the stalls and under carts. It could have been market day in a town square hundreds of years ago. The small thatched huts that surrounded the square looked surprisingly authentic. Perhaps it was not a faire but a movie set?

Whatever it was, it was very crowded, and the girl kept bumping into people as she walked.

There was the meat-pie vendor whose pies she caused to land on several unlucky shoppers: "Beslubbering boar-pig!" "Swag-bellied lout!" they complained.

And she nearly started a fight between two young fops in plumed hats and flouncy collars: "Clay-brained coxcomb!" "Mewling milk-livered maggot!"*

Momentarily she forgot about her transparent condition and asked a kind-looking woman for the name of the town they were in. Rather than responding, the woman walked straight into her, crashing their heads together. Then she spun around in confusion, cursing loudly.

The girl hardly felt the impact—her senses were still quite dull—but it was disconcerting nonetheless. She felt a bit guilty about wreaking such havoc, and yet she couldn't help admiring how skilled everyone here was at staying in character. (A theater camp for adult actors—could that be it?)

Avoiding further collisions as best she could, she made her way across the market, ducking here, weaving there, hoping for some sign that would tell her where she was.

She noticed that a small crowd had gathered in the center of the market. They cheered and jeered and generally seemed to be having a good time. Afraid

*As you might guess from their attire, a FOP is a fashionable young man—some would say too fashionable, but I say there is no such thing.

she might start a riot if she pushed her way in, the girl stood on tiptoe and tried to see who or what was causing the commotion.

First, she caught sight of three potatoes sailing in and out of view as they were repeatedly tossed in the air. Then she saw the silvery shimmer of bells dangling from the three pointed ends of a hat. Finally, she made out a wiry young man in a diamond-patterned outfit—a jester—standing on a box of some sort.* He was juggling and telling jokes that were, judging by the groans of the crowd, more confusing than they were funny.

She strained to listen.

"What dost thou say—that I have not sense?" he shouted at a heckler. "No, I have better, I have a sense of humor!"

The girl felt an unexpected jolt of recognition. What was it about him that seemed so familiar? Had she been a jester in her former life? She looked down at her jeans and sneakers—it hardly seemed likely. Perhaps she was raised in a circus, bouncing on the knee of a clown? That seemed like a better possibility. If she'd spent her childhood performing on a trapeze, that might explain why she was such a skilled climber. Then again, she really couldn't imagine herself in a sparkly leotard.

*A JESTER'S OUTFIT, BY THE WAY, IS KNOWN AS A *MOTLEY* BECAUSE IT IS SUCH A MOTLEY MIX OF COLORS AND DESIGNS.

*　　*　　*

When she reached a quieter corner of the market, she stopped to consider her options.

What to do next? She felt a sense of urgency, as though she had only a limited amount of time to accomplish a specific task. And yet, for all she knew, her time was infinite.

"Hail, young traveler."

The girl turned to see an old, straggly-haired woman sitting on a tree stump under an old, straggly-limbed tree. In front of the woman were a larger tree stump that served as a table and another, smaller stump for a companion to sit on.

With a start, the girl realized the old woman was staring directly at her.

"You can see me?"

The woman nodded. "I am a Seer. I have what they call *second sight*.... Sit. I will tell your fortune."

The woman was so fair-skinned, her hair so white, she was almost colorless. She was barefoot and wore a plain cotton shift.

Her only ornament: a gold-rimmed monocle that magnified her pale, watery blue eye.

"I don't really believe in that," said the girl, backing away.

"In what? Sitting?"

The girl hesitated. Who knew what she believed in? And what did it matter anyway? She might not believe in ghosts, but that didn't mean she wasn't one.

She felt in her pocket. "I don't have any money."

The woman smiled as if this were a grim joke. "Your money is no use here, I think. Please—" She motioned to the smaller tree stump. "What is your name, child?"

"I-I am...," the girl stammered, sitting. "I'm sorry, I don't know who I am."

"Don't worry, the cards will tell us."

"Am I...dead?"

The girl waited, tense. She was not at all certain she wanted to hear the answer.

The Seer peered at the girl through the golden monocle. While the Seer's left eye was closed, her right eye seemed never to blink.

"I don't think so," the Seer said finally. "In my experience, the dead are much more sure of themselves. They can be very tiresome that way."

"So then I'm not a ghost?" asked the girl, relieved, but only just.

"There are many kinds of ghosts. Only some are ghosts of the dead. Others are simply the appearance of someone far away. A few even come from the future."

"The future?" repeated the girl, growing more confused by the minute.

Looking down, she noticed the multitude of concentric rings that made up the large tree stump in front of her. From somewhere in her past, she heard a kindly man's voice (whose? she couldn't remember) telling her that each ring represented a year's passing and that you could read the age of a tree by counting the rings.*

"What year is it, anyway?" she asked.

But the Seer was no longer listening. Her eyes were closed and she was passing her hand over a deck of cards. The cards were well-worn and decorated with a pattern of moons and stars on their back sides.

As the girl watched, the Seer arranged ten cards facedown on the table. The girl rubbed her eyes. Unless she'd missed it, the Seer had never once touched the cards. Her hand had simply hovered over them.

Only after the middle card had flipped over — as if stirred by a breeze — did the Seer open her eyes and pick up her monocle.

The card was delicately painted with a picture of a slender youth standing against a backdrop of bil-

---

*THIS IS WHAT IS KNOWN AS THE SCIENCE OF *DENDROCHRONOLOGY*. BUT OF COURSE YOU KNEW THAT ALREADY.

lowing clouds. He was thrusting his sword forward while looking back over his shoulder.

"Ah, yes, the Page of Swords," said the Seer. "A stealthy card, the spy in the tarot deck. A natural for an invisible girl, yes? It means, I think, that you have been sent to this world on a mission."

"A mission? What kind?"

Ignoring the question, the Seer held her hand over a second card. By the time her hand moved away, the card had flipped over and was lying faceup across the first card. The second card bore a compass-like design framed in four directions by animals and crowned on top by a sphinx.

"Behold—the Wheel of Fortune." The Seer traced a circle in the air, and then an X. "You are at a crossroads. Which direction will you choose? This way you follow the angel, that way the eagle, this way the lion, that way the bull."

"How'm I supposed to know what that means?" asked the girl, staring at the card.

"Some say the Wheel means good luck, but do not trust it," said the Seer dismissively. "Your mission will go well or it will go badly. What is certain is that the Wheel will spin again."

"Thanks, that's really helpful," said the girl, who had lost her memory but not, evidently, her tendency toward sarcasm.

"The cards can only tell us what we already know," the Seer cautioned.

"But I don't even know where I'm supposed to be going. I don't know anything."

"Patience."

The Seer turned over another card. (Or was it that the card turned itself over?) This one was decorated with an Egyptian motif. It showed a somber-looking woman sitting with a scroll in her hand and a crescent moon at her foot.

"Here is your destiny — the High Priestess. She is the bearer of secrets. Is it perhaps a secret that you seek?"

"Yeah...I think...I think maybe it is," said the girl slowly. "*The* Secret."

She didn't know where the thought had come

from; nonetheless, a small flame had been lit in the darkness of her mind.

The Secret. She was seeking the Secret.

"The Secret, yes," said the Seer cryptically. "That is what we all seek in the end, isn't it?"

The Seer raised her hand slightly and another card was revealed. Unlike the others, it faced the girl rather than the Seer. The girl read the inscription: *Ace of Wands.*

"This fourth card takes us back to your distant past, to the foundation of your journey." The Seer shook her head sadly when she looked at the card. "See how it's upside down? It seems an old wrong must be righted. You will never rest until the wand is returned to its rightful position."

"What wrong? What wand?"

"It may be that something has been stolen from you. Or perhaps you have stolen from someone else?" The Seer shrugged. "Then again, sometimes a wand is just a wand."

"You mean like a magician's wand?"

"What other kind is there?" The Seer nodded with satisfaction as another card turned over. Here a robed man stood holding a wand aloft with his right hand while pointing downward with his left. *The Magician*, it read. "How else could you have gotten here — if not by magic?"

THE MAGICIAN

"How do I get out of here? That's what I want to know," said the girl, who was growing more irritable by the minute. "Or do I just click my heels and say, 'There's no place like home'?"

"*As above, so below.* As in this world, so in the other. This is why the Magician points upward and downward at the same time. I cannot tell you how to get from here to there. Only that your actions in this place will reflect in that one."

A sixth card turned over, and for the first time, the Seer looked surprised. "The Fool? But surely..."

THE FOOL

"What? Why is that weird?"

"The sixth card signals the goal of your quest. And yet the Fool is always the questioner. You." The Seer paused thoughtfully. "Perhaps it is you yourself you must find...."

The girl looked at the card. And now it was her turn to be surprised.

"What is it?" asked the Seer.

"A minute ago I saw a guy — a jester — who looked exactly like this. I kept thinking he looked familiar. And I think I just realized why...."

The Seer raised her eyebrows. "The cards are more helpful than you expected?"

"Yeah, maybe," the girl admitted. "Hey, um, what's your name? In case I want to find you again or something."

"Me? My name is Clara. But most people call me Cassandra." She laughed. "They say I too often predict disaster."

Cassandra. Cassandra. The girl repeated it in her head.

"I see the prophet's name is known to you. You are a student of Greek mythology?"

The girl smiled. "Not really, I just — I just know the name really well, that's all."

Cassandra. Her name was Cassandra.

The Magician. The Jester. The Secret.

Her memories fell into place one after another, like cards in a deck.

She was indeed on a mission. A mission into the past. A mission to find the Jester.

To find the Secret.

And to find herself.

She was the Secret Keeper, they had told her. It was time to learn what that meant.

When Cass's attention turned outward once more, the Seer was gone. Her tree stump perch was bare. And so too was her tree stump table. Save for a lone fly that flew away as soon as Cass noticed it.

Had she only imagined the encounter? Had it all been in her head?*

As Cass's eyes focused on the stump in front of her, the rings appeared to vibrate. Was she dreaming, or were there fewer rings now than previously? Did that mean that she'd gone further back in time? Or maybe the rings had represented her future and now she was solidly in the past?

She was about to conclude that she was slowly going crazy, that she had imagined the tarot card reading *and* the change in the tree stump, when she noticed a shiny object on the ground in front of her. The Seer's golden monocle.

Had the Seer left it for her intentionally? And if she looked into it, would she see what the Seer saw?

As she picked up the monocle, Cass noticed

---

*WITH ALL DUE RESPECT TO CASS, I'VE NEVER UNDERSTOOD THE REASONING BEHIND THE EXPRESSION "ONLY IN YOUR HEAD." AFTER ALL, SOMETHING CAN BE LOCATED IN YOUR HEAD AND NEVERTHELESS BE REAL. YOUR BRAIN, FOR INSTANCE, IS INSIDE YOUR HEAD. (UNLESS YOU'RE COMPLETELY BRAINLESS.)

something odd about it: it was made of two lenses, one on top of the other. It was, in effect, a *double monocle*.

A double monocle that gives you second sight — it makes sense in a way, she thought.

With only the slightest bit of nervousness — what could she see, after all, that wasn't already there? — Cass held up the Double Monocle to her eye and looked blinkingly through it.

Pietro's circus never looked very inviting in the early morning hours. Tent flaps were closed. The shades in the trailers and vans were pulled down. And then there was all the stale kettle corn, half-eaten hot dogs, and over-chewed wads of gum strewn across the ground.

By the time Max-Ernest made his way to the clowns' camper-van, the soles of his sneakers had doubled in thickness and long threads of cotton candy trailed through the dust behind him.

He hesitated at the door. If anybody knew where Pietro was, the clowns would, but interacting with the clowns was never easy. Screwing up his courage, he knocked — a little louder than he meant to.

"Who is it? — and don't wake up the whole neighborhood!" came the muffled reply.

Max-Ernest opened the door and immediately started coughing uncontrollably. The van was so smoky, there might have been a campfire inside.

"It's…Max…uh…Er…nest…," he managed to spit out between coughs.

The clowns, Mickey and Morrie, were sitting across from each other at a small folding table. As usual, they looked completely disheveled, shirts buttoned incorrectly, traces of clown makeup on their unshaven faces, as though they'd just woken up — or else hadn't slept in days. On one side of them sat Myrtle, the circus's bearded lady, a pink-and-green housecoat hiding her ample girth. On the other side sat Pietro, the old magician and secret leader of the Terces Society, his bushy gray mustache still showing the remains of his breakfast.

All four were smoking fat cigars. Large playing cards fanned out in their hands. A big pile of coins beckoned from the middle of the table.

"Well, if it isn't the two-named wonder!" joked Morrie, the shorter, fatter clown. "What do you think, Myrtle, would people pay to see him? Two names is almost like having two heads, isn't it?"

"Yeah, maybe we could promote him as a split personality. Dr. Max and Ernest Hyde," joked Mickey, the taller, skinnier clown.

"The only split personalities around here are going to be yours if you keep teasing that poor kid," said Myrtle.

She picked up an oversized yellow hammer off the floor and waved it threateningly. Max-Ernest was relieved to see that the hammer was rubber, one of the clowns' circus props.

He waved smoke away from his face. "Pi...e...tro...can...you...out...side?" he asked in a gasping whisper. It was still very hard for him to speak, but this was an emergency.

"Just wait the minute, Max-Ernest. This game, it is not over." The magician's Italian accent made all his words sound slightly comical and more than a little mischievous. As if a punch line were just around the corner.

"Just...for...a...sec...ond?"

Pietro shook his head. "I'm sorry, I cannot take my eyes off these clowns or they will steal the pot."

Myrtle nodded sagely. "Sticky fingers, these two..."

"Who—us little lambs? We never steal!" exclaimed Mickey.

"Why should we? We cheat plenty good!" agreed Morrie.

"But...it's...a...bout...Cass!" Max-Ernest protested.

Pietro put his finger to his lips, shushing Max-Ernest.

Helpless, Max-Ernest sat down on top of one of the clowns' costume trunks—a curly red wig spilled out the side—and resigned himself to watching the game.

"OK, my trick," said Myrtle.* "Leading with

---

*By TRICK, MYRTLE HERE DOES NOT MEAN A CARD TRICK OR MAGIC TRICK. SHE DOESN'T EVEN MEAN THE KIND OF TRICK YOU PLAY REGULARLY ON THE BULLIES AT SCHOOL. (AT LEAST I HOPE YOU DO.) RATHER, IN TRICK-TAKING CARD GAMES LIKE BRIDGE, SPADES, HEARTS, AND PINOCHLE, A TRICK REFERS TO A SINGLE ROUND OF CARDS.

wands. That would be the Ace of Wands," she added smugly as she laid the card on the table.

Pietro smiled appreciatively. "*Molto bene*, my bearded partner!"

Max-Ernest craned his neck to see the card. He had assumed they were playing poker, but he'd never heard of an Ace of Wands before.

"What...kind...of...cards...are...those?" he asked, interested despite himself.

"Tarot cards," said Mickey. "And what happened to your voice? Used to be nobody could shut you up."

On the counter next to Max-Ernest was an over-sized polka-dot notepad and an oversized candy-striped pen — more circus props. He picked up the pen and tested it on the notepad. (It worked, although it contained pink glitter-glue instead of ink.)

I HAVE LARYNGITIS, he wrote. And on the next line, *YOU MEAN LIKE CARDS FOR FORTUNE-TELLING?* Then he held up the pad for the table to see.

Morrie nodded. "Except when you gamble with them, you're not wasting your money!"

"That's right — you're contributing to the Clown Improvement Society!" said Mickey.

"In Italy, there is a game we play with tarot cards, many hundreds of years old," Pietro explained. "It is called the *Tarocchino*."

"Enough history lessons, old man," said Mickey. "Morrie?" He tapped the table twice, making sure Morrie saw him.

Morrie nodded discreetly. Or sort of discreetly.

"How sad! I'm fresh out of wands," said Morrie, sounding not very sad about it. He held up a card face-out for all to see. "Mr. Magician, I present my trump card...the Magician."

The real-life magician's eyes twinkled as he laid his card on top of Morrie's. "How about a clown for a clown? Or should I say, the Fool to trump a fool?"

"Wait, you can't play the Fool—that's like the Joker," said Mickey, outraged. "You're changing the rules...!"

"I am the only Italian in the room, no? I think I should know the rules. The Fool, he is wild. He trumps all."

Mickey threw the Two of Wands on the table, then pushed the pile of coins toward the magician.

"Cheater!" he grumbled.

A few minutes later, Pietro and Max-Ernest stood outside the trailer. Miserable, Max-Ernest was scribbling furiously with the candy-striped clown pen.

I DID EVERYTHING RIGHT AND SHE DIDN'T EVEN BLINK! SHE JUST KEPT LYING THERE. I

DON'T KNOW WHAT TO DO. THE DOCTORS SAY THE
LONGER SHE STAYS IN A COMA, THE LESS LIKELY
SHE'S EVER GOING TO WAKE UP.

He showed Pietro the pad, then added petu-
lantly: NOT THAT YOU CARE!

Pietro put his hand on Max-Ernest's shoulder. "I
know you are angry with me. You think I should not
be playing cards at a time like this. That I do not love
our Cass enough. But you must understand, the
cards, they were telling us something—"

Max-Ernest looked at him suspiciously.

I THOUGHT YOU WERE JUST PLAYING A GAME.

"That does not mean the cards have lost their
power."

BUT YOU DON'T THINK THEY'RE... Max-Ernest
hesitated before writing the word... MAGIC? YOU
DON'T ACTUALLY BELIEVE PEOPLE CAN SEE INTO
THE FUTURE, DO YOU?

He couldn't believe Pietro, his mentor and hero,
could be so superstitious. Pietro was a professional
magician—well, a retired professional magician—
not a wizard.

Pietro shrugged. "What is the magic? Most
people, they think it is what cannot be explained.
The magicians, we know better. The magic, it is what
has not been explained... yet. Here—"

He reached behind Max-Ernest's left ear and seemed to pull out a coin.

Max-Ernest almost rolled his eyes — it was the oldest trick in the book. But still he observed closely. Pietro rarely did magic tricks anymore, and it was always instructive to watch him.

Pietro closed his fist around the coin. When he opened his hand, there were two coins. He closed and opened his hand once more; and once more there was only one. Rather than lying flat, it stood on its edge — as if to show there was no coin underneath.

"Now, where do you think is the other coin?"

Max-Ernest smiled knowingly.

YOU'RE HOLDING IT BETWEEN THE BACKS OF YOUR FINGERS.

"That is the usual method, yes," admitted the magician.

But when he spread his fingers, there was no coin to be seen.

"This time it is something else."

He turned his hand over, keeping his fingers spread open. The second coin was standing upright on the back of his hand, seemingly perfectly balanced.

He turned his hand sideways and the coin did not move. Neither did the coin that was standing on

his palm. Both coins appeared to be weightless and/
or stuck to his skin.

"What is the trick, do you think?"

TAPE? GLUE?

The magician shook his head. "See for yourself."

He handed a coin to Max-Ernest, showing him
that it was not the slightest bit sticky.

Max-Ernest grunted in frustration. It wasn't in
his nature to be stumped.

"Do not be upset. We do not need always to
know everything right away," said Pietro. "The magician, he wants to understand, of course. How does
the elephant float in the air? What makes the illu-
sion? Is there a mirror or are there strings? OK, fine,
yes. This is the magician's job. But, Max-Ernest, if
you do not feel first the mystery, you do not see the
magic! You are like a musician who can make all the
sounds but does not hear the music.... Now, take
the other coin."

As soon as Pietro handed the second coin to Max-Ernest, it stuck to the first coin. Max-Ernest pulled them apart—they flew back together.

THEY'RE MAGNETS?

The magician nodded, smiling broadly.

Max-Ernest frowned, disgruntled.

ISN'T THAT CHEATING?

Pietro laughed. "You and the clowns with your cheating! It's a magic trick! What is the cheating? There is no cheating in magic, only in poker."

I STILL DON'T SEE WHAT THIS HAS TO DO WITH TAROT CARDS. OR CASS.

"Who knows? Perhaps there is some force field that directs the cards just as the magnetic field swirls around the magnets. Imagine, the people in the ancient world, what they thought the first time they saw the magnetism...."

As he spoke, Pietro took the magnetic coins back from Max-Ernest and made one dance in his palm by manipulating the other coin above the first. "Invisible strings pulling two things together—it is magic, no? The cards, I know they are a sign. Just because I do not understand their secret, that is no reason to ignore their message."

OK, wrote Max-Ernest, not totally convinced.

SO THEN WHAT WERE THE CARDS TELLING US?

The magician looked him in the eye. "Really? You are ready to listen?"

Max-Ernest nodded.

"Very well," said Pietro gravely. "Did you notice how the Ace of Wands, it fell upside down? This, I think, means a wrong must be righted. Or in this case, a stolen item returned."

WHAT STOLEN ITEM?

"Did you not take the Tuning Fork from your principal? What is her name? Mrs. Johnson. This thing, it is bad luck. It wants to be returned to its owner. That is why it will not help you."

IT'S A METAL OBJECT. HOW CAN IT WANT ANYTHING?

"Is a magnet not a metal object? Does it not want to point north? You ask for my advice. This is my advice. Give the Tuning Fork back to your principal."

FINE, I'LL GIVE IT BACK, wrote Max-Ernest, not at all certain he understood. BUT THEN HOW DO WE GET CASS BACK? I NEED THE TUNING FORK TO MAKE THE ANTIDOTE.

"You must get her yourself."

Max-Ernest stared in confusion. YOU MEAN FROM THE PAST? FROM BACK IN HISTORY?

"More or less. You must bring her home from her own head."

BUT HOW??

"You know her head better than anyone. Get inside it."

LIKE MIND READING?

"Yes, if you like to call it that."

Max-Ernest shook his head in disbelief. Pietro had given him many impossible assignments in the past, but this one took the cake.

"Listen, my friend. We both know you do not have the laryngitis."

The magician gently extracted the pen from Max-Ernest's hand and held it aloft as if it were one of his magic wands — or perhaps the Ace of Wands. "Your problem, it is not here" — he pointed the pen at Max-Ernest's throat — "it is here" — he pointed the pen at Max-Ernest's chest. "My heart is heavy, too. But you must be strong. This situation, it is very serious. It is not only Cass's life that is at stake. If she dies, the Secret, it will die, too."

Max-Ernest reached for the pen, but Pietro shook his head and made the pen disappear with another sleight of hand (not easy to do, considering the pen's large size).

"Speak."

Max-Ernest shrugged, resigned to using his voice. "I thought you didn't want anybody to find out the Secret."

"This is true," agreed Pietro. "But the only thing worse than people finding out the Secret, it is that we lose the Secret forever."

Max-Ernest looked at the ground, pondering the magician's words. Like everything about the Secret, they were paradoxical but, he knew, of monumental importance.

"OK, I'll be strong," he said after a moment, in as forceful a voice as he could muster. "And if there's any way to get inside Cass's head, I'll find it."

"Good. But first, return the Tuning Fork!" said Pietro, trying for a light tone he obviously did not feel. "And when this is all over, and our friend Cass is on her feet once more, I will teach you to play the *Tarocchino*."

With that last promise Pietro patted Max-Ernest on the back, then stepped back into the trailer to play another hand.

ALERT LEVEL:
90% CACAO, VERY DARK

A RECENT REPORT FROM ABROAD INDICATES THAT SOME OF THE BOOKS IN THE SECRET SERIES MAY HAVE BEEN TAMPERED WITH BY AGENTS OF THE MIDNIGHT SUN.

UNTIL PROVEN OTHERWISE, YOU SHOULD ASSUME THIS BOOK IS EQUIPPED WITH A DEVICE SUCH AS A RADIO FREQUENCY TRANSCEIVER OR GLOBAL POSITIONING SYSTEM THAT ENABLES THE MIDNIGHT SUN TO TRACK THE BOOK AND ANYBODY WHO HAPPENS TO BE HOLDING IT.

IT IS ALSO POSSIBLE THAT THE BOOK MAY BE TREATED WITH AN INVISIBLE INK OR POWDER DESIGNED TO RUB OFF ON THE READER, IDENTIFYING HIM OR HER AS A PERSON OF INTEREST TO THE MIDNIGHT SUN.

THERE IS NO WAY TO GUARANTEE YOUR SAFETY OR THE SAFETY OF THIS BOOK, BUT HERE ARE A FEW ORDINARY PRECAUTIONS YOU SHOULD TAKE:

☞ **NEVER LEAVE THIS BOOK LYING OUT IN THE OPEN.** (OF COURSE, YOU SHOULDN'T LEAVE IT TELLING THE TRUTH OUT IN THE OPEN, EITHER. THAT WOULD BE EVEN WORSE!)

☞ **IF IT IS NECESSARY TO CARRY THIS BOOK IN PUBLIC, DISGUISE THE BOOK.** THE MOST COMMON

WAY TO DO THIS IS TO BORROW A COVER FROM ANOTHER BOOK OR TO MAKE YOUR OWN COVER OUT OF A BROWN PAPER BAG, BUT I ENCOURAGE YOU TO USE YOUR OWN CRE-ATIVITY. DISGUISES, LIKE ROUTINES, SHOULD BE VARIED AS OFTEN AS POSSIBLE.

☞ **STAY ON THE LOOKOUT FOR ANY WHITE-GLOVE-WEARING STRANGERS AND EVEN—I HATE TO SAY IT—WHITE-GLOVE-WEARING FRIENDS.** REMEMBER, THE MASTERS OF THE MIDNIGHT SUN ARE SMART AND DEVIOUS. THEY MIGHT ADOPT DIS-GUISES THAT MAKE THEIR GLOVES LOOK INNOCUOUS—A BATON-TWIRLER COSTUME, FOR INSTANCE. OR THEY MIGHT WEAR OUTFITS THAT HIDE THEIR GLOVES ALTO-GETHER—LIKE A FULL-BODY MASCOT COSTUME AT A BALL GAME OR THEME PARK. IT IS BEST NOT TO TRUST ANY WALK-ING ALLIGATORS OR PURPLE DINOSAURS UNTIL FURTHER NOTICE.

☞ **DO NOT PANIC.** ANXIETY ATTACKS AND ASSOCIATED MALADIES LIKE DIZZINESS, NAUSEA, HYPERVENTILATION, SKIN RASHES, HIVES, AND INCONTINENCE, WHILE PER-FECTLY UNDERSTANDABLE, ARE NOT AT ALL HELPFUL.

☞ **USE COMMON SENSE.** IF SOMEBODY OFFERS YOU A THOUSAND DOLLARS FOR THIS BOOK, CHANCES ARE THEIR MOTIVES ARE NOT PURE. THEN AGAIN, A THOUSAND DOL-LARS IS A LOT OF MONEY. TAKE THE MONEY AND RUN.

☞ **IN THE UNFORTUNATE EVENT THAT YOU FIND YOURSELF CORNERED BY A MEMBER OF THE MIDNIGHT SUN, PICK YOUR NOSE.** REALLY. MOST MEMBERS OF THE MIDNIGHT SUN ARE VERY FASTIDIOUS. THE SIGHT OF SOMETHING SO DISGUSTING WILL LIKELY CAUSE THEM TO BACK AWAY IN HORROR, GIVING YOU A CHANCE TO ESCAPE. IF THAT DOESN'T WORK, YOU MIGHT

TRY TELLING THEM THEY HAVE SOMETHING STUCK IN THEIR
TEETH. MIDNIGHT SUN MEMBERS ARE EXTREMELY VAIN
AND THE THOUGHT OF SOMETHING DIRTYING THEIR
PEARLY WHITES SHOULD SEND THEM RUNNING TO THE
NEAREST MIRROR.

☞ **LASTLY, I AM AWARE THAT CERTAIN TEACHERS
AND LIBRARIANS AND EVEN SOME VERY IRRE-
SPONSIBLE PARENTS HAVE ON OCCASION
READ ONE OR MORE OF MY BOOKS ALOUD TO
ONE OR MORE CHILDREN.** IT GOES WITHOUT SAY-
ING THAT I HIGHLY DISAPPROVE OF THIS APPROACH. THE
ONLY THING WORSE THAN PEOPLE READING ONE OF MY
BOOKS TO THEMSELVES IS PEOPLE SHARING IT WITH OTH-
ERS. BE THAT AS IT MAY, I SUSPECT THAT ANY PLEADING ON
MY PART WOULD HAVE LITTLE EFFECT ON THE SITUATION;
THOSE RECKLESS READ-ALOUDERS WOULD ONLY READ
ALOUD LOUDER. PERHAPS, HOWEVER, A SUGGESTION OR
TWO WOULD NOT BE INAPPROPRIATE. IN THE EVENT THAT
YOU OR SOMEBODY YOU KNOW SIMPLY MUST READ THIS
BOOK ALOUD, PLEASE MAKE SURE THE BLINDS ARE CLOSED,
ANY RECORDING DEVICES ARE TURNED OFF, AND OF
COURSE THAT THERE IS PLENTY OF CHOCOLATE AVAILABLE
FOR EVERYONE.

THANK YOU,

P.B.

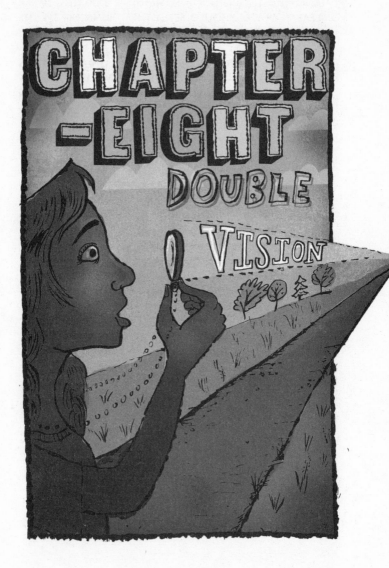

The Double Monocle gave her a headache.

Cass wasn't sure what she'd expected — to see all those ghosts the Seer was talking about? — but all she got was the dizzying experience of seeing double through a single eye.

Holding the monocle tight, she turned in a circle, surveying the world around her. As one object exited her vision and another took its place, the first object — a pitchfork, a donkey, a bale of hay — seemed to leave an afterimage. Like when you wave your hand through the air and it appears to leave a trail in its wake. A curious effect but hardly paranormal.

This is just double vision, she thought. Not second sight.

But when she put down the monocle, she noticed something rather surprising. Some of the things she'd been looking at were much farther away than they'd appeared through the monocle. To the naked eye, they were mere specks in the distance. She looked into the monocle again and confirmed that, yes, it functioned like an exceptionally powerful pair of binoculars.

As she moved the monocle away from her eye and then back again, she noticed something else: some things she was seeing through the monocle weren't visible at all otherwise. They were blocked by walls, by animals, by people. With the monocle she could see almost everything around her, no matter how far away or how covered up. Maybe not as exciting as seeing spirits, but to Cass thrilling nonetheless. And more useful.

Certainly, it would make finding someone much easier.

She turned in the direction in which she'd last seen the Jester. The crowd had not yet fully dispersed. With the monocle, she could see through the throngs of people at the market and yet she still could not see him. The box he'd been standing on was bare.

A quick glance around through the monocle was sufficient to confirm the bad news: he was gone.

Despair threatened to overtake her, but she stifled it with an act of will. She had been in plenty of situations more difficult than this, she reminded herself.

Of course, in most of those situations, Max-Ernest had been with her. More often than not she complained that he was just getting in the way, but now that he wasn't by her side, she suddenly felt helpless. She depended on his logical mind to solve puzzles and crack codes.

If he were here with her, what would he say that would help her find the Jester?

Well, what do we know about the Jester? she imagined Max-Ernest asking.

Dutifully, she started making a list in her head:

1. The Jester was the founder of the Terces Society.
2. He liked to rhyme and tell jokes.
3. He wore a silly hat with bells.
4. He worked for the King (if you could call being a jester *work*).
5. He had pointy ears like hers and he was her great-great-great- (she wasn't certain how many *great*s) grandfather.
6. He lived in a tent.
7. He knew the Secret.

Most of these things Cass knew from talking to her friend, the late great homunculus, Mr. Cabbage Face. Being five hundred years old, he'd known the Jester personally. He also was only two feet tall (or nearly) and born in a bottle, but that's another story — a story told in "The Legend of Cabbage Face."*

---

*IF YOU HAVE NOT READ "THE LEGEND OF CABBAGE FACE," YOU CAN FIND IT IN MY SECOND BOOK, *IF YOU'RE READING THIS, IT'S TOO LATE*. ONE WORD OF CAUTION: AS MR. WALLACE, THE TERCES SOCIETY ARCHIVIST, POINTS OUT IN THE BOOK, "THE LEGEND OF CABBAGE FACE" WAS WRITTEN BY SOMEONE WITH *LITERARY ASPIRATIONS*. THAT IS TO SAY, HE MAY HAVE TAKEN *LITERARY LICENSE*, EMBELLISHING FACTS OR PERHAPS EVEN MAKING UP THINGS ALTOGETHER. YOU SHOULD READ IT WITH A GRAIN OF SALT — IN OTHER WORDS, AS YOU SHOULD ANY SHORT STORY OR NOVEL (EXCEPTING THIS ONE!).

On the list, Number 4, *He worked for the King*, and Number 6, *He lived in a tent*, seemed to be the only items of information that might help at the moment.

The King, Cass assumed, lived not in a tent but in a palace or castle. (What was the difference, anyway?)* This palace or castle, Cass could hear Max-Ernest saying, would be the logical first place to look for the Jester. If the Jester wasn't there, she might find him in his tent nearby.

So the question was: where was the palace? (She dropped the words *or castle* for the sake of brevity. And because Max-Ernest wasn't really listening to her thoughts — not that she was aware of, anyway.) Being invisible, she couldn't very well ask for directions.

There were no signs, unfortunately. The market might have looked like a Renaissance faire, but there were no helpful markers stuck in the ground with arrows pointing one way to the King's palace, the other way to Ye Olde Pizza Stand.

Which way had she come from? That would be a place to start. Since she hadn't seen a palace on her way into town, maybe she should try the opposite direction?

---

*THE DIFFERENCE, AS MAX-ERNEST WOULD HAVE TOLD HER, IS THAT A PALACE IS A LUXURY RESIDENCE, DESIGNED TO COMFORT ROYALTY AND TO IMPRESS VISITORS; A CASTLE IS A FORTIFIED STRUCTURE BUILT TO WITHSTAND ENEMY ATTACK.

Before she could start retracing her steps, a trumpet sounded.

"Make way! Make way! The Duke is on parade and he brings gifts for the King!"

All at once the crowd of people in the market divided in two. Some grumbled in annoyance, others chattered with excitement, but everyone stepped aside as if there were no option but to obey.

A moment later, a long procession started passing through.

Cass surveyed the participants through the Double Monocle. First came a series of soldiers on foot—*footmen*, she presumed, unless the word had a more specific meaning? They held curving swords and wore puffy pants—*knickers*, Cass wanted to call them—that ended at the knee.

Then there were the knights on horseback. They were in full armor and gleamed in the sun. Long swords and longer javelins hung at their sides, ready and waiting for the next joust.

"Whoa, boy!" "Tally-ho!" they shouted to their horses.

Also on horseback were several finely dressed men and women who would simply be called *lords* and *ladies* in a Renaissance faire, but who in actuality, Cass figured, had more specific names and titles.

They did not call out to the crowd but rather chattered and gossiped among themselves, teasing one another and cooling themselves with fans, their stiff ruffled collars moving only slightly in the breeze.

Who were they? The Duke's family? Princes and princesses? Watching them pass by was like looking into a history book without being able to read the text. The images meant nothing without captions explaining them.

In the very middle of the procession was a large wooden chest studded with brass on all sides and held aloft by four muscle-bound soldiers. They grunted with effort and counted rhythmically— "one two three four, one two three four" —to synchronize their steps.

Around Cass, peasants grumbled at the sight of the chest:

"Gifts for the King, he says? More like duty for the King."

"'Tis not a gift if you demand it!"

"Ah, don't shed a tear for the Duke! He can afford it."

"'Course he can—he takes all our profits!"

I wonder what's inside that chest, Cass thought, edging closer to the procession. She examined the chest through the monocle. There was something about the lock—it was large and ornate and resembled a coat of arms—that told her more than simply money lay inside. In any case, the chest was headed for the King. So she would follow it to the palace. And, with any luck, to the Jester.

Her invisibility gave her great freedom of movement, and she was about to fall into place behind the last footman when a funny thing happened in front of her: a head—a man's head, to be more precise—peeked out of a barrel of onions that sat, seemingly abandoned, at the edge of the market.

Surprised—and momentarily overwhelmed by the scent of onions—Cass exhaled loudly.

The man wheeled around and looked straight in her direction. He was wearing a black mask over the top half of his face while the bottom half was covered by some rather angry-looking whiskers. He held a large axe in his hand. Were it not for the sticks of hay and assorted onion skins sticking out of his hair, he would have looked very sinister.

Cass tried not to flinch, reminding herself he couldn't see her.

Frowning, the masked man turned back and quietly stepped out of the barrel. He gestured silently to his right and Cass saw another man step out of a sack of potatoes. Still another man stepped out from behind an apple cart.

Afraid to make a noise, Cass watched, transfixed. It was clear that these three men were about to embark on some kind of illicit, probably criminal activity—but what activity in particular, she had no idea.

Suddenly the sound of a galloping horse drowned out all the other noise in the market.

Looking over her shoulder, Cass saw another masked figure thundering toward her on a tall black steed. The horse's neck was bent low, his long black mane flying in the wind. Matching the horse's posture, the rider was also bent forward, long dark hair flying. Around them, carts overturned, cages sprung open, people scattered, but horse and rider seemed to occupy their own universe, so fast-moving that in comparison, the rest of the market seemed to exist in slow motion. And yet with her monocle, Cass could see every inch of horse and rider as if time had stopped altogether.

The horse came closer—a living cyclone of clattering hooves, flared nostrils, and gleaming muscles—and for a brief second Cass caught a glimpse of the masked rider. It was a woman, a beautiful woman, her lips pursed in concentration.

"Anastasia…! Anastasia…!" The name rippled through the crowd, repeated like an incantation.

A moment later, the horse was hurtling toward the procession.

It all happened so fast, nobody seemed to know where to turn. There were screams and shouts and commotion. Soldiers waving swords. Horses spinning in circles. Ladies (and even a lord or two) fainting in fright.

Within seconds, the big wooden chest was on the ground. The bewhiskered bandit, a few onion skins still stuck to his hair, dropped his heavy axe down on the lid of the chest, breaking the big brass lock. The soldiers who'd been carrying the chest watched helplessly, their hands tied behind their backs.

Quickly and deftly, the masked woman — Anastasia — tossed ruby rings and emerald necklaces, silver goblets and golden candlesticks, to each of her masked cohorts in turn. Now on horseback themselves, they caught the glittering booty with outstretched hands, then urged their horses away from the market, in the direction of the neighboring woods.

"What's this—?" Her axe-wielding companion opened a small wooden box and held up a jagged black rock. The rock was about the size of a cantaloupe and had thin veins of gold running through it.

"It is ugly, but it must be very valuable," said Anastasia, ripping open a heavy bag and finding it full of gold coins. "Otherwise the Duke would not dare send it to the King."

As she spoke, coins started flying out of the bag and landing on the mysterious rock. Reins, spurs, chains, every bit of metal in the vicinity seemed to be drawn to it. Soon the rock was covered with a small mountain of metal.

Cass watched from the crowd. Through the lenses of the Double Monocle, the rock had a unique bluish glow. It seemed almost to pulsate. Was she imagining it, or could she feel the monocle being tugged in the rock's direction?

Anastasia stared at the rock. "I have never seen the like...."

Experimentally, her bandit colleague brushed away coins, making a clear patch. He brought his axe close to the rock — it stuck to the rock with a clang.

"What power!" he said, pulling them apart. "It is the stone of a sorcerer — do you think it is cursed?"

"Nonsense. There is a much simpler explanation, I am sure," said Anastasia. "Put it away, Thomas — there will be time to play later. Take the chest with you. It's nearly empty now."

Eyeing the rock with more than a hint of nervousness, the masked man — Thomas — carefully placed it inside his rucksack. Then he strapped the big wooden chest onto the back of the nearest horse, jumped on, and galloped away.

Meanwhile, Anastasia had raised another bag of coins above her head.

"And now I give back to the people what is theirs!" She spun the bag around with a flourish, raining gold coins on the cheering crowd.

"Anastasia...! Hooray for Anastasia...!" they chanted.

Her horse reared, tossing his thick black mane in the air so that it was backlit by the sun. As she brought her horse down onto four legs, the mysteriously generous thief tossed her own black mane in similar fashion. Then she, too, galloped away, following her bandit comrades into the woods.

Cass watched wistfully through the Double Monocle. She felt an unexpected yearning to follow after this daring woman and her band of thieves. But her job lay elsewhere.

With a sigh, she lowered the monocle. She turned back toward the procession — or what remained of the procession after the robbers had done their work — and prepared to follow it to the palace.

Hear Ye! Hear Ye!

All lads and lasses of the
Xyyyy School are hereby summoned to
Her Majesty's court at the
Renaissance Faire on Friday, October 10.

Be there, or a pox be upon you!
Prize for best costume will be awarded by
Queen Elizabeth herself.

School Field Trip sponsored by Medieval Days Family Restaurants.

Eat, Drink, and Be Medieval!

The yellow flyer showed a picture of a pair of knights jousting on horseback.

Max-Ernest shook his head. "Why doesn't anybody ever know the difference between Renaissance and medieval?" he muttered to himself. "They're almost exact opposites—"

The Xxxxx School visited the Renaissance Faire every fall; it was the first big event of the season, coming about a month after the start of school.

Usually Max-Ernest was excited for Ren-Faire. He'd never worn a costume, but he always found something to be interested in: whether it be solving obscure Renaissance riddles or distinguishing between English and Italian styles of armor. This year, he couldn't have been less interested in the annual field trip. As far as he was concerned, with Cass's life on the line, it was no time for merriment. And if he absolutely had to take a trip to the Renaissance, he would have preferred that it be to the real Renaissance—so he could retrieve Cass in person. That is, assuming she'd made it all the way back to the Jester's time and hadn't gotten stuck at her mother's high school prom.

Anything, however, would have been preferable to the trip he was currently embarked on.

It was the first day of school, and Max-Ernest was standing still in the hallway, stalling, while chattering students strode past him. Eventually he tore himself away from the bulletin board and stepped nervously into the administration office.

Behind the counter was a woman he didn't recognize. She was chewing gum—against school rules, Max-Ernest noted silently—and painting her fingernails.

"Hi," he said, his voice louder than intended. "I'm—"

"Max-Ernest, I know — Mrs. Johnson is waiting for you," said the woman in a nasally New York accent, not looking up.

"Oh. Um, who are you?"

"New school secretary," she said, popping a bubble. "Name is Opal. Like the rock." The secretary dangled her hand in front of Max-Ernest, showing off a gold ring inset with a milky, iridescent stone.

"Er, nice to meet you . . . ?"

"Likewise, I'm sure." She pronounced it *shoo-ah*.

Max-Ernest didn't know what to think of the new secretary. Even sitting down, Opal was very tall, and she had a big head of blond curly hair that made her look even taller. Her hands were exceptionally large, and her face wore a seemingly permanent smirk punctuated by a sizable mole on her right cheek. All in all, not a very reassuring presence.

"You sure she's not too busy?" Max-Ernest asked hopefully. "I'm sure there's a ton of stuff she needs to do. Maybe I should come back tomorrow. Yeah, that's a good idea — how 'bout that?"

"Sorry, Max-Ernest. No such luck."

Was it his imagination or was she stifling a laugh?

Max-Ernest took a tentative step in the direction

of the principal's door. The last time he'd seen Mrs. Johnson she had told him she never wanted to see him again. And for good reason. He and Cass and Yo-Yoji had stolen Mrs. Johnson's family heirloom, the Tuning Fork, and blackmailed her to boot. (It all had been for the noble purpose of saving Cass's mother's life, but that certainly didn't matter to Mrs. Johnson.) He would be lucky to leave her office with a semester's worth of detention; expulsion was more likely.

"She said not to knock," Opal added brightly. "Just walk right in."

Max-Ernest nodded weakly. His throat felt dry, his palms sweaty. Finally, he steeled himself and turned the doorknob.

"Max-Ernest, for shame! Didn't anyone ever teach you to knock?"

"Uh, sorry... Mrs. Johnson," Max-Ernest stammered, silently cursing the new secretary. It appeared that she had set him up.

"*We* will be most satisfied if you address us as Your Majesty, please," said Mrs. Johnson in an exaggerated English accent. "Well, don't just stand there, come in."

Max-Ernest couldn't help gaping. He almost

didn't recognize the woman standing in front of a full-length mirror. In place of her usual polyester pantsuit and matching hat she was wearing a long velvet gown and a rhinestone tiara. A black stone pendant on a black velvet ribbon hung around her neck; it was shaped like an inverted eye and polished to a glossy sheen.

"I, or rather *we*, will be Queen Elizabeth this year at the Renaissance Faire. And as you see, you have interrupted us in our royal chambers. Normally, the punishment for such an offense would be death."

"Sorry, Mrs.... I mean, Your Majesty."

"Much better. So, tell me what you think of the dress. Too plain? Too gaudy? It has only just arrived from the tailor."

"Um..." Max-Ernest looked down, unsure how to answer the question.

When he looked up, he gasped out loud. The pendant she was wearing appeared to be floating in the air.

"It's a magnet," said Mrs. Johnson, following Max-Ernest's eyes.

Oh, that explained it. Sort of.

The magnet was pointing directly at him. Or rather at the Tuning Fork in his pocket, he thought.

"A very *strong* magnet," she added. "It attracts

and absorbs all negative energies. It has transformed my, I mean, *our* life."

She patted the pendant and it settled back against her chest.

"You see, something terribly important has happened to us. We have received a message from... ourselves."

Before Max-Ernest could ask what that meant or declare that it made no sense or even ask just what message she had received, she continued: "And we went on a journey to a land far, far away. We call it the *I —*."

Max-Ernest didn't think he'd heard her correctly. "The *I love me?*"

"Well, there is that play on words, yes. But what we said was: the *Isle of Me*. The island of pure self that lies within us all...And what sent us on this trip from us to us, you ask?" She paused for emphasis. "The answer is: *you*. You and your friends."

"Me...er, us?"

Mrs. Johnson nodded. "In your own way, you've done me a favor."

Carefully adjusting her dress, she sat down behind her desk, a principal once more.

"After you took the Tuning Fork, I went through

a kind of withdrawal and I realized that the Fork had been ruling me — that I wasn't the master of my own isle, so to speak," she explained, dropping the royal "we" and the English accent at the same time. "It was time to put the *I* back in *me*."

"You mean the letter *I*? There is no *I* in *me*," said Max-Ernest, who was struggling valiantly to follow along. "Or do you mean put *the E-Y-E back in me?*" he asked, looking at the eye-shaped pendant hanging from her neck.

"Whichever. Both. I was speaking figuratively," said Mrs. Johnson impatiently. "Somehow, I knew the Tuning Fork would come back to me. And I wanted to be ready when it did. 'What force could protect me?' I asked *I*. What would draw the Tuning Fork away from me even as I was drawn to the Tuning Fork? And do you know what *I* told me was the answer to my problems?"

"A magnet?" Max-Ernest guessed, taking a seat opposite the principal. It was indisputably odd that the subject of magnets would be brought up by both Pietro and Mrs. Johnson in the space of two days, but Max-Ernest had a hunch this was the answer she was looking for.

"Very good." Mrs. Johnson looked impressed

and at the same time slightly disappointed, as if she'd been hoping to provide the answer herself.

"Naturally, being the principal of a magnet school, I had considered the significance of magnets before. But I had never considered they might have a personal application," Mrs. Johnson continued.* "And lo and behold, what should I find in my attic? In a box of things that belonged to my Great-Great-Great-Aunt Clara? The same woman to whom the Tuning Fork belonged, incidentally? The one everybody says was a witch?"

"The magnet?"

"That's right—the very magnet I am wearing around my neck."

She held up the pendant for Max-Ernest's inspection. At close range, it seemed to be some sort of black stone with a thin vein of gold running through it.

"I have decided no longer to be ashamed of my ancestor but to embrace her memory," continued Mrs. Johnson. "It may be there is much to learn from her so-called witchcraft.... Now, I cannot wait any

*OOPS. I BELIEVE I JUST LET SLIP THAT OUR HEROES' SCHOOL WAS A MAGNET SCHOOL. OR RATHER, MRS. JOHNSON DID. OH WELL. TOO LATE. THAT PARTICULAR CAT IS OUT OF THE PROVERBIAL BAG....

YOU PROBABLY KNOW WHAT A MAGNET SCHOOL IS. PERHAPS YOU ATTEND ONE YOURSELF? A MAGNET SCHOOL IS DESIGNED TO ATTRACT STUDENTS FROM ALL OVER A SCHOOL DISTRICT WHO MIGHT NOT OTHERWISE GO TO SCHOOL TOGETHER; THIS IS WHAT IS KNOWN AS *DIVERSITY*. TO ACHIEVE THIS GOAL, MOST MAGNET SCHOOLS SPECIALIZE IN A CERTAIN SUBJECT. BUT OUR HEROES' SCHOOL WASN'T AN ART MAGNET OR A SCIENCE MAGNET OR A SPORTS MAGNET. IT WAS JUST A MAGNET—OR AS

longer. Do you have the Tuning Fork? I take it that's why you wanted to see me."

She looked anxiously at him, craning her neck, inspecting his pockets for bulges, trying to peek into his schoolbag.

"Yeah, it's right here, Mrs. Johnson."

This time she didn't bother to correct him on the name.

As soon as Max-Ernest brought out the Tuning Fork, Mrs. Johnson's eyes were drawn to it — as if her eyes were magnets themselves.

The pendant around her neck was floating again, straining against the chain. Max-Ernest, meanwhile, felt an invisible force pulling him toward the principal.

"You see its power —?" She gasped.

Tearing her gaze away from the Tuning Fork, she stood up and walked around her desk to Max-Ernest. "We will make a circuit, you and I," she said, grasping him by the hand and pulling him out of his seat. "We will draw out all the negative energy and create a positive flow."

MAX-ERNEST CALLED IT, A *MAGNET* MAGNET. FOR YEARS, MRS. JOHNSON HAD BEEN TRYING TO COME UP WITH A MORE SPECIFIC MISSION FOR THE SCHOOL. AS THE PRINCIPAL WITH PRINCIPLES, HER FAVORITE IDEA WAS THAT THE SCHOOL BE A MANNERS MAGNET. BUT THE STUDENTS DISLIKED THIS IDEA SO MUCH THAT THEY REBELLED WITH A "MANNERS BOYCOTT." YOU CAN IMAGINE WHAT THAT WAS LIKE. IT QUICKLY BECAME KNOWN AS THE REVOLTING REVOLT BECAUSE OF ALL THE BURPING, NOSE PICKING, MOUTH-FULL-OF-FOOD OPENING, AND, I'M SORRY TO REPORT, FARTING. MRS. JOHNSON GAVE IN VERY QUICKLY.

Positive or negative, all Max-Ernest could think about was that he and the principal were holding hands. *Holding hands!* He gritted his teeth and prepared to wait it out.

At least it looked like he wouldn't be expelled.

ack on your feet, gents! Do not tarry, m'ladies."

The knights and the footmen, the lords and the ladies, and the entire procession reassembled relatively quickly, albeit grumblingly, after the robbery — rather as if it all had happened before. Cass got the sense that the masked woman and her band of thieves regularly set upon travelers in the area — like bandits who staked out stagecoach routes in the Old West.

Miraculously, nobody appeared to have been hurt in the fracas.

Cass slipped in among the last of the footmen and was soon following the procession down the road in the direction, she hoped, of the King's palace — and of the Jester himself.

The trip took hours and the procession became increasingly bedraggled. Sweat trickled down noses and made shirts stick to backs. Mud splattered breeches and filled soldiers' boots. Humans and animals alike complained of aches and pains, thirst and hunger. Despite her ghostly state, even Cass was beginning to feel the toll.

Eventually, however, the bumpy road gave way to smooth stone, and the wild countryside was replaced by carefully tended gardens. A matching formality overtook the procession. Backs stiffened, soldiers fell into stride with each other, flags were held erect. The lords and ladies or whoever they were in the finer clothing stopped and primped themselves.

Even before she saw it, Cass knew they were nearing the palace.

While the palace was not a white and sparkling fairy-tale castle on a hill, nor an austere fortress with a moat and a drawbridge, it was nonetheless grand, and certainly it was very impressive to Cass. A vast red-brick edifice, it stretched out on either side the length of several city blocks and boasted row after row of white-framed windows that blinked in the flickering sunlight like hundreds of eyes on an enormous face.

After the procession had passed through the palace's outer gates and into its expansive grounds, some of the soldiers and footmen peeled away, presumably heading for their barracks, while others escorted the more important travelers toward the twin towers that buttressed the palace's arched front entrance.

Cass shivered, reminding herself that she had nothing to be afraid of — except failing her mission. She peered through the Double Monocle into the courtyard that lay beyond the entrance. A group of dignitaries waited. Could the Jester be among them?

Woof woof! Ruff ruff! Bow wow! Yap yap! Grrrrrrrrr... *

Cass was about to follow the others past the lines of royal guards and into the palace's interior courtyard when she was suddenly descended upon by a dozen barking beagles. The beagles nipped angrily at her heels, somehow sensing that the invisible girl was an interloper, unwelcome on royal grounds.**

A tired-looking man in leather breeches — their trainer, Cass guessed — trotted up to the beagles.

"Terrence? Bailey? Hunter? What are you little gits up to? Found a groundhog, have you? Or another partridge fallen?" he asked solicitously, almost as if the dogs were his master and not the other way around. "No need to fight over the spoils. Plenty of delicious treats waiting for you in the kennels! Come on now, quit your barking."

To the trainer and anyone else around, it must have looked very odd — the beagles circling for no apparent reason, pawing at the air. Her invisibility

*I'M AFRAID I'M NOT SURE WHICH OF THESE DOG SOUNDS IS EXACTLY RIGHT. YOU WILL HAVE TO CHOOSE THE ONE YOU LIKE BEST. WHILE IT IS DIFFICULT TO RE-CREATE DIALOGUE THAT TOOK PLACE HUNDREDS OF YEARS AGO, IT IS PERHAPS MORE DIFFICULT TO RE-CREATE THE SPEECH OF ANIMALS... FROM ANY ERA. DID YOU KNOW THAT IN ALMOST EVERY LANGUAGE, A DOG'S BARK IS WRITTEN DIFFERENTLY? IN AFRIKAANS, FOR EXAMPLE, A BARK IS A *BLAF*; IN ESPERANTO, IT'S A *VOJ*; AND IN SWEDISH, IT'S A *VOFF*.

**I CALL THESE DOGS *BEAGLES* BECAUSE OF EASE OF FAMILIARITY. IN POINT OF FACT, HOWEVER, THEY WERE *TALBOT HOUNDS*, A PREDECESSOR OF THE MODERN BEAGLE.

had protected her until now; Cass didn't want to press her luck. Desperate, she tried to shoo the dogs away from her—a difficult task to perform without making any noise.

Fortunately, the trainer was able to coax them away with a few treats he happened to be carrying in his satchel.

Unfortunately, by the time all the dogs had been rounded up, the procession had disappeared and the gate was clanging shut. Cass had missed her chance to get into the palace.

Trying not to be discouraged, she started walking the perimeter of the royal residence.

Where would she find the Jester? Did he have regular work hours or did he come and go as he pleased? (She imagined being a jester was something like being a stand-up comedian, but more mobile—like being a walking comedian.) She remembered a red-and-white-striped tent. Did he pitch his tent on royal grounds or did he hide it out in the woods somewhere?

Being invisible, she figured it wouldn't be too much of a risk to climb through an open window, but it was chilly out, and every window she saw was shut. She was, however, able to look inside a few windows where curtains were not drawn, and she saw some of the palace rooms. Cass knew that some people, like her antiques-collecting grandfathers, would have given their right arms to see the furnishings inside, but to her, all the rooms looked the same: filled with uncomfortable-looking chairs and gold-framed paintings that were either dark and scary or silly and heaven-ish. Nowhere did she see a wiry man wearing a three-pointed hat with bells.

After turning a corner, she noticed a stairwell on the side of the building. Walking down the short flight of steps, she found a small iron door — the first door she'd come across since the front entrance. She tried the handle. It was locked.

As she turned away, the door opened, nearly pushing her to the ground.

"Ow!" she exclaimed, the sound obscured by the clanging of chains.

Recovering from the blow, Cass turned to see a uniformed soldier dragging a small creature out the door — a monkey, Cass assumed at first glance.

A scowling man in a dark cloak presided from the doorway. "Let him sleep in the kennels. If he will not speak, he is no better than a dog!"

The cloaked man spit on the creature's back and then slammed the door before Cass could slip inside.

Dismayed, she looked down at the whimpering creature at her feet.

"Come on, you heard your master," said the soldier, tugging on his collar. "It's the kennels for you."

The creature had exceptionally large eyes, and to Cass's shock she found they were staring directly at her. He could see her! But the greater shock was that she knew those eyes very well....

"Mr. Cabbage Face!" she cried out before thinking better of it.

The creature looked at her oddly, as if he didn't quite understand.

But she was certain of it: although he was even shorter (if that was possible) than when she'd last seen him, and although there were fewer folds in his leathery skin, the creature in front of her was none other than a younger incarnation of her long-lost old friend, the homunculus. She would recognize him anywhere, she thought: the huge hands (for grabbing fistfuls of meat), the huge nose (for sniffing out roasts and sweets), the little torso with the big belly (for filling with meal after meal). The homunculus was literally one of a kind. The reason he could see her, she suspected, was that he was not entirely mortal.

The soldier drew his sword. "Who's there?"

How awful to see her friend in chains! How was

she going to free him? That was all she could think of.

Cass put her finger to her lips. The homunculus nodded slightly. He wouldn't give her away.

Shrugging his shoulders, the soldier sheathed his sword. "Guess it's that blasted ringing in my ears again...."

He gave the homunculus a tug. "Let's go, dog."

The homunculus grunted in complaint but started shuffling after him, chancing only a quick backward glance at Cass.

What is the homunculus doing at the palace? she wondered, silently following. And why is he being dragged to the kennels?

Then she remembered "The Legend of Cabbage Face."

In the story, the homunculus's creator, Lord Pharaoh, brings the homunculus to an audience with the King. When the homunculus won't perform on command, Lord Pharaoh grows angry and punishes him by sending him outside to sleep in the mud with the hogs.

Was it possible she was witnessing in real life the events she'd previously only read about?

In that case, Cass realized with a chill, the cloaked man she saw in the doorway must have been the dreaded Lord Pharaoh — the brilliant but evil alchemist who was not only the father of the homunculus but also the founder of the Midnight Sun!*

As for the hogs, the writer of the story had obviously gotten that part wrong.

Not *hogs*, she thought.

Dogs.**

*LORD PHARAOH, OF COURSE, WAS NEITHER LORD NOR PHARAOH BUT RATHER A SWISS DOCTOR WHO HAD RENAMED HIMSELF ONCE HE BECAME A MASTER ALCHEMIST. ABOUT LORD PHARAOH'S NAME, YOU MAY RECALL THAT MAX-ERNEST ONCE ASKED, "ISN'T THAT REDUNDANT? LIKE *KING KING*?" FUNNY, ISN'T IT? — GIVEN THE WAY MAX-ERNEST SEEMS TO REPEAT HIMSELF SO OFTEN.

**IT'S WORTH NOTING THAT IN HIS OLD AGE, THE HOMUNCULUS HIMSELF CLAIMED TO HAVE DINED WITH THE KING'S *HOGS* (AS OPPOSED TO *DOGS*). I THINK THIS FAILURE OF MEMORY ON HIS PART CAN BEST BE ASCRIBED TO THE PHENOMENON KNOWN AS "BELIEVING YOUR OWN PRESS." SOMEWHERE ALONG THE LINE, HE MUST HAVE READ "THE LEGEND OF CABBAGE FACE" AND ACCEPTED THE LITERARY VERSION OF HIS LIFE AS THE TRUTH.

t was lunchtime, and Max-Ernest was still pre-occupied with his bizarre encounter with Mrs. Johnson in her Renaissance Faire costume. What a powerful magnet that must have been to float like that, he thought. He had to admit Pietro was right. To someone who didn't know about magnetism, it would look like magic.

Automatically, he headed for his regular lunch spot: the Nuts Table.

Only as he was sitting down at his usual seat did he become aware that he was about to commit that capital schoolyard crime: having lunch alone.

He stared at the empty seats around him: Cass's directly across the table and Yo-Yoji's to his right. For years he hadn't thought twice about eating by himself. But now that he'd experienced the pleasure of having friends to eat with, lunch didn't seem like lunch without them.

What to do?

He wasn't very hungry, and in any case he hadn't taken a lunch with him to school that day. (In past years, he'd always had two lunches: one packed by his mother, one by his father. Lately, neither parent seemed to remember he might sometimes need to eat.) The only thing he had with him as far as food goes was a single chocolate bar — and that had to last until he got home. Besides, it had been in his pants pocket and was almost certainly melted. He needed to put it someplace cool and let it harden again.

Should he get up? He would look pretty silly, considering he'd just sat down. Besides, he had nowhere to go. At least not until after school.

He glanced down at the blue plastic surface of the Nuts Table as if his instructions might be written on it; and in fact there was plenty of graffiti etched into the plastic, but nothing helpful (or even repeatable).

Max-Ernest, it is fair to say, was at a loss.

I'm lonely, he thought with a sense of discovery.

I feel bad.

In an odd way, that felt good.

Usually, being bad at feelings, Max-Ernest didn't *feel bad*, he *felt badly* (the same way he threw badly, although Yo-Yoji had helped a little with that). But today, you could say, he was feeling bad *well*. That is not to say he was feeling well, exactly, but rather that he was doing a good job of feeling bad.

He was so pleased with this formulation that he almost repeated it aloud, but — sadly — there was no one to hear it.

The two other kids at the Nuts Table, Daniel-not-Danielle and Glob, didn't count. For one thing, they were sitting at the far end of the table and he would have had to shout. For another, they hadn't so much as said hello to him. (Then again, Max-Ernest hadn't said hello, either. Hello wasn't really done at the Nuts Table.)

Daniel-not-Danielle was a soft-spoken caramel-skinned boy with exceptionally long dreadlocks that he refused to cut, despite the fact that they were always covering his face. Although he would have preferred to call himself by his given name, Daniel, he'd had to correct the pronunciation so many times that the correction itself became his name.

Glob was a pimply and very pale-skinned boy who was even lower on the school pecking order but who enjoyed an inordinate degree of power in the "convenience food" industry. His junk food–reviewing website — The Glob Blog — was read by thousands of fast-food fans, and his opinions, it was said, could make or break a product in its first week.

Max-Ernest knew them as he knew everyone at the Nuts Table, but he didn't *know* know them. That is, he wasn't friends with them. On the other hand, he wasn't enemies with them, either.*

---

*THE ONE TIME HE'D SPOKEN TO GLOB, MAX-ERNEST HAD MENTIONED THAT *GLOB* AND *BLOG* WERE ANAGRAMS. "THEY HAVE ALL THE SAME LETTERS. LIKE WHEN YOU TRY TO FIND WORDS IN SCRABBLE OR BOGGLE. ACTUALLY, COME TO THINK OF IT, BOTH WORDS ARE CONTAINED IN THE NAME *BOGGLE*. HOW 'BOUT THAT?" HE'D MEANT THE COMMENT TO BE COMPLIMENTARY, BUT GLOB HAD TAKEN OFFENSE. "SO WHAT! GLOB BLOG IS STILL MINE. I CAME UP WITH IT MYSELF. I'VE NEVER EVEN PLAYED THAT," SAID GLOB, AS IF MAX-ERNEST HAD IMPLIED THAT GLOB HAD STOLEN THE NAME OF HIS BLOG FROM A GAME OF BOGGLE.

As an experiment, Max-Ernest moved several seats closer to the two boys in question. They didn't welcome him, nor did they protest.

He took this as a positive sign.

"I thought he was an aristocrat, like a lord or a count or something—from England," Daniel-not-Danielle was saying in a voice just barely above a whisper. "But then I heard he was an ex-convict who just got out of juvenile hall because of DNA evidence!"

At first, hearing the words *lord* and *count*, Max-Ernest assumed they were talking about what everyone at school was talking about: the Renaissance Faire. But as he listened in on Glob and Daniel-not-Danielle, he realized their topic was something else altogether: apparently, their school had been graced with the presence of an important new luminary.

"He's neither. He's a child actor," said Glob, munching on a new, experimental variety of lime-green, spearmint-flavored, breath-freshening popcorn. (Food companies were always sending Glob free samples of the latest Exploding Cherry-Bomb Bubble Gum and Nacho-Cheese Extreme Potato Chips in the hopes of a favorable mention on his website.) "He's on hiatus."

Daniel-not-Danielle looked distressed. "He hates us? But he doesn't even know us."

"No, idiot, *hiatus*. He's on hiatus. It's what they call summer vacation when you're on a TV show. Except when my blog goes on the food channel, we won't really have a summer vacation because cable is on a different schedule." He pulled a half-eaten popcorn kernel out of his mouth and inspected it. "These things are totally disgusting, but you kind of want to keep eating them—it's weird."

"Oh," said Daniel-not-Danielle. "Well, either way, he's definitely a genius. They say he's fluent in twelve languages. Like even Belgian."

"That's impossible," said Max-Ernest, cutting in. He was finding himself increasingly resentful of this brilliant new student.

"Why? Because it's more languages than you speak?" Glob asked. (His sarcasm was a little less sharp than it might have been, owing to his mouth being full of green popcorn.)

"No. Because there's no such thing as Belgian."

"Is so. What about Belgian waffles?"

"What about them? Waffles don't speak any languages at all, last time I checked. The point is, in Belgium they speak French and also Flemish, which is actually a kind of Dutch. How 'bout that?"

"Whatever," said Daniel-not-Danielle. "So maybe he speaks Flemish."

"Yeah, and don't dis Belgian waffles," said Glob. "Medieval Days Restaurant gave me, like, a hundred bucks' worth of coupons to try theirs. Now they're gonna sponsor my blog during Ren-Faire. And this time they're paying cash!"

Max-Ernest turned away. He felt like a jerk. Why was he bothering to talk to them? And why had he gotten so worked up about this aristocrat or actor or whatever-he-was new kid? He was supposed to be focused on saving Cass and saving Cass alone.

Suddenly, Max-Ernest missed her intensely. If a moment ago he was feeling an ache, this was more like a searing pain. With Cass he could argue about Belgium for hours and not feel like a jerk. She might laugh at him for obsessing about the differences between, say, Flemish Dutch and Dutch Dutch, but whenever she laughed *at* him she was always laughing *with* him at the same time. If that made any sense.

"Wait — that's him!" said Glob.

"He's not coming to the Nuts Table, is he? Now *that's* impossible," said Daniel-not-Danielle.

Glob and Daniel-not-Danielle were openly staring at a boy who was walking — no, sauntering — toward them. Even at a distance, there was no mistaking him for anybody else at school. Instead of jeans and a T-shirt, he wore a striped suit and a bowtie, and instead of a backpack, he carried a brief-case, giving the impression of a dapper businessman rather than a middle-school student. Sunlight illu-minated his golden curls and created bright sparkles in the large glass lens that covered his left eye.

"It's not impossible. Anybody can sit here," said Max-Ernest stubbornly, although he knew what Daniel-not-Danielle meant. "Besides, it's always possible he's really allergic to nuts," he added.*

"What's that over his eye? Is it a magnifying glass or something? Maybe we can use it to light a fire," said Glob excitedly.

"It's a monocle," said Max-Ernest. "It's like glasses for one eye. Rich guys used to wear them in the old days." And some magicians, he thought. Which was how he knew about monocles.

"He is — he's totally coming to our table," said Daniel-not-Danielle.

Indeed, he was waving in their direction.

"Hullo, Max-Ernest, my dear fellow!"

Daniel-not-Danielle and Glob turned in unison toward Max-Ernest. Judging by their expressions, the only thing they thought more unlikely than the new boy visiting the Nuts Table was that he should know Max-Ernest by name.

---

*OFFICIALLY, THE NUTS TABLE WAS THE TABLE FOR KIDS WITH NUT ALLER-GIES, AND FOR A LONG TIME MAX-ERNEST HAD WONDERED WHY IT WASN'T CALLED THE NO-NUTS TABLE. RECENTLY, MAX-ERNEST HAD FIG-URED IT OUT: THE OTHER KIDS AT SCHOOL THOUGHT THAT THE KIDS AT THE NUTS TABLE WERE, YOU GUESSED IT, NUTS.

⚠ **EMERGENCY DRILL** ⚠

ATTENTION, READER:

WE ARE SORRY TO INTERRUPT YOU IN THE MIDDLE OF A CHAP-
TER BUT AS YOU KNOW, EMERGENCIES ARE NOT ALWAYS
SCHEDULED AT CONVENIENT TIMES. INDEED, THEY ARE NOT
SCHEDULED AT ALL. THAT IS WHY THEY ARE EMERGENCIES.

THE AUTHOR OF THIS BOOK HAS HIRED US, THE **T**EAM OF **E**MER-
GENCY **A**GENTS, **S**PECIALISTS, AND **E**NGINEERS — MORE POPU-
LARLY KNOWN BY OUR ACRONYM, **T.E.A.S.E.** — TO CONDUCT
THIS DRILL IN ORDER TO ENSURE THAT YOU ARE PREPARED FOR
A GENUINE EMERGENCY. ALTHOUGH THIS IS ONLY A DRILL,
YOUR FULL COOPERATION AND PARTICIPATION ARE IMPOR-
TANT FOR YOUR OWN PROTECTION AND THE PROTECTION OF
OTHERS. ALSO, IT IS NECESSARY IF WE ARE GOING TO BE COM-
PENSATED FOR OUR WORK. (PSEUDONYMOUS BOSCH, THAT
CHEAP @$%@#%$&!!, REFUSES TO PAY US IN ADVANCE.)

YOUR RESPONSE TO THE DRILL WILL BE TIMED AND COMPARED
TO OTHER READERS' RESPONSES. THIS IS FOR INFORMATIONAL
PURPOSES ONLY. HUMILIATION OF PERCEIVED LOSERS IS NOT
OUR INTENTION — ONLY A PERK.

REMEMBER OUR SLOGAN: IF AT FIRST YOU DON'T SUC-
CEED, YOU'LL NEVER HAVE ANOTHER CHANCE.

READY?

HERE IS THE SCENARIO FOR THE DRILL AS SUPPLIED TO US BY THE
AUTHOR OF THIS BOOK. WE TAKE NO RESPONSIBILITY FOR ITS
LIKELIHOOD OR VERACITY. BY PARTICIPATING, YOU AGREE NOT

YOU ARE ON THE SCHOOL BUS. YOUR BEST FRIEND IS HOME SICK AND YOU HAVE THE SEAT TO YOURSELF. YOU ARE QUIETLY READING A BOOK — *THIS* BOOK, THE BOOK IN YOUR HANDS NOW, ALTHOUGH NO ONE ON YOUR BUS WOULD KNOW IT BECAUSE YOU HAVE, OF COURSE, DISGUISED THE BOOK AS DISCUSSED EARLIER.

IF YOU MUST READ A SECRET SERIES BOOK IN PUBLIC, EVEN SOMEPLACE SAFE AND FAMILIAR-SEEMING, LIKE A SCHOOL BUS, IT IS BEST TO GLANCE UPWARD EVERY ONE OR TWO MINUTES TO MAKE SURE YOU ARE NOT BEING OBSERVED BY ANY POTENTIAL MIDNIGHT SUN MEMBERS. SADLY, YOU HAVE GOTTEN A LITTLE OVERINVOLVED IN THE STORY (SHAME ON YOU!) AND YOU HAVEN'T LOOKED UP IN MORE THAN TEN MINUTES.

NOW IMAGINE THIS: SUDDENLY REALIZING YOUR ERROR, YOU LIFT YOUR HEAD AND GLANCE OUT THE WINDOW. RUBBING YOUR EYES AND SHIELDING THEM FROM THE SUN, YOU DON'T AT FIRST SEE ANYTHING AMISS.

GRADUALLY, YOU REALIZE THE BUS IS STOPPED AT A CROWDED INTERSECTION. THE POWER IS OUT AND THE TRAFFIC SIGNALS ARE REPEATEDLY BLINKING RED. A TRAFFIC COP IS STANDING IN THE MIDDLE OF THE INTERSECTION, DIRECTING TRAFFIC. WAIT A SECOND, SHE — WELL, OF COURSE, SHE'S WEARING WHITE GLOVES! IT'S PART OF HER UNIFORM. PERFECTLY NATURAL. NO CAUSE FOR ALARM. NONETHELESS, YOU CAN'T HELP EXPERIENCING A SMALL SHIVER.

SURVEYING THE STREETSCAPE FURTHER, YOU ARE SURPRISED TO SEE A MANHOLE COVER OPEN AND FLIP OVER ONTO THE ASPHALT. A CONSTRUCTION WORKER IN A YELLOW HARDHAT AND AN ORANGE JUMPSUIT CLIMBS OUT FROM UNDER THE

STREET. HE IS ALSO WEARING WHITE GLOVES. PROBABLY THEY ARE WORK GLOVES, YOU THINK. BUT STRANGE THAT THEY ARE WHITE. NOT VERY PRACTICAL FOR CONSTRUCTION. WELL, THAT'S HIS PROBLEM. NO REASON TO PANIC.

AT FIRST YOU THINK IT'S A TRICK OF THE LIGHT, BUT THE MAN SITTING AT THE BUS STOP ON THE FAR SIDE OF THE STREET ALSO APPEARS TO BE WEARING WHITE GLOVES. ON SECOND INSPECTION, YOU CONFIRM THAT, YES, HE IS, IN FACT, WEARING WHITE GLOVES. BUT WHY? GIVEN THE BLACK SUIT AND THE MUSIC STAND LEANING AGAINST THE BENCH NEXT TO HIM, MAYBE HE IS AN ORCHESTRA CONDUCTOR? CONDUCTORS WEAR GLOVES. THERE IS NO REAL EVIDENCE HE IS A MEMBER OF THE MIDNIGHT SUN, AFTER ALL.

AND YET. COMMON SENSE TELLS YOU: TWO PEOPLE WEARING GLOVES MIGHT BE A COINCIDENCE, THREE PEOPLE IS CAUSE FOR CONCERN.

YOUR CONCERN HEIGHTENS WHEN A MARCHING BAND SUDDENLY EMERGES FROM BEHIND A LINE OF CARS AND STARTS CROSSING THE INTERSECTION RIGHT IN FRONT OF YOUR SCHOOL BUS. THERE ARE OVER A HUNDRED BAND MEMBERS — TRUMPETERS, TUBA PLAYERS, DRUMMERS, THE WORKS — ALL IN RED UNIFORMS DECORATED WITH GOLD BRAID.

AND ALL WEARING WHITE GLOVES.

YOU LOOK AT THEIR FACES, HOPING FOR A SIGN THAT THEY ARE A REAL MARCHING BAND — MAYBE A HIGH SCHOOL MARCHING BAND — AND NOT AN ARMY OF EVIL ALCHEMISTS. BUT THEIR EYES ARE COLD. AND THEIR SKIN, WHILE YOUTHFUL, IS PALE AND ALMOST TOO TAUT. IN YOUR IMAGINATION, THEY TRANSFORM FROM A HANDSOME, HEALTHY MARCHING BAND TO A BAND OF SKELETONS, MARCHING ON THE DAY OF THE DEAD.

BY NOW, YOUR PULSE IS RACING. YOUR MIND IS SWIMMING WITH FEARFUL THOUGHTS. THE BUS IS STOPPED AND CANNOT MOVE WITHOUT PLOWING THROUGH THE BAND. THIS IS THE CRUCIAL MOMENT. YOU HAVE SEEN THEM. BUT THEY HAVE NOT YET SEEN YOU.

IT IS TIME TO ACT.

THE DRILL STARTS...

NOW.

PLEASE DOCUMENT ALL YOUR ACTIONS SECOND BY SECOND ON A TIME CARD. VIDEO FOOTAGE OF YOUR DRILL IS WELCOME BUT SHOULD NOT BE CONSIDERED A SUBSTITUTE FOR YOUR WRITTEN SUBMISSION.

SEND TO:

T.E.A.S.E.
P. BOSCH EMERGENCY DRILL
ATTN: DRILL SERGEANT

ax-Ernest squinted, trying to make out the features of the boy waving at him. In truth, he was just as surprised as the others.

"Don't tell me you don't remember your old comrade-at-arms!" the boy protested when he reached the Nuts Table. He smiled dazzlingly and removed his monocle. "It's only been a year since our last teatime tête-à-tête."*

"A year and a half," corrected Max-Ernest, finally recognizing him — but only barely. "Actually, a year and eight months."

"Ah, there's the Max-Ernest we all know and love! Always exact, isn't he? Don't make a mistake around him — he'll catch it every time," said the boy, chuckling.

The other two boys at the table laughed in appreciative agreement. The new kid had a peculiarly old-fashioned way of speaking, but he was so relaxed and self-confident that it didn't seem weird so much as adult and sophisticated.

"Aren't you going to introduce me to your chums?"

It took a moment for Max-Ernest to understand the question, because first of all, he'd never heard the word *chum* spoken aloud (only read it in old books

*IN FRENCH, *TÊTE-À-TÊTE* MEANS *HEAD-TO-HEAD*, AS IN A HEAD-TO-HEAD (OR HEART-TO-HEART) CONVERSATION. IN ENGLISH, IT MEANS YOU LIKE TO PEPPER YOUR SPEECH WITH PRETENTIOUS FRENCH PHRASES.

about a pair of brother detectives),* and second of all (as we established earlier), Daniel-not-Danielle and Glob weren't his chums in the first place.

"Um, OK. Daniel-not-Danielle, Glob, this is, uh, Benjamin Blake," said Max-Ernest. "He used to go here."

At least it *appeared* to be Benjamin Blake.

When Max-Ernest had last seen Benjamin, he'd been several inches shorter and had looked years younger. But it was the way he spoke now more than the way he looked that represented the biggest change. The old Benjamin had mumbled his words to such an extent that almost nobody could decipher them. What's more, whenever somebody bothered to figure out what he was saying, it turned out that his ideas were even less intelligible than his words. As an extreme synesthete, his senses were all entangled with each other, and his thoughts were a confused jumble of colors and sounds, tastes and smells.**

Today his speech was a study in perfect elocution. He sounded, not to mention looked, like the star of an old black-and-white movie. Most surprising

---

*As a rule, Max-Ernest disliked fiction. He didn't understand the point of reading about something that wasn't true. But he made an exception for mysteries, because they were like puzzles or riddles, only longer. The Hardy Boys books had been his favorite mysteries when he was younger. Now he preferred Edgar Allan Poe and Sherlock Holmes.

**If you haven't heard of synesthesia, you might consider consulting the first book in the Secret Series. But I warn you, it will still mean confusion — a confusion of the senses, that is.

of all was his manner; once shy and awkward to the point where he nearly couldn't function in normal life, he was now all cheerful insouciance and casual savoir faire.*

"I thought you were at a spec—I mean, a different school now," said Max-Ernest when he'd recovered from his initial shock.

He and Cass had been told that Benjamin was going to a "special" school for kids with disabilities. Because of Benjamin's value to the Midnight Sun, they were supposed to be keeping an eye on him for the Terces Society. (At one time, the Midnight Sun had believed Benjamin's unique brain chemistry might be the key to unlocking the formula of the Secret.) But they'd figured a school like that would keep him safe, so they had pretty much allowed themselves to forget about him. With a flush of guilt, Max-Ernest realized they'd never even checked to make sure Benjamin had enrolled. He could have been anywhere for all Cass and Max-Ernest knew. The Midnight Sun had kidnapped Benjamin once before; it was a stroke of luck they hadn't kidnapped him again.

"Oh, but I was at a special school—very special," said Benjamin. "The New Promethean Academy. It

---

*I COULD TELL YOU WHAT *INSOUCIANCE* MEANS IF I CHOSE TO, BUT I CAN'T BE TROUBLED AT THE MOMENT—IT'S FAR TOO SUNNY A DAY. (HINT: THE OPPOSITE OF INSOUCIANT IS ANXIOUS AND STRESSED OUT.) AS FOR *SAVOIR FAIRE*, IT MEANS *KNOW WHAT TO DO* IN FRENCH. IN ENGLISH, IT MEANS THE SAME THING *TÊTE-À-TÊTE* DOES, I.E., THAT YOU HAVE A PREDILECTION FOR PRETENTIOUS FRENCH PHRASES.

was sort of a *finishing* school. You know, to teach proper social decorum and so on and so forth. But in my case you could say it was a *starting* school as well. I feel they really brought me to life."

Max-Ernest couldn't disagree. Although he wasn't sure that he didn't prefer the old, nonliving Benjamin.

"May I sit down?"

Max-Ernest nodded and Benjamin took Cass's seat. (It was very likely the first time in the history of the Nuts Table that somebody had asked permission before sitting.)

Max-Ernest tried to think of something to say to the old-friend-now-stranger in front of him. "So... are you going to enter a painting in Renaissance Masters this year?"

Renaissance Masters was the name of a student art competition held in conjunction with the Renaissance Faire. Benjamin Blake had won the year he'd entered it.

"No, I don't paint anymore."

"Really?"

Max-Ernest was surprised. In the past, apart from being a prizewinning artist, Benjamin had loved painting. Painting was almost the only way he could communicate with the outside world.

"Oh, art is a childish pursuit, don't you think? Unless you're a truly great artist, I mean. If you're not going to be Michelangelo or Raphael, what's the point? I detest mediocrity."

"Yeah, me, too," said Max-Ernest reflexively. Then he thought about it for a moment. "Except how do you know if you're going to be great at something if you don't try? Michelangelo didn't know he was going to be Michelangelo until he was...Michelangelo. How 'bout that?"

Benjamin smiled witheringly. "So encouraging! So wise! You sound like one of my poor little parents."

Max-Ernest blushed. He had to admit, it did sound like something a parent would say. "Anyway, some people thought you were great."

"Sure, compared to most kids. But my destiny lies elsewhere." Benjamin held his monocle to the light and peered into it for a moment, as if his destiny might lie inside it.

Max-Ernest noticed that there were two lenses, one on top of the other. That was why the monocle had bulged slightly out of Benjamin's eye socket. "Wow, I've never seen a monocle like that. It's like a visual oxymoron. You know, because *mono* means *one* but it's got *two* lenses. Actually, you could say it's a *visual* visual oxymoron. You *see* the contradiction in terms, so it's visual in that sense. But it's also visual in the sense that you look through it. How 'bout that?"

"Huh. I never thought about it that way," said Benjamin, quickly bringing it back up to his eye. "Does the second lens make it stronger or something?"

"Something like that... Now, on to serious matters. How is our friend Cassandra? I am so concerned about her. She's still in the hospital, I take it?"

Max-Ernest frowned. "How did you know she was in the hospital?" he whispered. He looked over at Daniel-not-Danielle and Glob, making it clear that they weren't meant to be included in the conversation. They turned away (but somehow I doubt they stopped listening).

"I thought everybody did. I didn't know it was supposed to be a secret."

Max-Ernest regarded his old/new schoolmate with alarm. If an outsider like Benjamin knew about Cass, then anybody might. Even the Midnight Sun. Max-Ernest wasn't sure what they would do with the information — kidnap Cass from the hospital? poison her IV? — but he didn't want to wait to find out.

His mission was more urgent than ever.

"Anyway, don't tell anyone else — she wouldn't want people to talk about it," he said. "And don't worry about her — she'll be OK soon."

"I hope so! My goodness, what would happen to all the disasters in the world if our dear Cass wasn't around to predict them?"

Max-Ernest nodded his assent. Although his powers of sarcasm detection had improved greatly over the last couple of years, if there was any sarcasm in Benjamin's voice — and I'm not saying there was — it was far too subtle for Max-Ernest to discern.

Lunch ended shortly thereafter. As the reunited friends parted ways, Benjamin coughed and lowered his voice.

"Max-Ernest, old chum, I don't want to embarrass you, but there's a piece of paper stuck to your back. . . . May I?"

Gravely and politely, Benjamin unpinned the paper and handed it to Max-Ernest.

Max-Ernest groaned. It was a classic schoolyard prank — one played on him dozens of times over the years. There were two words written on the paper:

KICK ME

"Thanks," he said through gritted teeth.

"Don't mention it." Benjamin gave a little bow, then sauntered away.

Max-Ernest was about to toss the offending paper in the trash when he noticed that there was writing on the back side. It looked like some kind of travel advisory.

WARNING:
L TRAIN – ORD, FARE CHANGING.
BRING OLIVES, NOT N-WORDS.

The wording was so strange that Max-Ernest immediately suspected he was looking at a coded message from the Terces Society. Travel-derived encryptions were a personal favorite of Pietro's. But what did it mean? Max-Ernest could tell at a glance it wasn't a keyword code or any kind of simple alphabet substitution.

ORD were the call letters for Chicago O'Hare Airport. Was he meant to go there? Why? How?* Presumably, there was an L (short for *elevated*) train in Chicago that led to the airport. But as for the fare changing, why should he care? He didn't even know how much the old fare had been.

BRING OLIVES, NOT N-WORDS. Max-Ernest

---

*WITHOUT GIVING TOO MUCH AWAY ABOUT HIS LOCATION, I CAN TELL YOU THAT MAX-ERNEST WAS NOWHERE CLOSE TO CHICAGO O'HARE AIRPORT, AND GETTING THERE ON HIS OWN WOULD HAVE BEEN VERY DIFFICULT FOR SOMEONE HIS AGE, TO SAY THE LEAST.

figured the key to decoding the message lay in that last sentence, simply because it was the oddest. *Olive* was a word/name that occurred often in palindromic form — e.g., *EVIL = OLIVE*. The most likely solution, Max-Ernest concluded, would involve if not a palindrome then at least an anagram. *WORDS = SWORD?* But then what about the *N*?

The n-word was usually *no*, but the plural suggested the meaning had to be something else. Bring olives, not *nuts?* Not *newspapers?* Not *nuclear bombs?*

Uncharacteristically, Max-Ernest gave up and slipped the message into his back pocket. Normally, a message from the Terces Society would be a top priority for him, and he would forgo all other activity until it was decoded. But this one would have to wait, he decided. He had a more pressing matter to attend to: Cass.*

A moment later, in the library, Max-Ernest wrote an e-mail to Yo-Yoji, telling him about the unlikely return of Benjamin Blake. And about how desperate he was to bring Cass back to the present.

Get inside Cass's head, Pietro had instructed him. He had to figure out how right away.

---

*ALSO, IT'S JUST POSSIBLE THAT MAX-ERNEST'S FEELINGS WERE A BIT HURT. PIETRO, OF COURSE, LOVED PRANKS, BUT THE *KICK ME* SIGN SEEMED UNNECESSARILY MEAN. COULDN'T THE MAGICIAN HAVE LEFT THE MESSAGE IN SOME OTHER WAY? I THINK MAX-ERNEST MAY HAVE DELAYED DECODING THE MESSAGE AS A SILENT AND FRANKLY INEFFECTIVE MEANS OF RETALIATION.

ompared to the horrifying description of the pigpen in "The Legend of Cabbage Face," the royal kennels didn't look like such a bad place to stay the night. Indeed, they were rather splendid.

The kennels occupied a long brick building designed to resemble the palace in miniature. Inside, the walls were painted with murals of dogs frolicking in the woods and giving chase to a frightened fox while chubby canine cherubim smiled down at them. Each of the King's prize beagles had his own tufted velvet pillow trimmed with gold braid so thick and opulent, you would have expected to see it hanging from the canopy above the King's own bed. Meanwhile, each beagle meal was served in a silver tureen with a royal crest engraved in the center and the beagle's name engraved on the rim.

And such meals!

As the visibly hungry homunculus was dragged in by the soldier, the regal beagles were feasting on all sorts of meats and poultries dripping with delicious fats and juices. Cass noticed the homunculus's eyes linger on a standing rib roast currently being devoured by the first and fattest and clearly most favored in the line of dogs—Terrence III, according to his bowl. Is this where Mr. Cabbage Face develops his obsession with crown roasts? Cass wondered.

As the homunculus passed by, his mouth watering, Terrence looked up from his bowl and casually let fall a rib from his teeth. It landed at the hungry homunculus's feet, and the homunculus gratefully reached for it. But Terrence snatched it back, snarling, before the homunculus made contact.

The homunculus winced as if he'd been hit.

Then, as if once weren't enough, the overfed beagle again dropped the bone in front of the homunculus — and again snatched it back before the homunculus could reach it.

Cass shook her head in disbelief. What kind of dog intentionally tortured someone like that?

Alas, the luxurious life of a regal beagle was not for a lowly homunculus. Once the soldier handed him over to the trainer, it became clear there were other plans for the homunculus. He was not to sleep on a velvet pillow or even to sleep at all, the trainer instructed, but rather to spend the night cleaning the kennels of any, shall we say, royal remains that happened to sully the kennels' polished marble floor. The trainer gave the homunculus a shovel and a mop and made sure he knew that if there were any spots on the floor in the morning, the homunculus would dearly regret it.

Cass waited until all the other humans had left,

or perhaps I should say until all the other *humanoids* had left (considering we're dealing with an invisible time-traveling girl and a tiny boy-man made in a bottle) before addressing the homunculus.

"You don't recognize me, do you...? No, of course, you don't. We haven't met yet. We won't meet for five hundred years," she said as much to remind herself as to enlighten him. "I'm Cassandra. If that's too long, you can call me Cass. Almost everybody does."

The homunculus stared at her, perplexed. He seemed unable to understand her words and even less to understand her intentions.

"You don't know it, but we're going to be good friends one day. Well, sort of good friends. I have to admit there's a part of me that will always be a little freaked out because you're a cannibal."*

Perhaps she shouldn't have mentioned that, Cass thought. It might influence him to try cannibalism sooner.

---

*I FEEL DUTY-BOUND TO POINT OUT HERE THAT WHILE A TRUE GOURMAND, THE HOMUNCULUS IS NOT IN FACT A CANNIBAL, AT LEAST NOT IN ALL SENSES OF THE WORD. IT IS TRUE THAT HE SOMETIMES EATS PEOPLE (ROASTED VILLAINS, MOSTLY), BUT SINCE HE IS NOT FULLY HUMAN HIMSELF, HE IS, ARGUABLY, NOT FULLY CANNIBALISTIC. IN ORDER TO BE A CANNIBAL, PROPERLY SPEAKING, HE WOULD HAVE TO EAT OTHER HOMUNCULI (WHETHER ROASTED, JELLIED, OR RAW). JUST AS A CANNIBAL SQUIRREL EATS SQUIRREL STEW, NOT HUMAN RAGOUT. UNFORTUNATELY, HE IS THE ONLY HOMUNCULUS IN EXISTENCE THAT I KNOW OF. ERGO, HE COULD NOT BECOME A CANNIBAL NO MATTER HOW HARD HE TRIED. NO, LET ME AMEND THAT: HE COULD EAT HIMSELF. AND KNOWING HIM, IN CERTAIN CIRCUMSTANCES, HE WOULD.

It was a strange experience, meeting an old friend with whom you share so many memories, and realizing that this person doesn't remember any of them. She didn't know how much to tell the young Mr. Cabbage Face, how much to let him learn later on his own. According to the Prime Directive, she shouldn't be interfering with his normal development; but were the rules for interstellar space travel the same as for intrabrain time travel?*

"Anyway, we have to figure out how to get you out of here," she said, changing the subject. "Remember, if anybody comes, don't say anything to me. They can't see me.... But you can talk now, if you want."

Cass couldn't understand why he wasn't saying anything. Although the homunculus in her memory wasn't always the most talkative creature in the world, he could talk up a storm when he got going on one of his stories. And the insatiable Mr. Cabbage Face was downright garrulous when you plied him with food and drink.

"Well, first things first—let's get you food, right?"

Although all the beagles had licked their bowls clean (seemingly relishing eating in front of the

---

*THE PRIME DIRECTIVE, A FAVORITE CONVERSATION TOPIC AT THE NUTS TABLE, IS THE FIRST RULE GUIDING THE STARFLEET ON *STAR TREK*. IT HOLDS THAT A SPACE TRAVELER MUST NOT INTERFERE WITH THE NATURAL DEVELOPMENT OF A PLANET THAT HAS NOT YET GAINED THE CAPACITY FOR INTERSTELLAR SPACE TRAVEL. OF COURSE, THIS IS A RULE THAT GETS BROKEN AGAIN AND AGAIN.

starving homunculus), Cass was able to find six left-over roast chickens on a counter.

"Here you go, Mr. Cabbage Face. Six chickens coming up. That should be enough — even for you."

The beagles yelped in protest, seeing chickens they felt rightfully to be theirs carried away by invisible hands. But the homunculus, showing unexpected spirit, snarled so viciously into Terrence's ear that not only Terrence but all the dogs sank into their velvet cushions, whimpering with fear.

"I guess some dogs can dish it out, but they can't take it," said Cass, shaking her invisible head.

The not-quite-two-foot-tall homunculus ate the six chickens almost faster than Cass was able to hand them to him. Soon there was a familiar pile of bones in front of him, each bone gnawed furiously and with every drop of marrow sucked out.

Cass smiled. Some things never changed. Or rather, never would change over the next five hundred years.

"OK, satisfied now?" she asked after the homunculus had devoured his last bite.

Crouched on the floor, a last bone in each hand, the homunculus looked up at her, unblinking. He either didn't understand the question or didn't know how to answer.

"Right. You're never satisfied. I know." Cass sighed, leaning against the counter. "What I mean is, did you eat enough so we can think about something else now — like what's next?"

Cass was torn about what to do:

In "The Legend of Cabbage Face," she remembered, the Jester finds the homunculus in the pigpen. After offering the homunculus food, he persuades the homunculus to speak. And it is the Jester who frees the homunculus — from the pigpen and from Lord Pharaoh.

Would she be toying too much with fate if she freed the homunculus herself? And shouldn't she be waiting for the Jester, anyway? Meeting him was her reason for being here. He was why she had eaten the chocolate and journeyed five hundred years into the past.

On the other hand, what if the Jester never showed up? The story had already been proven unreliable. Wasn't the homunculus's freedom the most important thing?

"I really don't know what to do, but if you don't say something, I might just have to leave you here," said Cass, not meaning it. "I'll tell you what — if you talk, I'll make sure you get one of those crown roasts like the dog had as soon we get out of here, OK?"

The bribery was a desperate tactic, but it had worked in the past. Or rather in the future.

"Come on, think of those juicy bones. I know you can speak."

"I c-can," he whispered.

"What's that? I didn't hear you."

"I can," said the homunculus more loudly. "I *can* speak."

"Well done!"

Cass froze. Who had said those last two words?

She heard the jingling of the bells on his hat before she saw him.

The Jester.

"I knew thou couldst speak. I came on purpose to make thee squeak!"

He entered, the dogs barking snappishly after him but still too scared to get up from their cushions.

"I thought to make many trips. But I see I've already loose'd your lips!"

Cass stared. She couldn't believe she was standing in the same room as the Jester, the founder of the Terces Society, her only known ancestor. Her previous encounters with him—also chocolate-induced—had been so fleeting and dreamlike, he hadn't seemed real.

He looked much as Cass remembered—round freckled cheeks, orange curls peeking out of his hat—

but at the same time much younger. Of course, his most striking feature was identical to *her* most striking feature: the big pointy ears.

The Jester grinned, nearly twirling around, he was so pleased with himself.

"Like magic I give thee the gift of speech. I need not lift my hand to reach!"

What could she possibly say to him that would measure up to the importance of the occasion? True, she was invisible, but she would just have to make him overlook that.

And *she* would have to try to overlook the fact that he was taking credit for getting the homunculus to talk. (Normally, this was the kind of thing that made her furious.)

The Jester glanced around, making sure he and the homunculus were alone.

"We have only the animals for audience," he whispered. "So I may tell you my secret."

Cass's ears pricked up. Was she about to hear the Secret already?

"I tire of this palace place. Like you, I seek to be my own master. Lord Pharaoh keeps you on a leash. So the King keeps me. Though you see not the chain, I feel no less the pain."

He studied the homunculus's face for a reaction,

then continued, "I have a most daring plan. By cover of night, we shall flee. Far from king and pharaoh, where we shall both be free."

The Jester paced excitedly, gesturing with his hands.

"What then, you ask? Where go our feet? What shall we eat?" The Jester smiled. "Ah, but this is the best part. 'Tis a dream come true. We shall perform together! Think on it—the Human Fool and the Wise Monster. I shall make them laugh, you shall make them weep. And together we shall make a big gold heap!"

He formed the heap of gold with his hands, then rubbed them together with anticipation.

"So, my little friend—what say you?"

The homunculus opened his mouth, then clamped it shut. Whether because there was nothing to say or too much.

The Jester nodded. "You speak no more tonight. Good. You are my ideal friend, for I talk without end. You see, I never learned to hold my tongue, only to fold it—"

He started to fold his tongue in demonstration, then, seeing the homunculus's blank expression, he gave up.

"What? I do not make you laugh...? You're right, there was little fun in that pun. How's this, then — did you hear the one —? Oh, what's the use? I can no more tell a joke than flap my wings and fly. A fine jester am I!"

He sank down to the floor and slumped against the wall, his enthusiasm draining away.

"But you, you are a living miracle," said the Jester bitterly. "The talking homunculus. To see you, people would travel the world. And what am I? A fool! Not even a full-fool, I am a half-wit. An idiot. No wonder you will not have me. I do not deserve to work with a talent such as you...."

The Jester lifted his head, clenching his jaw in determination.

"Well, if I must, I'll strike out on my own. I am used to working alone. I am a professional, after all. And you, what have you ever done? It wasn't you that made you! You are not your own miracle, you are Lord Pharaoh's," said the Jester scornfully. "I offer you the benefit of my professional expertise, and you spurn me without so much as an 'if you please...'"

He put his head in his hands, the picture of despair, while the homunculus watched, baffled.

"Forgive me, I know not what I say," came the Jester's muffled apology. "You have done no wrong."

Now sitting on the counter, Cass contemplated the Jester in chagrined disbelief. Was this really the great man she'd read and heard so much about? Only her experience listening to Max-Ernest prepared her to follow the Jester's wild leaps in logic. As for his radical mood swings, she was fairly certain Max-Ernest would diagnose the Jester as bipolar.

The Jester looked over at the homunculus again and took a deep breath. "It is time for my confessional: I am no more a professional. I do not run from the King, the King has run me out. Now that Lord Pharaoh has his ear, he says my sense of humor is in doubt. 'Tis true, tonight I ate my last of the royal repast."

Tears ran down his cheeks and it was all Cass could do to resist the impulse to offer him a reassuring hug.

"Yesterday, I was the King's jester. Today I am merely the King's yester."

Pulling himself together, the Jester stood and addressed the homunculus once more.

"I hoped you would be my partner, but I will no longer try to barter. Let them not say of me that I failed to set you free."

Eyes shining, he put his hand to his heart, overwhelmed by his own noble nature. "If I cannot be a proper fool, at least I shall be a proper man!"

His words were punctuated by the bang of a door and the renewed barking of the beagles.

"Hark! What do I hear?"

Footsteps. The unmistakable synchronized footsteps of the King's soldiers.

Cass quickly surveyed their surroundings. The closest thing to an exit was a window above the counter, large enough for a homunculus but too small for a full-size human. She reached up and pushed it open.

"Look—an open window!" The Jester pointed, as if he'd personally discovered it.

"Wait. Your collar—," said Cass aloud to the homunculus before she could stop herself. She was worried that the chain dangling from the homunculus's collar would catch on the window.

A large pair of gardening shears were sitting nearby. In a flash, she clipped his collar off.

"Ah, good, I'm glad you are rid of that!" The Jester, confused about what he'd just seen and heard, shrugged it off. "Now, you climb through the window, and I...I will stay and face the King's soldiers," he said in an exaggeratedly strong voice.

The homunculus did not have to be told twice. He sprang up onto the counter like an oversize frog and climbed out the window just as the soldiers stormed in.

Lord Pharaoh followed.

"Where is he?" he demanded, towering over the Jester. "What have you done with my homunculus?"

"He's not yours," replied the Jester. "He is his own self's. And I have done nothing but what any man would do who has a heart."

"You may have a heart but you have no brain. Arrest this baboon!" Lord Pharaoh pointed to the Jester's hat. "I do not want to hear those bells jingle again unless they're deep inside the palace dungeon!"

As Cass watched helplessly, the soldiers hog-tied the Jester and dragged him out of the kennels, leaving Cass alone with the jeering barks of the regal beagles.*

---

*A FINAL NOTE ON DIFFERENCES BETWEEN LEGEND AND REALITY:
IF YOU HAVE NOT READ "THE LEGEND OF CABBAGE FACE," YOU MAY SKIP THIS FOOTNOTE. IF YOU *HAVE* READ IT, YOU WILL NO DOUBT NOTICE SEVERAL DISCREPANCIES BETWEEN THAT STORY AND THE CHAPTER ABOVE. ASIDE FROM THE DOGS/HOGS CONFUSION, WHICH CASS HERSELF NOTED, THERE ARE TWO MAJOR DISCREPANCIES THAT I FEEL I SHOULD ADDRESS. THE FIRST CONCERNS THE NAMING OF THE HOMUNCULUS. IN "THE LEGEND OF CABBAGE FACE," THE HOMUNCULUS ADMITS TO THE JESTER IN THEIR VERY FIRST CONVERSATION THAT LORD PHARAOH'S HOUSEKEEPER OCCASIONALLY CALLS HIM "HER LITTLE CABBAGE FACE," AND THE JESTER SEIZES ON THAT AS THE HOMUNCULUS'S NAME. AS FAR AS I KNOW, NO SUCH EXCHANGE OCCURRED IN REALITY—AT LEAST NOT AT THE TIME DESCRIBED. THE OTHER DISCREPANCY CONCERNS THE SOUND PRISM, THE MAGICAL BALL OF SOUND THAT THE JESTER PLAYS LIKE AN INSTRUMENT IN "THE LEGEND OF CABBAGE FACE" AND THAT CASS, MAX-ERNEST, AND YO-YOJI USE YEARS LATER TO SUMMON THE HOMUNCULUS. WHY DOES THE JESTER NOT HAVE THE SOUND PRISM IN THE TIME OF THIS BOOK, WE CANNOT HELP ASKING. I HAVE NO WAY OF KNOWING FOR CERTAIN, BUT I THINK THE EXPLANATION FOR BOTH DISCREPANCIES IS THE SAME. THOSE THINGS SIMPLY HAPPENED LATER. THAT IS TO SAY, THE HOMUNCULUS WAS NAMED LATER IN HIS LIFE, AND THE JESTER ACQUIRED THE SOUND PRISM LATER IN *HIS*. I BELIEVE THE AUTHOR OF "THE LEGEND OF CABBAGE FACE" MUST HAVE COLLAPSED TIME FOR HIS OWN LITERARY PURPOSES. MANY AUTHORS DO THIS. THAT IS WHY MEMOIRS IN PARTICULAR ARE NOTORIOUSLY UNRELIABLE.

om, Dad, do you have any books on mental telepathy or second sight or anything like that?"

Max-Ernest found his parents sitting in what was now their joint office. Their desks arranged so that the back of one desk touched the back of the other, they stared moonishly into each other's eyes without having to so much as turn their necks. Once two separate offices, the room was ringed by a ragged line of cracks and splinters where the two offices had been joined together. On the floor were broken pieces of lumber and chalky chunks of mortar — a hazardous mess — but they didn't appear to notice any of it.

Or perhaps they were too in love to care.

Max-Ernest coughed loudly. "Hello, Mom. Hello, Dad. I'm right here, two feet away from you. I know you can hear me...."

In the old days, Max-Ernest couldn't keep his parents off his back. These days, he had trouble just trying to get their attention.

"I asked if you had any books on mental telepathy — you know, like on psychic phenomena or any extrasensory brain stuff?"

Both his parents were psychologists, and they were surrounded on all sides by shelves full of books on everything to do with the human brain as well as books on animal brains and even robot brains, so it was a good bet they would have plenty of books on the subjects Max-Ernest mentioned. But like many people who collect things, they were very possessive of their books. The rule was that Max-Ernest had to ask for special permission if he wanted to borrow one. Then he was supposed to write the name of the book in a ledger, so his parents wouldn't lose track of it.

"Why would I need a book on mental telepathy? I can read your mind right now," said his father, not turning away from Max-Ernest's mother.

"There's no need to read about mental telepathy—I already know what you're thinking," said Max-Ernest's mother, not turning away from his father.

When they were divorced (but still living in the same house) Max-Ernest's parents had gotten into the habit of repeating each other's sentences as though the other parent weren't there. Unfortunately, now that they were back together, the habit persisted. It made speaking to them very disorienting—even for Max-Ernest, who was used to it.

"So does that mean I can borrow some books or not?"

"Oh, come on now, Max-Ernest," said his father, never averting his gaze from Max-Ernest's mother.

"There's no need to pretend. Your thoughts are written all over your face."

"Oh, please, Max-Ernest," said Max-Ernest's mother, never averting her gaze from his father. "It's clear as rain what you're thinking. Don't play dumb."

"Remember, we're not only your parents," said his father. "We're psychologists."

"Don't forget, we're mental health professionals," said his mother. "Not just the people who gave birth to you."

Max-Ernest looked at them in confusion. "What are you guys talking about? I'm not thinking anything."

"It's not what you're thinking so much as what you're feeling," corrected his father. "Don't forget about your feelings, son."

"We're talking about emotions," corrected his mother. "Not everything is always rational, Max-Ernest. Not even you."

"OK, what am I feeling, then?" asked Max-Ernest, resigned. He sat down on the long couch reserved for his parents' patients. But he refused to recline the way their patients did. That was going too far.

Surreptitiously, he scanned the shelves for books

that might contain what he was looking for. One title caught his attention: *Second Sight: Seeing With Your Third Eye in Four Easy Steps, Fifth Edition*. The book was level with his shoulder, tantalizingly close.

"It hasn't escaped our notice that you've been a little, shall we say, depressed," said his father, finally turning to face Max-Ernest.

"Don't think we haven't seen that dark cloud you've been carrying around," said his mother, finally turning as well.

Brilliant, thought Max-Ernest. My best friend is in a coma. It really takes a genius to figure out I'm depressed. Even *I* figured that out.

But he didn't say that. He figured listening to his parents was the price he had to pay if he wanted to borrow their books. They had to get back to the books at some point.

"We can tell you've sensed what's going on," said his mother. "Many children do."

"Like many kids, you've guessed without our having to tell you," said his father.

Guessed what? he wondered. Were they getting remarried? Or re-divorced? Or splitting up the house but staying together? Or not staying together but keeping the house? It had to be something like that. Although Max-Ernest had no idea which was most likely. Or which he would prefer. All the scenarios were equally problematic.

Max-Ernest inched closer to the book on second sight. Maybe he could sneak it off the shelf.

"Call it fraternal telepathy if you like," said his mother.

"It's a sixth sense that siblings have," said his father.

Max-Ernest frowned, unable to grab hold of the book with his parents' eyes trained on him. *Fraternal?* Like fraternal twins? And *siblings?* What siblings? He was an only child. Only-childhood had pretty much defined his childhood. Were they going to tell him he had a secret twin somewhere? Or an older sibling who had died at birth?

His father smiled knowingly at him. "Tell us, Max-Ernest, when did you first realize your mother was pregnant?"

His mother smiled the same way. "Be honest, how long have you known you were going to have a brother?"

"A...bro...ther?"

Max-Ernest stared at his parents, his mouth open, momentarily forgetting all about his book-sneaking mission.

He was going to have a brother? How could he

not have seen this coming? Where had he been that such a big development could escape him?

"Yes, the baby you sensed is a little boy," said his mother. "We understand if you feel replaced in our hearts."

His father nodded wisely. "Children in your situation often feel like somebody else is taking their place."

"It's completely expected that you would be jealous," agreed his mother.

"Your mood is a natural reaction to your circumstances," added his father.

They thought he was depressed about the baby? Had they forgotten about Cass? His parents used to obsess about every aspect of his life. Did they care nothing about what was happening to him anymore?

He was so taken aback he didn't bother to correct them.

"Please try to keep your anger in check," cautioned his father. "No pouring mayonnaise on the baby in the middle of the night!"

"Control yourself," cautioned his mother. "We don't want to wake up and find you standing over the baby with an empty jar of mayo!"

"OK. No mayo," said Max-Ernest, forcing a smile.

He assumed they were joking — at least he hoped

they were—but he still couldn't believe they were talking to him like this. As if he were a two-year-old boy so jealous of his soon-to-be baby brother that he would pour his least favorite substance all over him. Besides, didn't his parents know he was so horrified by mayonnaise that he wouldn't even be able to touch the jar?

"Good. I'm glad we've had this conversation," said Max-Ernest's father. "And in case you're worried, we want to assure you that your little brother will be in good hands. We've learned from our mistakes—that's a promise."

"Good. I'm happy we've come to an understanding," said Max-Ernest's mother. "And not to worry—your little brother will be safe with us. Everything we got wrong with you, we're going to get right this time—we promise."

His father took his mother's hand, smiling at her. "*He's* not going to spend his childhood bouncing from doctor to doctor, making him a neurotic mess."

Max-Ernest's mother smiled back at Max-Ernest's father, grasping his other hand with hers. "We won't turn *him* into a nervous wreck, searching and searching for a condition that may or may not have a cure!"

Reminding himself that he was supposed to be focusing not on his own life or his brother's but on

Cass's, Max-Ernest tried his best not to listen to what his parents were saying. The idea that they felt they had failed with him was somewhat upsetting, of course, even for somebody bad at feelings, but this was not the time to be upset. Right now he had to concentrate all of his attention on the task in front of him:

Robbery.

With his parents' attention fixed on each other, he quickly pulled the book on second sight off the shelf and put it behind his back. He breathed a silent sigh of relief. So far so good.

"We aren't going to be breathing down *his* neck every moment," continued Max-Ernest's father.

"We won't be fighting over every second of *his* life," continued Max-Ernest's mother.

"Our *new* son is going to have a nice, normal childhood!" concluded Max-Ernest's father.

"Our *new* son is going to be a nice, normal kid!" concluded Max-Ernest's mother.

Max-Ernest swallowed. Despite his best efforts, he was unable to completely, entirely, one-hundred-percent-ly ignore his parents. He knew they didn't think he was normal. Otherwise why would they have spent all that time and money searching for a cure for his condition? But it was different to hear them say it out loud.

Never mind, he told himself. A *normal* person wouldn't be able to prevent a comatose girl from disappearing into her ancestral past. A *normal* person wouldn't be able to save Cass. Cass didn't think he was normal, but she didn't *want* him to be normal, either. She was relying on him to be just who he was. She had faith in him. She had told him so. And living up to that faith was the only thing that he should be thinking about.

His parents were beaming so hard and happily at each other that he suspected he could walk right out, book in hand, without their noticing.

And that's exactly what he did.

And then he ate some chocolate.

And then some more chocolate.

And then some more.

And some more.

And some...
    hmmgh...

more.

ass stepped out of the kennels too late to see where they'd taken the Jester. Approaching the palace, she scanned her surroundings with the Double Monocle as if it were a pair of field binoculars, but—no luck.

As for the homunculus, knowing him, Cass figured he'd probably gone in search of the palace kitchens and was at that very moment devouring a roast pig twice his size. Unless he was too scared to stay so close to Lord Pharaoh. In which case, Cass supposed, he was long gone.

She'd come so near to achieving her goal: to meet the Jester and ask him about the Secret. About who she was. But now she felt further away from achieving her goal than ever. Not to mention, what kind of secret could the Secret be if it was the Jester's secret? It hardly seemed likely that such a nutty, moody man would hold information important to the fate of the entire world.

Lost in speculation, Cass didn't at first notice the maid holding a pail out the window above.

Cass got a whiff just in time to jump out of the way before the contents of the pail poured out in a long, unpleasant stream. I won't say what those contents were, but if you know what a chamber pot is, you can guess. (Remember, this was before the invention of indoor plumbing.)

Cass expected there to be a great splattering next to her, but as it turned out, the chamber pot had been emptied directly into what looked like a stone well in the ground.

The stench issuing forth from this well (if a well it was) would have been enough to make most people steer clear. But the light coming out of it made Cass curious. Pinching her nose, she looked over the edge.

She couldn't see much, but she could see enough. There was indeed a pool of water at the bottom, but the water was filled with waste. From somewhere down below came the faint cries of prisoners as well as — was she just imagining it? — the even fainter jingle of the Jester's hat.

This royal privy, it appeared, was also the palace dungeon.

But how to get in? She could try rappeling herself down to the bottom, but then where would she land? Cass remembered lowering herself into the pyramid at the Midnight Sun Spa, only to be greeted by flames licking at her feet. The pool of waste would almost be worse.

Thankfully, Cass found another route. Not far away was a larger stairwell descending underground;

it almost certainly led to the dungeon. A heavy iron gate blocked her way down, but she figured if she waited long enough, somebody would eventually open it.

Sure enough, a posse of six soldiers soon arrived with their new prisoners: two men from Anastasia's team of bandits, their masks now hanging loose around their necks.

"You can lock us in iron, but it is you who are slaves to the King!" shouted one.

"Think you can keep us any longer than last time? I wouldn't bet on it!" shouted the other.

Cass felt a not entirely sensible sympathy for the bandits and briefly considered using her invisibility to help them in some way, but she decided her efforts were best directed in the service of the Jester.

She stayed close to the soldiers until she was inside the gate, then she paused to let them get ahead.

Following in their footsteps, she found herself in a long and winding passageway that normally would have been too dark to navigate without a torch. With the aid of the monocle, she could see every crack and crevice and had no trouble at all. Unless you call having to avoid rats and cockroaches and one particularly large spider trouble.

She knew she was close when she had to hold her nose.

Now very dimly lit by a few candles burning on the walls, the corridor widened until it became a kind of underground rotunda with the pool of waste in the center and prison cells surrounding it.

Not far ahead of Cass, the soldiers slammed a cell door shut on the bandits. She pressed against the wall as they passed her on their way out.

The cell doors were made of iron, crusted with rust, and had only small openings through which to communicate with the inmates. Cass stood on tiptoe and looked into the first cell. It was dark and difficult to see, but she was almost certain there was no one inside.

Before she could get to the second cell, Lord Pharaoh stormed out of it, holding a candle. He was accompanied by a prison guard.

"If you don't tell me where that creature went, you'll spend the rest of your days in here, I swear it!" he shouted to the cell's inhabitant; then he started striding away in Cass's direction.

"I know not where your monkey went," came the reply from the door. "I know only where you're going. And my advice is not to bring that cloak. You'll be much too warm. In fact, you'll be burning!"

Cass slunk back against the wall—but not in time. Lord Pharaoh brushed against her, jarring her arm and causing her to drop the monocle.

Luckily, the glass did not break, but it hit the stone floor with a loud enough clink to catch Lord Pharaoh's attention. "What's that?"

Cass stood frozen, her heart beating in her chest. The monocle glinted in the torchlight.

Lord Pharaoh picked up the monocle and turned it over in his hand. "How curious, a *Double Mono-cle...*"

And then it happened. He put the monocle to his eye and looked straight at her. "Curious, indeed," he said with a sinister smile.

He reached out and grabbed her arm. She tried to push him off, but he was too strong. "I thought for a second you were just a trick of the eye. But now I see you have the trick of touch as well."

Cass stared back at the man staring at her. Enlarged by the Double Monocle, his dark green eye looked ominous and reptilian. She wanted to make a retort—to say something smart and stinging to this awful man—but she found she was too afraid.

"Why is it when I look at you, I think I see the future?" mused Lord Pharaoh. "You are not of this time, am I right?"

"What is it?" asked the guard nervously. "A ghost?"

Lord Pharaoh snickered. "If she is a ghost, she is but a sniveling girl ghost. There is no need to fear her."

He tightened his grip on Cass. "This is a very intriguing glass you have.... What else do you bring from your invisible world? Empty your pockets. Now. Or I will have the guard do it."

Cass obeyed, but there was nothing in her pockets, save for a crumpled wrapper. Lord Pharaoh unfolded it, revealing a tiny triangle of chocolate.

Cass let out a little gasp — it was the last uneaten bit of Señor Hugo's special time-traveling recipe. She'd forgotten that there was any left.

Lord Pharaoh sniffed the chocolate, then touched it with his tongue. "What is this? Some kind of spice?"

"It's chocolate," Cass answered, surprise momentarily overcoming her fear. Then she remembered that the New World treat had yet to be imported to Europe.

"It is vile. But unique. I shall have to study it further," said Lord Pharaoh, rewrapping the remains.

Cass looked for signs that Señor Hugo's chocolate was having an effect on him — with any luck, Lord Pharaoh would fall to the ground unconscious — but apparently the one taste had been too small to make a difference.

"As for you — let's throw you in with the Jester for now. Later we shall learn how best to kill a ghost."

He lowered the monocle and inspected it briefly. "I have a distinct feeling the future will be much brighter without you," he concluded, replacing the monocle — this time with an expression so satisfied one might have expected him never to remove the monocle again.

Cass choked back a sob. Without the monocle, she'd never be able to escape.

The bells on the Jester's hat jingled in defiance of the darkness.

"Who's there?" he asked. "Though I cannot see your face, I wouldst know what unlucky soul has entered this gloomy place."

Cass peered around the cell, trying to make out the form of her fellow prisoner. The only light came from the small opening in the cell door.

There was a glimmer that she thought might be one of the bells on the Jester's hat. She crawled toward it.

"Um, hi. My name is Cassandra, but everybody calls me Cass."

"Cass?" the Jester repeated in surprise. "You are but a lass if my ears do not lie. Why is such a child as you in a place like this? What did you do wrong? Or is it, rather, what did you do right? If I am here, then this prison must be reserved for the best and most bright."

Cass giggled. Evidently, the Jester's mood was on an upswing again.

"It's kind of a long story, but, well, I think part of the reason is that—" She took a breath. She might as well just say it. "I'm invisible, and Lord Pharaoh wants to find out why."

The Jester laughed. "'Tis a good joke but no real riddle. We are all invisible in the dark. Come now, tell me the true story. Or if not true, then at least a better one."

"No, really, you wouldn't be able to see me even if there was light. See, watch. Let me take your hat—"

By now, Cass had located the Jester. Before he could protest, she pulled his hat off his head.

"Look, see how that little bit of light is shining on this bell. Now, feel my hand. It's there, right? Now I'm moving my hand over the bell. See how there's still light on it? No shadow."

"A nice trick, I admit," said the Jester, impressed.

"If you can do this sort of magic in the daylight, we might put on a show together."

"It's not a magic trick. That's my friend Max-Ernest's department."

"He must be a great magician, your friend. Does *he* want a partner? I will give him one coin for every ten we make. Oh, I'm feeling like a rich man already, I shall make it two—"

"Forget about Max-Ernest. He's a really difficult partner—trust me, I should know. The point is, the light shines through me because I'm invisible."

It was important that she convince him, Cass decided. For one thing, she didn't want him to die of shock if the cell was ever illuminated and he couldn't see her. On a more practical level, if he first accepted the fact of her invisibility, it would be easier to make him believe what was even more unlikely—that she was a visitor from the future.

"Here, now I'm putting my hand over your eyes and you can still see, right?"

The Jester didn't say anything, just nodded.

"You are a ghost, then? A spirit?" he whispered after a moment. "I have not met such a one before."

"I don't know; that's hard," said Cass. "I think it depends on how you define *ghost*."

The Jester shuddered in the darkness. "I know what you are—you are no ghost; you are that voice in my head they warn about."

He reached for his hat and put it back on his head, as if it might squelch her voice. The bells shook mockingly.

"You see, despite my vanity, I fear for my sanity," he whispered. "When they call me mad, I always laugh and tell another joke, but in secret I worry about my mental yolk. . . . That is a pun, by the way. The brain is like the yolk in the egg of your head, but also your mental *yoke* is your mental tether, your sense of reality—there, see how I ramble—"

"Wait. Stop. I'm not a voice in your head, I swear. If anything, you're in mine. I mean, I think I might be dreaming you . . . in a way."

"What? What are you saying? You confuse me more, you wily wraith! Very well, you sneaky specter—do not spare me!"

He stood, warming to his theme. "Take me, oh gods of the insane—I will be your slave. If you will have me, I will rave and rave! For in madness lies escape from this horrid prison. If I must live in the dark, I will imagine I am a lark. These walls will not see me die, for in my mind I will fly. My flesh may rot but I need it not . . . !"

"Would you just stop talking for a second!?" Cass demanded in the firm voice she reserved for when Max-Ernest went off on his longest and most ridiculous tangents. "You're not crazy—you're just making *me* crazy. Now listen, this is going to sound really weird, but I come from the future, hundreds of years from now. Actually, I'm your great-great- and a bunch of other *great*s granddaughter."

"Ha! Are you not satisfied to turn my mind to jelly? Must you spread it on toast and eat it, too?"

"Wait—feel my ears." Cass reached for the Jester's hand and made him touch the points of her ears. "See, they're just like yours."

"That they are," said the Jester agreeably. "But it proves not that you are my future self, merely that you, like me, are half elf."

Cass froze, her heart beating in her chest. Could that be true, as incredible as it sounded? Was that her secret? Was that *the* Secret?

"Are you really... part elf?" she asked.

The Jester chuckled. "Now it is *your* mind that is lost! No, I am not, and none is that I know."

"Oh," said Cass, relieved and disappointed at the same time. "Well, elf or not, I am your descendant. I'm ninety-nine percent sure, anyway."

The Jester sighed. "Perhaps you are; I myself am sure of nothing."

Calm again, the Jester sat down next to Cass.

Now's the time, she thought. She was about to ask about the Secret when a loud crash echoed in the corridor.

ax-Ernest couldn't have been in a worse mood.

Reading the purloined book hadn't helped him get any closer to reading Cass's mind.* As far as he was concerned, *Second Sight: Seeing With Your Third Eye in Four Easy Steps* might as well have been written by someone who really had three eyes—it was that silly.

After that particular book proved to be of little value, he'd managed to secure his parents' permission to comb through their bookshelves. The imminent arrival of Max-Ernest's baby brother seemed to have made them relax their guard.

"Just keep an eye out for any baby how-to books we might have missed," said his father.

"Let us know if you see any more books about raising babies," said his mother.

Max-Ernest sat on the office floor for hours, reading book after book not on babies but on extrasensory perception—some logical and scientific, but most too fantastical for his taste—and he learned a fair amount of fascinating trivia. *Bilocation*, for instance, was the condition of being in two places at once (just as he'd often had to be when his parents lived in separate places). *Dowsing* was a form of divination that involved the use of a wire or pendulum

---

*PURLOINED, AS EVERY ASPIRING BOOK THIEF SHOULD KNOW, MEANS STOLEN. THERE IS A FAMOUS STORY BY EDGAR ALLAN POE CALLED "THE PURLOINED LETTER." IN THE STORY, NOBODY CAN FIGURE OUT WHERE

to locate a missing object (he wondered whether Mrs. Johnson's using a magnet to locate the Tuning Fork would count). And *scrying* was using an object such as a crystal ball or a mirror to see faraway events (which is pretty much what you're doing when you're watching television, Max-Ernest reflected; not really all that impressive).

There were many theories about the hows and whys and wherefores of mental telepathy. But it all sounded more or less like hogwash to Max-Ernest, and in any case he found no instructions for reading the mind of a comatose girl. Most of what he read advised him to start by looking into someone's eyes (Cass's were closed), studying that person's facial expressions (Cass made very few), or listening to his or her voice (Cass was pretty much silent).

Why do they call it mind *reading* and not mind *seeing* or mind *hearing*, Max-Ernest wondered, if all they can tell you is to look and listen?

As a master decoder and puzzle-solver, Max-Ernest was used to finding a single key, a set of rules, a rubric with which to solve any problem that confronted him. The books advised him to rely on his intuition, which frustrated him greatly.

What's an intuition, anyway? he grumbled to himself. An intuition is nothing. It's a hunch. It's

---

THE PURLOINED LETTER HAS BEEN HIDDEN — UNTIL POE'S HERO, THE DETECTIVE DUPIN, REALIZES IT'S BEEN SITTING ON THE MANTELPIECE RIGHT IN FRONT OF EVERYBODY'S NOSE.

not logical. It has no basis in anything. I don't have intuitions. I have ideas.

His reading did lead to a couple of unexpected discoveries, however. The first involved Mrs. Johnson's magnet pendant. One of the so-called magical objects Max-Ernest read about was a *lodestone*, a naturally occurring magnet. He had thought Mrs. Johnson's pendant looked like a stone, and now he was sure of it. Not that the information was useful in any way. Somehow he doubted that he could wake up Cass by waving a black rock over her face.*

The other discovery involved the KICK ME sign; with the help of a book called *The Open Mind*, Max-Ernest was finally able to decode the message on the back.

"Negativity is your enemy," the book advised him. "Remember, the N-word is a dirty word. Just say no to *no*. Cut it out of your vocabulary." Max-Ernest had no intention of cutting *no* from his vocabulary; it was one of his favorite words. But he could cut N-words out of the coded message, he thought. BRING OLIVES, NOT N-WORDS. Perhaps that meant to cut all the N-words — that is, all the words containing the letter *N* — out of the message.

---

*EVEN TO GEOLOGISTS, A LODESTONE — ALSO KNOWN AS MAGNETITE — IS SOMEWHAT MYSTERIOUS. MOST NOW BELIEVE A LODESTONE GAINS ITS MAGNETIC FORCE WHEN IT IS STRUCK BY LIGHTNING, BUT NOBODY KNOWS FOR CERTAIN.

When he did so:

WARNING.
L TRAIN – ORD. FARE CHANGING.
BRING OLIVES, NOT N-WORDS.

became

~~WARNING.~~
L ~~TRAIN~~ – ORD. FARE ~~CHANGING~~.
~~BRING~~ OLIVES, ~~NOT N-WORDS~~.

or

L – ORD. FARE OLIVES.

At first glance, the shortened message made even less sense than the original. Then it hit him. The message was phonetic. Properly spelled, it was:

LORD PHARAOH LIVES.

Max-Ernest experienced only the briefest satisfaction at having solved the puzzle before growing angry. What kind of message was this? It was like something you'd see written on a bathroom wall. ELVIS LIVES. Or

MY FAVORITE SPORTS TEAM/ROCK BAND/WHATEVER RULES. It was a slogan, not a real message.

One thing was certain: it wasn't from Pietro. Come to think of it, as much as Pietro loved a practical joke, he would never put KICK ME on Max-Ernest's back; Pietro was far too soft-hearted. It was the Midnight Sun taunting him with the name of their alchemist hero and founder, Lord Pharaoh. That was the only possible explanation. The message had no meaning other than to show Max-Ernest how close they could get to him without his knowing.

And that, clearly, was very close.

So who put the message on his back? That was the question he was asking himself the next morning as he walked through school, instead of thinking about his oral report on jesters in Shakespeare's plays for language arts. (They were doing a Shakespeare unit in preparation for the Renaissance Faire; Max-Ernest had volunteered to cover jesters, not realizing that it meant he was actually supposed to read the plays the jesters appeared in.)

Glob and Daniel-not-Danielle, marginally friendlier now, nodded to him as he passed the Nuts Table. The KICK ME part he could easily imagine them writing.

But agents of the Midnight Sun? Not witting ones, anyway.

The most obvious candidate—really the only candidate—was Amber. Officially, she was the nicest girl in school. Unofficially, she was an agent (although hardly a full-fledged member) of the Midnight Sun.

By the time he reached Amber sitting at her usual table in the very center of the schoolyard, he had already:

a) convinced himself that she was the culprit,
b) imagined all the brave and scornful things he would say to her when he saw her, and then
c) decided not to confront her after all. It would give her too much satisfaction.

Unfortunately, Amber, who usually didn't relish talking to Max-Ernest any more than he relished talking to *her*, chose this of all mornings to flag him down for a conversation. "Max-Ernest! Hel-lo! Come over here!"

He did his best to act as though he didn't hear her.

Alas, Amber would not be put off. "Max-Ernest! Yoo-hoo! I know you can hear me!"

Ignoring Amber was fast becoming more

confrontational than answering her would be, so Max-Ernest stopped and turned in her direction. But he didn't say anything, just waited, his expression very plainly saying, *Yes, what do you want?*

Across the table from Amber, her friend Veronica watched, eager to see what would happen.

Amber smiled widely. "Aren't you even gonna say hi?"

"Um, I wasn't really planning on it," replied Max-Ernest.

Undaunted, Amber smiled even wider. "Well, I am! Hi, Max-Ernest! How was your summer?"

"Why are you saying hi to me? You don't talk to me. You hate me," said Max-Ernest neutrally. *Or is it just because you want to see if I know it was you who left the message?* he wondered silently.

"Come on, all that stuff that happened between us is so three months ago. Can't we be friends? Ask anybody, I'm really nice."

Veronica nodded vigorously. "She totally is."

"Some people think I'm the nicest person in school, did you know that?"

"Yeah, I did. But that doesn't mean they're right."

"Gosh, what did I ever do to you? I mean, seriously."

"Well, let's see..." Max-Ernest was about to start

answering the question, beginning with the time Amber accused him and Cass of liking each other (*like* liking, that is, which Max-Ernest felt should be called *more-than-like* liking, and which in any case should never be applied to him and Cass!), continuing with the time Amber helped the Midnight Sun capture their friend the homunculus, and ending with the KICK ME sign, but then he thought better of it.

"I think you know," he said.

"So now I'm psychic or something?" Amber laughed. "Actually, I am. Me and Veronica are doing fortune-telling today. We didn't want to have to wait all the way till Ren-Faire to find out everybody's futures. So, can I tell your fortune?"

"No."

"Pretty please."

"Why?"

"Why not? Are you scared?"

Max-Ernest didn't have the energy to argue. Besides, maybe Amber knew something about what the Midnight Sun was up to. She might inadvertently reveal something useful if he allowed her to read his cards.

"OK, but just so you know, I don't believe in this stuff."

"Sit—"

Max-Ernest expected to see tarot cards again, but the deck Amber shuffled in front of him was the normal playing-card variety—albeit with sparkle-pink back sides.

"OK, the first card is the romance card. Let's see if it tells us you like somebody or not...."

She peeled the top card off the deck, looked at it, and smiled.

"Oh, it's the Ten of Hearts. That's a big yes. Ten out of ten. Totally in love! Who is it, Max-Ernest? Don't be shy. You can tell us."

"It's nobody," said Max-Ernest, red-faced.

Why did I consent to do this? I must have had a temporary lapse of sanity, he thought. I'd better have my cerebral cortex examined. There could be damage. Would laparoscopic surgery be in order?

"Oh, come on, the cards don't lie. Besides, we all know who it is...." Amber smiled mischievously. "Cass, are you listening?"

A small crowd had gathered around, including, among others, Daniel-not-Danielle and Glob. Ordinarily, Amber wouldn't have allowed anybody from the Nuts Table to linger so close, but evidently this was a special occasion.

"Cass, I think you have a not-so-secret admirer!" she called out. "I think he's ready to propose!"

Glob, who was sampling a new brand of bubble gum called The Volcano, laughed so loud he spit out his entire wad of gum, which proceeded to erupt on the asphalt.

"The next card says what the next big event in your life is," Amber continued in not quite as loud a voice. "What do you guys think it will be? Will Max-Ernest and a certain girl be getting married soon? I won't say who, but she has really big, I mean, beautiful ears...."

She removed the next card from the top of the deck and studied it. Her face turned serious.

"Oh no. Is somebody sick?" she asked Max-Ernest, sounding very distressed. "Because this card is the Queen of Spades, and it means somebody you love is going to die." Amber scanned the crowd around them. "Come to think of it, where is Cass? Did she come to school today? I hope she's OK...."

Max-Ernest felt sick to his stomach. He wanted to say something angry and defiant, but he was utterly unable to speak.

Benjamin Blake, who had joined the group just after Amber started telling Max-Ernest's fortune, stepped forward.

"May I see that, Miss —?" asked Benjamin in his exaggeratedly formal way.

"My name is Amber."

"Well, then, may I please see that card, Miss Amber?"

"What do you mean? What card?" asked Amber, flustered.

"The one in your hand, of course."

"Why?" Amber held the card to her chest, not allowing anybody to see it.

"Because it's not the Queen of Spades. I don't know why you would make up something like that— surely you don't think it's amusing that somebody whom Max-Ernest cares for would die? Nonetheless, it's a fact that you lied. The card in your hand is the Three of Clubs."

"How would you know?"

"If it's the Queen, show it to us."

Seemingly unable to help herself, Amber peeked at the card in her hand—and was apparently so startled she dropped the card on the table.

Max-Ernest grabbed it before she could. Sure enough, it was the Three of Clubs. He held it up for all to see.

"Sheesh, Amber. That was kind of uncool," Daniel-not-Danielle piped up unexpectedly from under his dreadlocks.

"Yeah, way uncool," agreed Glob. "What happened to that whole 'nicest girl in school' thing?" He

curled two fingers of each hand, making the interna-
tional air quotes sign.

Daniel-not-Danielle, Glob, and the half dozen
or so others standing around walked away, shaking
their heads.

"Come on, old chum — time for class," said Benjamin Blake.

He pulled the still-reeling Max-Ernest away,
Amber and Veronica glaring after them.

"How did you do it?" asked a slightly more cheerful
Max-Ernest over lunch, when they were again sitting
at the Nuts Table. (This time, Benjamin hadn't asked
permission to sit.) "Did you force a card in Amber's
deck when she wasn't looking?"

Benjamin shook his head. "I don't even know
what that means."

"You know, to set it up so she has to take it. So
she has no choice."

"Well, then, no, I didn't force it."

"But you *did* see her cards before she did? You
must have...."

"No."

"Did you have a mirror?"

"Nope."

"Somebody signaling you?"

Benjamin shook his head.

Max-Ernest looked at him, equally impressed and confused. "Then I give up—how did you know what card she was holding?"

Benjamin smiled mysteriously. "A magician never reveals his tricks. You of all people should know that, Max-Ernest. Didn't I hear that you wanted to be a magician? Or a stand-up comedian-slash-magician or something like that?"

"That's how I know there's no way to do that trick. Or no regular way."

"Then maybe I was really reading Amber's mind. Have you considered that possibility?"

"Yeah right, sure," said Max-Ernest.

Then he thought again about what Pietro had said. Was he too quick to discount the possibility of real mental telepathy? Pietro had suggested that Max-Ernest should be more open to things he didn't understand.

Besides, if there was any chance that Benjamin knew something about mind reading, Max-Ernest had to find out what it was; Cass's life was on the line.

"Wait a second. Who told you I wanted to be a magician?"

"Oh, everybody knows."

"Yeah, but who told you?"

"Like I said, everybody—"

"That's exactly what you said about how you knew Cass was in the hospital. And maybe everybody knows I want to be a magician, but not everybody knows about Cass. Almost nobody knows that."

"So? What are you trying to say?"

"You're—"

"What? What am I?"

He couldn't say it. It sounded too incredible.

Max-Ernest decided to try an experiment.

You're reading my mind, he thought as clearly as he could. *You can actually read minds.*

Benjamin didn't say anything for a moment, just studied Max-Ernest through his monocle. Then he nodded. "Yes, old chum, I can."

Max-Ernest stared. Here was proof, if any more were needed.

"You need not look so surprised. It's just like your friend Pietro says about things that appear to be magic. It's not that mental telepathy cannot be explained. It's just that it hasn't been explained *yet.*"

"Don't tell me—you read that in my mind, too?"

Benjamin nodded. Max-Ernest shook his head in amazement.

"OK, explain telepathy, then. Does it have

something to do with your synesthesia? Is that how come you can do it?"

"Not directly, no. At New Promethean they trained me in mind control. It's amazing what you can do if you concentrate hard enough. I'm afraid that's all I can tell you right now."

"Because you don't really know how you do it or because you're not allowed?"

"Both."

"Who taught you?"

"Special teachers," said Benjamin vaguely. "Experts."

"Can you teach me?"

"Sorry. No can do, old chum."

"Well, is mind reading more like reading or more like seeing?" Max-Ernest asked with more than a hint of desperation. "Can you at least tell me that?"

This question had been plaguing Max-Ernest ever since he read the book on second sight. If mind reading was a kind of reading, then there was hope; it meant there was a code he might crack. If mind reading was a kind of seeing, truly a sort of second sight, well, he wasn't sure how he would go about it.

"Hm…" Benjamin paused. "You have to see words to read them, right?"

"Not if you're blind and reading Braille — then

you touch them," Max-Ernest pointed out. "Or somebody could spell a word for you out loud. Then you'd be hearing it first. And I even know of two brothers who spelled words for each other with smell signals.* How 'bout that?"

"How 'bout that?" echoed Benjamin.

"So which is it, then? Do you look into some-body's mind or do you read it?"

Benjamin shrugged. "Both. Neither. It's too hard to say."

To say Max-Ernest was frustrated is an under-statement. Here at last was somebody with a proven ability to read minds, but he, Max-Ernest, was no closer himself to being able to read Cass's mind!

Aargh, he thought. What am I going to do?

"Well, I could do it for you," said Benjamin calmly. "I mean, if you'd like."

Max-Ernest almost jumped, he was so startled. He was going to have to be more careful of his thoughts in the future.

Benjamin laughed. "Don't worry. I don't usually look into people's minds without their permission. Or read them, I mean. I consider it very impolite."

"That's...good...I...guess...," said Max-Ernest. "So you really think you could read Cass's mind, even though she's in a coma?"

---

*THE BROTHERS WOULD BE PIETRO AND DR. L (THEN LUCIANO), OF COURSE. WHEN THEY WERE ONLY ELEVEN YEARS OLD, THEY USED THE SYMPHONY OF SMELLS TO COMMUNICATE IN SMELL-CODE AS PART OF THEIR CIRCUS ACT.

Benjamin smiled. "I can try."

"Would you?" asked Max-Ernest, a flicker of hope lighting up his eyes. "I'm...I'm really scared she's not going to wake up. Pietro—er, somebody I know—thinks getting into her head is the only way."

Benjamin removed his monocle and examined it thoughtfully.

"Are there a lot of people around in the hospital? That might be a problem. I think it would be best if I were alone with her."

"We could try to get in after hours. There are still night nurses around and janitors and stuff, but it would be easier to get a few minutes by ourselves.... The problem is, we won't be allowed in 'cause we're not family."

"We could create a diversion," suggested Benjamin.

"And then slip in when they're not looking? That could work."

"What if we cut off the electricity in the hospital for a few minutes? The darkness would give us cover and we'd have time to get to her room."

Max-Ernest shook his head. "Too hard. How would we ever cut off the backup generators? Besides, there are patients on life-support machines. We don't want to kill anyone, do we?"

Benjamin furrowed his brow as if this were a real question. "No, I suppose not. That might cause problems...."

"Hey, I know, maybe I could create the diversion!" said Max-Ernest excitedly. "I could pretend to be having an epileptic fit. Then all the nurses would have to help me, and you could sneak into Cass's room. How 'bout that? I've seen a couple epileptic fits before. I think I could make it look pretty realistic."

Benjamin looked impressed. "I think that's a capital idea!"

Max-Ernest's heart sank. "Oh wait, then I wouldn't be able to be in the room with you. Forget it."

"You know, I hate to say it, but that...might be better," said Benjamin hesitantly. "No extra brain waves to distract me. Believe me, you have a lot of brain waves."

"I do?" asked Max-Ernest, curious.

Benjamin nodded. "Most I've ever seen."

"Hm. I guess that makes sense," said Max-Ernest, flattered. "Not to brag or anything, but I always have a ton of thoughts in my head. Sometimes it drives me crazy."

"I know the feeling." Benjamin extended his hand. "So it's a deal, then?"

"It's a deal."

They shook hands as solemnly as jewel thieves planning a heist.

Later, as they discussed the finer details — drawing floor plans, diagramming exit strategies — Max-Ernest wondered if what he was doing was very wise. Saving Cass was supposed to be *his* job, after all, not Benjamin's. Pietro hadn't said anything about somebody *else* going inside Cass's head.

What if Benjamin saw something he shouldn't see? Cass was hunting for the Secret. If she'd found it, would it be visible or readable or whatever-the-word-was to Benjamin?

Max-Ernest pushed the thought aside. Benjamin might be listening in.

Not only that, Benjamin was on their side — he had to be. The Midnight Sun had kidnapped him and nearly sucked his brains out. Cass and Max-Ernest had rescued him from a fate worse than death. If Benjamin suspected that Operation Mind-Read had anything to do with the ongoing battle between the Terces Society and the Midnight Sun, he would only be inspired to help out that much more. As for the Secret, there was no reason to believe Benjamin had ever heard of it. And if by some quirk of fate Benjamin found the Secret in Cass's head, chances were he'd have no idea that it was of any consequence at all.

Besides, Max-Ernest half-acknowledged to himself, it was a nice feeling, having a partner again. A friend.

And he didn't want it to end.

I must say, it was a stroke of bad luck that Max-Ernest didn't look at his e-mail that afternoon.

As it turns out, at the very moment that Max-Ernest and Benjamin were shaking hands, Yo-Yoji was replying to the e-mail Max-Ernest had written earlier about Benjamin. Here is the subject line of Yo-Yoji's reply:

Subject: DUDE, YOU BETTER READ THIS RIGHT NOW!!!

Unfortunately, Max-Ernest wouldn't see Yo-Yoji's message until late that night. Of course, I could reproduce it for you now. But I think it's best that you experience events in the same order Max-Ernest did.

This book is much more fun that way.

At least for me.

For you, I imagine, it makes the book much more stressful.

n axe crashed through the cell door.

Anastasia stepped through the splintered wood, holding a candle in front of her. Next to her: her bewhiskered colleague, Thomas, holding his axe.

"Burnes? Gatewood? Are you in here? I told you they couldn't keep you two for long!" Anastasia called into the darkness, eyes glinting above her mask. Her long hair fell heavily over her shoulders.

The Jester blinked, obviously surprised to see this mysterious woman standing in the cell doorway.

"Sorry, m'lady, it's just me and—" He looked in Cass's direction but of course didn't see her. "Just me."

"And who is this Just Me?" Anastasia looked at the Jester sitting there with his hat askew. "Please tell me you are not a jester and that that is just a disguise! Does the King dare insult me by locking up my men with fools?"

"Do not worry," said the Jester dryly. "I'm not a real jester...anymore. The King saw to that."

"Come on. Nobody's in here—," said Anastasia's bandit colleague.

"That's right, Thomas. Nobody. Merely a tool of royalty who is now abandoned property. This is the thanks he gets for making a monarch laugh while his subjects starve? Well, just deserts, I say! How does the saying go? If you lie down with dogs, you will rise with fleas?"

"If you saw how comfortably the King's dogs lie, you would lie down with them, too!" declared the Jester. "Their pillows are very fine indeed. As for the royal fleas, they do not bite but merely scratch when you complain of itch. They are but servants in miniature livery."

Cass stifled a laugh. But Anastasia did not appear to be listening. With a last contemptuous look at the Jester, she swung her hair around and left, leaving the cell door open.

"Let's go!" whispered Cass.

"What? Oh. Yes," answered the Jester, his eyes still focused on the spot where Anastasia had been standing. "I'm glad you're here. I thought maybe I'd imagined you after all."

"No. I'm right here. In the flesh. Well, in the invisible flesh —"

She gave him a tug.

Outside their cell it was chaos.

Every door in the dungeon had been opened in the search for the captured bandits, and the cheers of the escaping prisoners rang through the corridors so loudly, it sounded like they were in some kind of underground sports stadium.

Cass hesitated before following the other prisoners out of the dungeon.

"Ugh. Those poor guys..."

All the prison guards had been thrown into the central cesspool. Mouths gagged, hands bound, they stood up to their shoulders in muck, watching with mute rage.

The Jester chuckled. "Why the angry faces, gents? Are you not slugs in your native element? That smelly mud to you should be mother's milk!"

A few of the guards lunged toward him — only to slip deeper into the cesspool. From the looks in their eyes, the guards were all thinking about what they would do with the Jester if they ever got their hands on him again. And they weren't planning to pat him on the back.

"C'mon—"

Cass clutched the Jester's hand as they ran up the stone stairs and out into the moonlit night.

Just outside the exit, the bandits were waiting on horseback, a few riderless horses at the ready.

"Look—let's get on that gray one over there!" whispered Cass, pointing to a horse standing by a wall a few feet away. The horse whinnied invitingly.

The Jester hesitated. "I have a terrible fear of horses...."

"Oh great," Cass groaned. "Could you be more like Max-Ernest if you tried? I don't think so."

"What?"

"Never mind. There's no time to be afraid. We have to get out of here!"

"Don't worry," said the Jester, standing tall. "I conquered the fear long ago. The first time I escaped from prison—"

"You were in prison before?" asked Cass, alarmed. "What did you do?"

"Nothing. I was referring to my parents' house. It was far worse than this place—"

Unexpectedly agile, the Jester hopped onto the gray horse and pulled Cass up after him.

Anastasia reined her black steed next to them.

"You, Jester—what are you doing? That's not your horse!"

The Jester laughed. "You're a fine one to talk, Madame Thief! I would bet a king's ransom that that horse you're sitting on is not yours, either. But if you like, I will give this one back after we have escaped."

Anastasia was about to offer a retort when a dozen soldiers on horseback appeared from behind the palace, heading in their direction.

"Very well," she said, displeased. "Follow us. But if you lose that horse, you will pay with your life. Men—!"

She whistled, and the bandits took off in a thunder of hooves.

Cass woke with a stiff neck and with a sharp twig poking into her back. Above her, a maple tree made patterns of green and gold. It was day.

Raising her head slightly, she spied a few burlap tents and a trail of smoke wending upward. Instinctively, she reached for the Double Monocle, then remembered it was gone. Oh well, she had survived without X-ray vision in the past (or rather the future); she would have to again. Rubbing her eyes, she looked out at the campsite in the old-fashioned way.

It was the *bandits'* campsite, she deduced when she saw a surly-looking man, Thomas, striding toward her, his black mask hanging around his neck and his axe swinging on his thigh. She was about to greet him when he walked right past her, humming in the way one does only when one is alone. She'd forgotten for a moment he couldn't see her.

Feeling like a spy, she watched him stop at a tree a few feet away. When a tiny stream started trickling in her direction, she had the awful realization that he was relieving himself of the previous night's drink.

She scooted to safety just in time.

As the bandit returned to camp, the Jester walked up to Cass. Or rather to his hat, which was sitting on a rock five feet away from her. It was the first time Cass had seen him bareheaded in the daylight. His orange curls sprang up in all directions like coiled wires.

"Cass?" he whispered to the hat. "Are you up?"

"Yes, but I'm over here to your right," she whispered back.

"Where?" He looked around, confused. "I left my hat as a marker."

"I move around a lot when I sleep. Wait. Stay there...." She got up and walked over to him.

"Here I am," she said, picking up his hat.

The Jester stepped back in surprise as the hat appeared to fly into the air and land on his head.

"Ah, I see that you are," he said, recovering. "I brought you breakfast."

He held up a metal cup full of some kind of gruel-like porridge.

"I wasn't sure if you ate real food or if you only needed invisible sustenance," said the Jester, watching the cup move in the air.

"I'm starving. But this is disgusting. What is it?"

The Jester laughed. "Do they not have frumenty where you come from...? Well, enjoy it. Those selfish thieves have a pile of treasure that would be the envy of dragons, but I had to beg and plead for that little tin cup."*

"They're not selfish. They steal from the rich to give to the poor. Like Robin Hood."

The Jester laughed. "Who? All I know is that I'm poor and they aren't giving any treasure to me. I think the only reason they let me have that cup was that it was stuck to their lodestone. Have you ever seen a lodestone?"

"I don't think so...."

"Marvelous thing," said the Jester. "Metal sticks right to it as if it were glue."

"You mean it's a magnet?"

The Jester's face froze. "Quick, give the cup back to me!" he whispered.

*FRUMENTY, IN CASE THEY DON'T HAVE IT WHERE *YOU* COME FROM, IS MADE FROM BOILED WHEAT. SOMETIMES CONSIDERED ENGLAND'S OLDEST DISH, IT WAS A MAINSTAY OF MEDIEVAL COOKERY, TRADITIONALLY SERVED WITH VENISON OR PORPOISE. (YES, VENISON, AS IN DEER, AND PORPOISE, AS IN *DOLPHIN*!)

"But I'm not done!"

"Just give it to me—Anastasia's coming." He grabbed the cup so hard he spilled frumenty all over himself.

"Practicing for a comedy?"

Anastasia regarded the Jester with arched eyebrows. Without her mask, she was even more beautiful, but no less formidable. "I think next time perhaps you should use an empty cup for rehearsal."

"It's not the same," said the Jester, playing along. "I need to feel the spill to play the role."

"And yet you need not a real actor with whom to say your lines? I saw you talking a moment ago. He is very talented, I thought. He who can speak to the air."

"Watch and I shall pluck a whole world from the air. My comedy is my magic, my jokes are my spells."

"Perhaps," said Anastasia, turning serious. "But your spells have no place here. They do not protect us against the King's men. Nor do they clothe the poor."

"Yes, but they feed the soul."

"We want to feed the hungry. That is our only goal."

"Must their food be so somber? Do not the poor deserve a merry dinner?"

"So they can forget their hunger? Forget injustice?"

"No, so they can laugh at it. 'Tis not the same."

The bandit shook her head. "The men and I have agreed, you must go. On foot. Do not forget, the horse is ours. You have five minutes. If you are not gone when I return, we shall remember how close you were to the King and we shall be much less generous with you."

The Jester watched her leave, uncharacteristically quiet.

Cass looked from the big porridge stain on his shirt to the glum expression on his face. "Sorry if I made you look silly. I should have given you the cup back faster."

The Jester shrugged sadly. "To her I will always be silly, I think, no matter how I look."

He forced a smile. "Do not worry — a jester is not a jester who is not sometimes seen talking to himself. Is that not our job — to throw balls from our right hand to our left, and to throw jokes from the left side of our mouth to the right? A jester no more needs an audience than a puppy needs a kitten to chase his tail. Or is it the kitten who does not need the puppy? Or the bird...? What I mean is, I have no more need of Anastasia than a, well..." He stammered, confused by his own analogy. "I am perfectly merry without her, that is all. I never said I wanted to marry her!"

"Who said you did?" asked Cass, slightly mystified.

"Nobody! — I am perfectly capable of chasing my own tail and running in circles all by myself. That is all I am trying to say," said the Jester, flustered. "Now, my invisible friend, where do we go from here?"

Cass glanced around the woods. She had nowhere else to go. Her goal was to find the Jester and she'd found him.

It was time to ask about the Secret.

Midnight was the mopping hour at the hospital.

When he got to room twelve in the PICU, the janitor looked up from the shiny floor and peered through the door as he did every night. It was sad to see such a young girl lying there like that in the dim green light of the heart monitor. But she was a strong one, he felt. A fighter. He could see it in those pointy ears of hers. He was rooting for her.

He was about to push on when he noticed her lips moving. It's probably nothing, he thought. Just a twitch. Nonetheless, he leaned his mop against the wall and stepped into the shadowy room.

Her eyes were closed, her face almost completely still. And yet there was no doubt — she was murmuring to herself.

By putting his ear close he was able to make out a few whispered words:

"The Secret... What is the Secret...? You have to tell me the Secret...you have to..."

The janitor shivered. What he wouldn't have given to see inside the girl's head just then! There was something about the way she said the word *secret* that made him think she was talking about the Secret of Secrets, the secret of life itself.

But that wasn't the point with somebody in her

condition, he reminded himself. It wasn't *what* she'd said. It was that she'd said it at all.

Should I tell someone? he wondered. He wasn't sure exactly how significant it was that the unconscious girl had spoken. Had he witnessed a breakthrough? Or did she talk to herself every night?

Just in case, he hurried over to the nurse's station. Nobody was there.

It was then that he noticed the flashing light.

An emergency. Downstairs.

He was reluctant to leave the girl, but he knew he should immediately go down to help.

Tomorrow he would leave a note about the young patient in room twelve. For now, her whispered words would have to wait.

ELLLLLLLLLLLLLLLLLLLLP!!!!!!!"

As Max-Ernest ran screaming through the familiar double doors of the emergency room, he was overwhelmed with a flood of memories. He felt almost sentimental remembering the time he'd come in for a Slurpee-induced brain freeze so intense, he'd been convinced that he had frostbite of the parietal lobe.* The night he forgot that he'd eaten red beets and was so alarmed by the color of his pee that he called 9-1-1 and started dictating his last will and testament to the phone operator. The super-size genetically mutated head lice that turned out only to be cookie crumbs left on his pillow after a midnight snack. The extra-strong strain of poison oak, which he was certain had spread from the outside to his liver if not to his kidneys. The splinter he was positive was tapeworm. The hiccups that proved he had lung disease. The runny nose that meant he had a cerebral hemorrhage. The athlete's foot that indicated incipient skin cancer or possibly elephantiasis...

In the past, due to the frequency of his medical complaints, Max-Ernest had been accused of such things as paranoia and hypochondria, not to mention alarmism and hysteria. But there was another way to look at it, he decided as he ran through the waiting room — a blur of fluorescent lights, hobbling

*IF YOU'RE CURIOUS, THE PARIETAL LOBE IS THE PART OF YOUR BRAIN THAT INTEGRATES THE FIVE SENSES.

patients, crying babies. What all his ailments had in common was that they were products of a powerful creative imagination. He had a surplus of brain waves, according to Benjamin. That was his problem.

And a good thing it was, too, because he would need to summon all of his paranoia power and more in the next few moments. Only a true Superhero of Hypochondria, a Master Presenter of Medical Symptoms, a World-Class Worrier, a True Warrior of Words, could create an emergency big enough to draw hospital staff from the upper floors.

"HELP! HELP! HELP!" he screamed again and again at the top of his lungs, grateful that he no longer seemed to have any trouble exercising his vocal cords.

And then he dropped to the floor, writhing and flailing his arms.

As soon as the first orderly rushed over, Max-Ernest started fluttering his eyelids and looking upward so that the whites of his eyes showed.

And then, the *pièce de résistance*, he bit down — and his mouth erupted with foam.*

Watching through the window, Benjamin smiled. Max-Ernest was a skilled actor — though not, Benjamin reflected with satisfaction, as skilled an actor as Benjamin himself.

*Glob had given Max-Ernest his last sample of The Volcano gum after Benjamin did a little judicious Globby mind reading and gently threatened to tell the world what he found out.

Turning away from the delightfully comic spectacle of Max-Ernest's staged epileptic fit, Benjamin walked quickly toward the hospital's main entrance.

Inside, a light was flashing over the front desk. The nurse behind the desk stood with her back to the door, listening to the intercom.

"All available staff to Emergency, please. All available staff."

Quickly glancing around the room to confirm that it was empty of incoming patients, the nurse left her post and rushed off in the direction of the emergency room.

It was just as they'd planned.

Or rather just as Benjamin had planned. There were one or two key parts of the evening's agenda that he had conveniently failed to mention to Max-Ernest. If all went swimmingly, Max-Ernest would never know what an important moment he was missing. Not until it was too late, anyway.

Consulting Max-Ernest's scrupulously detailed map, Benjamin proceeded toward the third elevator from the right.

The one marked PICU.

Thank you, Max-Ernest, he thought. And to think, I'm supposed be the one helping *you*! When

---

Out of respect for the deal they struck, I won't reveal Glob's shameful secrets here. All I will say is that while insignificant, they were plentiful.

this is all over, I'll have to send you a present. Some new magic tricks, perhaps?

He had a hunch Max-Ernest would soon be wanting nothing more than to disappear in a puff of smoke. Poor Max-Ernest...

By now, three nurses, two orderlies, and a doctor were standing in a circle around the tragically ill boy lying on the floor. Would-be patients in waiting-room chairs stared with a mixture of curiosity (what is *wrong* with that guy?) and resentment (why is he getting so much attention when I've been here for three hours?).

"Yes, that's right—I'm having chest pain and shortness of breath," gasped Max-Ernest, wheezing noisily. "It's...very...short...see—"

He knew those were the things that were supposed to command the most immediate attention in a hospital, but for some reason the doctor didn't seem to see it that way.

"Those aren't necessarily symptoms of epilepsy," said the doctor, regarding him skeptically from above.

"I know—it's unrelated. My asthma. Combined with an allergic reaction, I think."

"To what?"

"Vinyl. The flooring is vinyl—see."

"You're having an allergic reaction to the floor in here?"

"Yes. The floor is highly toxic. I think you should consider replacing it."

"That doesn't explain why you're here in the first place. Or was your reaction anticipatory?"

Max-Ernest nodded vigorously. "Well, that and the fact that I was undergoing cardiac arrest."

The doctor leaned down to feel Max-Ernest's pulse. She put a stethoscope to his chest and listened intently.

Max-Ernest breathed in and out as fast as he could—to no avail.

The doctor smiled, standing. "Well, you can rest easy—I'm very confident you're not having a heart attack."

"Oh, that's just because I have white-coat syndrome. You know, when you see a doctor and suddenly your symptoms disappear—but then they come back when the doctor's gone?"

"Actually, white-coat syndrome, otherwise known as white-coat hypertension, is almost the exact opposite of what you're describing," said the doctor smoothly. "It's when the sight of a doctor induces high blood pressure in patients who otherwise exhibit normal blood pressure. For some reason, I don't think that's your problem."

Max-Ernest silently cursed himself. How could he have gotten that wrong? It was so unlike him! He must be nervous.

"I think the only white coat we need here is one to put on you." The doctor gestured to the orderly. "Straitjacket, please!"

Max-Ernest turned pale. He knew all about straitjackets from reading biographies of Houdini and other escape artists — and that's how he knew he wouldn't be able to escape from one. "I'm not crazy! I just have Munchausen syndrome," he said desperately (referring to the medical disorder that consists of fabricating medical disorders). "I can control it, I promise!"

"You no more have Munchausen syndrome than I'm a munchkin in Oz," declared the doctor, towering over Max-Ernest.

The nurse from the reception area strode in. She looked down at Max-Ernest in surprise. "Max-Ernest?! What are you doing here? Are you OK?"

Max-Ernest jumped to his feet. "Nothing! It's nothing. I'm fine."

Not waiting for a response, he sprinted toward the exit.

Taken by surprise, the nurses and staff watched him go for a moment before running after him.

"Hey, we have to be fast," Max-Ernest whispered, entering Cass's room. "Benjamin, can you hear me—?"

Benjamin, who had been leaning over Cass, stood up straight, startled. His monocle fell to the floor. Fumbling, he picked it up and restored it to its place covering his eye.

"Sorry if I scared you," continued Max-Ernest. "They figured out I was faking. They even figured out I was *faking* faking. Like that I didn't even have real Munchausen syndrome. It was fake Munchausen. Which, if you think about it, is a *fake* fake *syndrome* syndrome....Anyway, they'll be here any second—" He stopped, seeing Benjamin's expression. "What happened? Is she OK? Were you able to see inside her head?"

"Yes, for a second, I almost...saw..." Benjamin seemed to be in some kind of trance, as if still half inside Cass's mind. "I almost...I almost reached her....And then you..." He trailed off.

"You mean you...? Wow, that's great!" said Max-Ernest, excited. "If I stall the nurses for another minute, would that be enough time to...to reach her?"

Benjamin nodded, staring down at Cass. "I think so...."

"OK. Maybe I can just run around the floor and make them chase me. How 'bout that?"

"Yes...yes. Good idea..."

Max-Ernest hesitated in the doorway, staring at Benjamin. He was thrilled that Benjamin was on the verge of success, and yet he felt strangely uneasy.

"What did you see before...or almost see?"

"The Secret," said Benjamin softly. The jagged line of Cass's heart monitor reflected eerily in the monocle — a moving crack in the glass lens. "She was thinking about the Secret, I could tell. I was so close...."

"The Secret? What do you know about the Secret?" asked Max-Ernest, his guard immediately up.

"Oh, I don't know about it at all, really," said Benjamin quickly. He looked up at Max-Ernest, regaining his composure. "It's just that I couldn't help picking up from you that Cass was looking for the Secret — *a* secret, I should say. There are so many secrets in the world, after all!"

"Right. I guess I should have tried to hide it more....," said Max-Ernest. But I did try to hide it — my mind couldn't be *that* transparent! he thought.

"Perhaps, but I would have seen anyway."

But you said you never looked into people's minds without asking, Max-Ernest thought, but he didn't say it out loud.

"Now go," said Benjamin. No longer in his trancelike state, he appeared completely alert — on edge, even. "I need to be alone. It's very important."

Max-Ernest stared at his friend. Or rather at the boy he'd thought was his friend.

He couldn't trust Benjamin; he knew it now with certainty.

"Um, you know what, I don't think there's time, after all. The nurses'll be here any second. We better get out while we can."

"Just give me one minute with Cass, old chum. I'm afraid I really must insist. Let me worry about the nurses." Benjamin took a step toward Max-Ernest. It was clear that if Max-Ernest didn't leave, Benjamin was prepared to push him out the door.

"No, I don't think so...."

Max-Ernest started looking around the room for an object — a broom or mop maybe? — with which to protect himself and Cass if necessary.

"Max-Ernest? What is going on here? I need an explanation or I'm going to have to call security right now!"

The boys turned.

The nurse from reception was standing in the doorway with her hands on her hips, the janitor behind her.

The jig, as they say in the crime business, was up.

Three minutes earlier, Max-Ernest would have been bitterly disappointed to see them show up. Now, he was relieved.

"Sorry, wrong room," said Benjamin quickly. "Looking for my grannie!"

He rushed out without looking anybody in the eye.

Max-Ernest was unable to leave so quickly. He had to talk to a hospital administrator first.

Thankfully, the nurse persuaded the hospital not to press charges (as some had wanted), or even to have Max-Ernest committed to the mental ward (as others had suggested). Grief over Cass, she said, was responsible for his crazy behavior.

Nonetheless, Max-Ernest left the hospital totally despondent. Time, he knew, was running out. And he seemed further away from saving Cass than ever.

And yet when he got home and saw Yo-Yoji's e-mail, he was flooded with relief. While Cass's condition was critical, at least one tragedy — a potentially drastic one—had been averted. As it turned out, Max-Ernest had been right not to trust Benjamin—more right than he possibly could have known:

From: ohnoitsyoyo@xxxxx.com
Subject: DUDE, YOU BETTER READ THIS RIGHT NOW!!!
To: mdash@xxxxxxxxx.com

Jfstnm, Lro, u r lnfmc pjayne darenr tdam am afr cuftar fm bromt ob ky latdrook kfrror...Gust cot laih brok Bugf ame saw yr n-kafj alout Lnmgakfm. Soumene so rameok, tdn way dn idamcne, so F efe a jfttjn makn snarid. Modtfmc... Lut tdnm F joohne up tdat sidooj dn wnmt to, ame cunss wdo's "dnae ob sidooj" at Mnw Prokntdnam...A cuy makne...eruk rojj, pjnasn...Juifamo Lnrcako. Ud-dud. Er. Brnahfm' J!!! Ynp, Lnmgakfm's sidooj was rum ly Kfemfcdt Sum! Eummo wdat ft knams...Spy??? Enbfmftnjy MOT COOE. Ajnrt ajnrt ajnrt! Pjz tnjj kn wdnm u cnt tdfs so F iam rnjax ame co laih to lufjefmc cakn jnvnjs.*

Lates! Y-Y

\m/ (>.<) \m/

(Rock On!)

---

*For the code-challenged, a translation of this message appears in the appendix alongside Yo-Yoji's first e-mail.

rom time to time, some of my more adoring fans (OK, OK, some of my more suspicious readers) ask me if it is really and truly true that I almost drowned in a jar of mayonnaise when I was a young child. I'm not certain in which of my many, many major media interviews they happened to read this story (OK, OK, it was the interview I conducted with myself at the end of my second book, and who better to conduct it, I ask you) but it is time I settled the question once and for all.

The answer is: yes, I did.

Here is how it happened:

The True Origins of My Mayophobia
A Personal Digression

As hard as it is to believe now, there was once a time when yours truly, Pseudonymous Bosch, was just a Baby Bosch. An innocent infant who knew nothing of secrets, let alone *the* Secret. Who had never heard of the Terces Society or the Midnight Sun. Who had not yet even tasted his first bite of chocolate.

This unformed child, this unfinished project, this unbaked loaf, this unsculpted clay, this unwritten novel, this baby was I.

Do not think for a second that I am trying to gain your sympathy, but I was not a happy baby. What with my parents always fighting over me (oh, did I mention the tragedy of my broken home?) and my insides always fighting with themselves (oh, did I mention the curse of my acid stomach?), I spent so much of my babyhood crying inconsolably that fights seemed to break out wherever I went.

No, I am not looking for your sympathy, but a crying baby has no friends. None. You try listening to a baby cry for five minutes or ten minutes or twenty minutes or for months and months on end as I cried. See if you don't want to throttle the poor little lamb.

Not for the crying baby the clucking and the cooing of Grandma Jo. The sneaking of sweets by Grandpa Carl. The pinching of cheeks by Aunt Martha. At best it's a pitying glance and a shake of the head. You're lucky if nobody throws a shoe at you.

No, really, honestly, I am not looking for sympathy. Keep your tissues to yourself. Don't send me flowers or consolation cards. I have no use for your well-meaning words.

Well, not now, anyway. Back then I suppose it might have been nice if just one person had smiled at me. If a single solitary individual had taken just the slightest bit of interest in that red-faced baby boy with the yellow snot running down his nose and the heat rash on his toes.

You see, had someone taken just a little itty-bitty bit of interest, he or she might have discovered the little green pea, hardened and blackened over time, lodged between the folds of my little baby thigh. It had stuck to my skin somehow and caused a small but persistent pain, an icky-itchy-sticky-scratchy-pushy-pully feeling in my leg that never went away, day or night.

Call me the Princess and the Pea. Make fun of me all you like. But that pea bothered me for nearly a year. It was the reason I was crying. Or the main one. Who knows what would have happened if some kindly person had thought to look into my thigh and remove that pea the day it got stuck there. Who knows what a smiley, bouncy baby I would have become. All the smiling and bouncing that would have been bestowed upon me.

Ah well, then I wouldn't be the same person

now, would I? Our hard-luck knocks define us. Those peas in our thighs, they make us who we are.

But I digress from my digression.

Both my parents worked, and neither had time to take care of me. And yet, due to my incessant crying, they were unable to find me a nanny who would stay more than a week. Some lasted less than an hour. One, memorably, quit after only a minute. By the time my first birthday came around, there were no nannies or babysitters or even semi-responsible ten-year-olds left within a hundred-mile radius who would put up with me.

And so the unthinkable happened: my parents were forced to take me along on my birthday dinner.

They should have known better.

While, as usual, my parents spoke nary a word to each other, my crying grew so loud at the restaurant that the waitress begged my parents to let her take me into the kitchen.

Naturally, I only cried louder once she took me away from my parents. The waitress tried giving me all kinds of sugary, salty, and otherwise unhealthy treats, but nothing would shut me up. Thinking maybe I needed a diaper change, she rather roughly threw me onto the hard, cold, wet, stainless-steel kitchen counter and lifted my tender little baby legs. I wailed and wailed, but lo and behold, she found what no one had found before:

the pea.

By now, however, it had been there so long that it had practically grown into my skin. It looked like some kind of blackish-bluish-brownish-greenish wart—something you were more likely to find on a witch's cheek than on a baby's thigh—and it gripped into me so hard the waitress even wondered if it wasn't a sort of parasite or leech. Unable to remove it with her bare fingers, she searched desperately for a lubricant, preferably industrial-strength.

Can you guess where this is going?

The nearest item within reach: a vat of mayonnaise the size of a smallish garbage can, just large enough, in other words, to hold a baby.

In her defense, she sought only to dunk my lower body. But when my toes hit the cold mayonnaise, I started wriggling like an eel. She simply couldn't hold me. Once I fell in, there was no way to pull me out with her hands. I was far too slippery.

I waved and waved, I shook this way and that, but I only succeeded in sinking further. I coughed and sputtered, gasping for air but sucking in mayonnaise. It went up my nose and got into my eyes. It filled my ears and got under my nails.

Soon I was entirely submerged in the chilly, slimy, smelly, gelatinous, high-caloric, cholesterol-raising, bacteria-collecting, botulism-inducing, absolutely disgusting, and utterly gross white goo.

In only seconds, I would be no better than a tuna sandwich: drowned in mayonnaise.

Luckily, the sous chef happened to be working on his famous Thousand Island salad dressing at the time, and—thank the gods, or rather, the Green Goddess—he needed an extra cup of mayo. Just as I was about to suffer the humiliating fate of a fish stick, he reached in and gripped me by the neck with his salad tongs.

While I wriggled in the air, crying like a newborn, the sous chef deftly squeezed the pea between his thumb and forefinger and twisted hard. The pea snapped off of my thigh, leaving a red-raw circle about the size of a dime. (Just like twisting the end off a string bean, the chef said.) It hurt, of course, but the relief was immediate.

I stopped crying and stared with fascination at

the object that had caused me so much pain and distress. Shrunken to the size of a peppercorn, it sat on the stainless-steel counter, taunting me with its very smallness.

Perhaps because I felt a desire to vanquish my enemy in a dramatic fashion, or more likely just because it was there, I reached for the pea and, before anyone could stop me, I did what babies do: I swallowed it.

That's when I started crying again. Not because the pea bothered my stomach, but because, free of other distractions, I noticed I was still covered with that slimy white substance I'd nearly drowned in. Sensing my discomfort, the sous chef hastily wiped it off. Then he handed me over to the grateful waitress and went back to work.

Now I don't want to brag, but everybody complimented him on his salad dressing that evening. It seems I added a certain piquant *je ne sais quoi* to the flavor—not to mention a certain yellowness to the color—that only a baby can provide.*

Ever since then, I have felt a warm affinity for sous chefs—and a morbid fear of mayonnaise.

---

*Please don't ask me what *je ne sais quoi* means; I'll just say it means I don't know what.

ass wasn't sure she'd heard the Jester correctly.

"Really? You don't know the Secret?"

"I promise, I don't know the Secret. I have never heard of the Secret," said the Jester. "*You* are the invisible girl. *You* are the time traveler. *You* are the only secret I know. I should be asking *you* for the Secret."

Yes, unfortunately, she'd heard him correctly.

She was crestfallen. Here she'd come so far to ask him the question, and he didn't know the answer. He seemed barely to understand the question. Her mission was a failure. Beyond that, her role in the Terces Society — her whole purpose in life — would now be in jeopardy. How could she be the Secret Keeper if she had no secret to keep?

She glanced around the woods, as if the Secret might be hidden behind a tree. But she saw nothing more illuminating than a pinecone sitting on a rock.

"But what about the Terces Society?" she persisted. "You're the founder of the Terces Society. And the whole point of the Terces Society is to protect the Secret. It's the secret society of the Secret!"

"Sorry, I know nothing of any secret society. If I am the founder, I have not founded it yet."

"Well, what about my parents? Who are they?" asked Cass, increasingly desperate. "At least you must know that. I came all this way to find out who I am. I thought you knew. All I know is I'm supposed to be the Secret Keeper."

"If you come from the future, how could I know who your parents are? You haven't been born yet," said the Jester with indisputable logic. "You make no sense—even a fool like me can see that!"

"You're serious, you don't know anything? I don't understand—"

The Jester shook his head, muttering. "Either you are not here, after all, and I am nothing but a madman talking to the wind. Or you have been sent on purpose to make me go mad. It is the same either way."

Cass slumped against a tree trunk. "I can't believe I came all this way for nothing! What am I supposed to do now?" She tried to choke back a sob, but failed.

"Oh, it can't be so bad as that," said the Jester. The sound of her crying had shaken him. "Where are you? Give me your hand so I may pat your head."

Reluctantly, Cass nudged him on the arm.

"Oh, there you are—you can't keep moving around like that! It's disorienting. Now, there, there—"

He patted her invisible head as promised. "How

is that? I have not much experience comforting little children. Only making them laugh until they get tired and cross. When they start to cry I send them away — 'tis bad for business."

"I'm not a little child, but you're doing fine," said Cass, sniffling.

"Here's an idea," said the Jester. "Are you sure it is not another jester you are looking for? I hear the King of France has a very funny fellow in his employ." His face clouded. "And that lucky dog still has a job!"

Cass shook her head. "No, it's you. We've met before. I mean, I think we have. But it was different, you were older, some of the time, anyway...."

"Ah, well, that explains it, then," said the Jester, brightening. "You've simply come back in time too far, that is all. It may be that I will discover the Secret tomorrow, or next year, or not until I am an old man. And this society of yours may not arise for many moons after that. You just have to go home, then come back again — to my future!"

"I'm not sure I can do that," said Cass sadly. "I don't even know if I can go home in the first place."

Home. She wanted to go home now. Desperately. Even if she was going home empty-handed. There was no sense delaying any longer. It would only make the disappointment worse.

But how? How was she supposed to go home?

She was depending on Max-Ernest to bring her back, but shouldn't he have done it by now? He'd made the antidote before. How hard could it be to make it again? Or had it not really been that long?

How much time had passed in her own world since she'd left? She had no way of knowing whether it had been seconds or minutes or hours or years. In her real life, she could be ninety years old by now, for all she knew. Her friends and family might all be dead. She might not recognize her own home — or even her own self.

Max-Ernest had warned her there might be a problem like that. Why hadn't she listened? She, not the Jester, was the true fool.

By the time they heard the barking it was too late.

The regal beagles, roused from their velvet pillows and made for once to work for their roast beef, had sniffed out the bandits' trail and had led the King's soldiers directly to the campsite. The bandits had been taken by surprise — the man on watch had been drunk on mead, Cass gathered from Anastasia's cursing — and they were outnumbered.*

Now the camp was surrounded, and all the ban-

*MEAD, WHICH YOU HAVE PERHAPS HEARD OF WITHOUT QUITE KNOWING WHAT IT WAS, IS A SORT OF WINE MADE FROM HONEY. ITS ORIGINS DATE BACK TO THE EARLIEST CIVILIZATIONS; IT WAS VERY POPULAR, FOR EXAMPLE, AMONG THE ANCIENT GREEKS. I WOULD NOT TRY IT IF I WERE

dits had bayonets at their backs. The regal beagles circled watchfully, as if they were herding sheep.

Only the Jester and Cass, about forty feet from the camp, remained free, unseen by the soldiers and as yet unsniffed by the beagles.

"How proud you must feel, hounds, catching your prize fox!" cried Anastasia. (By *hounds*, mind you, she referred not to the beagles but to the soldiers.) As scornful as ever, she seemed oblivious to the fact that her throat could be cut at any second. Cass couldn't help admiring Anastasia's bravery under pressure. "I see the King needed only to send one hundred of his best men to capture ten thieves! And you call yourselves soldiers?"

"Soldiers, yes, and trained killers each of us. Tell us where the treasure is and we will make your deaths quick and easy," declared a rather pompous soldier with thick gold braiding on his uniform and beads of sweat on his brow, clearly the Commander. "And if you lead us to that two-foot-tall dung heap they call the homunculus, we may even spare one or two of you. Lord Pharaoh has offered a big reward for his little monster."

"Come on," the Jester whispered urgently. "Let's get out of here before they see us." He nodded in the

---

YOU, HOWEVER. IN THE LEGEND OF BEOWULF, THE NORSEMEN WHO WERE ATTACKED BY THE MONSTER GRENDEL WERE FAMOUSLY DRUNK ON MEAD. APPARENTLY, THE MEAD GREATLY HINDERED THEM IN BATTLE— ALTHOUGH IT MAY HAVE DULLED THE PAIN A LITTLE.

direction of the nearest soldier, who was shifting on his feet, perilously close to turning around. "Or smell us —" The Jester nodded toward the beagles, who were sniffing the ground suspiciously, as if they were just then catching the scent of a renegade jester and an invisible girl.

"What do you mean — we can't just leave them!" Cass sputtered.

"Easy for you to say — you're invisible."

"But that's just...wrong."

"Why? Did not the Bandit Queen command me to leave? I am but following her orders."

"Yeah, but she freed us from the dungeon, remember? And she gave us her horse. We owe her our lives!"

"*Lent* us the horse, you mean, and very grudgingly, I might add."

"I kind of thought you liked her."

"Liked her?"

"Yeah, you know, *like* liked," said Cass, automatically raising her eyebrows to make the point, even though the Jester couldn't see them. (Having a conversation when you're invisible is like talking to a blind person; you have to communicate everything with your voice.)

"*Like* liked? What does that mean — that I like

her twice? But I don't like her even once — I *loathe* her thrice!" protested the Jester, but he made no further movement toward leaving. It was clear Cass's words had had their intended effect.

"OK, you go stall them," she said, going into the operations mode she had practiced so often with Max-Ernest and the Terces Society. "I'll try and see if I can untie anybody."

"And how do you expect me to do that?"

"I don't know...go juggle or tell jokes or chase your tail or something. You're a jester, right?"

The Jester opened his mouth to reply but remained silent. He sensed Cass might have already gone, and while it was one thing to be *perceived* as talking to yourself, it was quite another actually to do it.

He took a breath and then boldly stepped forward.

"Soldiers! Salutations!"

The dozen closest soldiers reeled around, drawing their swords. The beagles ran toward him in a pack, yapping madly.

"Who goes there?" shouted the Commander.

"What—? Who—? Nobody!" cried the Jester, jumping to and fro to keep the beagles from sinking their teeth into his ankles. "I mean to say, 'tis I who go there! You see, here...I...go!"

The soldiers laughed.

"Look, men — the King's jester! More lately the King's prisoner!" shouted a young soldier. "And now he is the beagles' dinner!"

"What happened, Jester?" shouted another. "Why did you reject our hospitality? Was the dungeon floor too hard for your liking? The food too cold?"

"Oh the floor was fine, and the food, too," the Jester offered, moving aside just as a beagle was about to bite into his shoe. "It was the prison guards — their smell offended!"

"You're a cocky one to joke when you are surrounded by so many men!" snarled the Commander.

"Men? And yet you tie up a lady?" The Jester gestured toward Anastasia, who was shaking her head in disbelief. Evidently, she didn't think the Jester was helping her cause.

"Do not worry," replied the Commander. "She will not be tied for long. It is only her head the King wants. We brought this platter special —"

He raised his hand in the air and a younger soldier ran up with a silver platter. "We are instructed to bring back her head sitting on it. Perhaps there is room for yours as well."

"My head would be honored to be in such noble

company. But please do not face her toward me. I fear she will bite off my nose — if these beagles do not get to it first."

The Jester grinned at Anastasia, who glared back with ferocity. Indeed, it looked as if she might bite the Jester if she could.

ear ye! Hear ye! Attention, all lords and ladies, brave knights and beautiful maidens, the Renaissance Faire is just a month away. After your day of frolic and revelry, come for a royal repast at your local Medieval Days Family Restaurant!"

It was Glob and Daniel-not-Danielle, dressed as not quite medieval, not quite Renaissance, not quite modern-day heralds, in green tights and jester hats. They held plastic trumpets in their hands and wore sandwich boards over their shoulders advertising Medieval Days Family Restaurants:

> It's not just for dinner,
> it's joust for dinner!

Kids walking by on their way into school snickered and jeered.

"Nice tights!"

"Are you supposed to be lords or ladies?"

"Laugh all you like, dudes—they're paying us a hundred bucks each to do this, plus free soda all day!" shouted Glob, holding up a can. "What part of *mucho dinero* don't you understand? And what are *you* getting for wearing your old, smelly jeans? That's right—the big zero. *Nada!*"

"Will you stop shouting? You're just making it worse," whispered Daniel-not-Danielle, who was busy arranging his dreadlocks so not a centimeter of his face showed to passersby.

"They're not going to like it when they see what I write on my blog," grumbled Glob. "I'm going to live-blog Ren-Faire, and none of them will escape my wrath!"

"They don't care about your blog, man."

"Do you know how many direct hits I had last week? Like, thousands," replied Glob, outraged. "Hey, Max-Ernest, you want in? I've got another one—" Glob pointed to an extra sandwich board leaning against the wall, a pair of green tights hanging over it.

Max-Ernest shook his head violently and kept walking.

"Fine. See if I ever offer you a job again!"

Max-Ernest had returned to school with a sense of dread.

Benjamin had been his only hope for saving Cass. And now he knew that Benjamin was their worst enemy. According to Yo-Yoji, Benjamin had been Dr. L's student at the New Promethean Academy. And now he was a spy—a mole—for the Midnight Sun in their very own school.

Given the choice, of course, Max-Ernest would have avoided ever seeing Benjamin again — or school, for that matter. But even if he couldn't get inside Cass's head, her voice was always in *his*, telling him not to give up, to remember the Terces Society and the vows they had made to protect the Secret.

Why, Max-Ernest wondered frequently, does she have to be just as bossy in my imagination as she is in real life?

At this very moment, he was having a silent conversation with Cass that went something like this:

C: *Don't let Benjamin out of your sight. If the Midnight Sun went to the trouble of training him and planting him in our school, he won't give up so easily.*

M-E: How am I supposed to tail Benjamin? As soon as I get near him, he can read my mind!

C: *Just concentrate on different thoughts. Pretend that you don't know about him. That you're still friends.*

M-E: But I don't even know how to be friends. I was never friends with anybody.

C: *Oh, you weren't?*

M-E: You don't count.

C: *Thanks a lot.*

M-E: You know what I mean.

C: *No, I don't. And I think Yo-Yoji would be pretty insulted to hear that, too. . . . All I know is, you better find out Benjamin's next move before he finds out yours.*

M-E: Easy for you to say. You're just lying there doing nothing.

C: *Doing nothing?! You mean in a coma? You want to trade places?*

"You should try to keep it down when you talk to yourself, Max-Ernest. You don't want people thinking you're crazy, do you? Not that they don't already..."

Max-Ernest spun around. Opal, the new school secretary, was standing in front of him, hands on her hips, laughing at him. Or at the very least grinning all the way up to the big mole on her cheek.

Max-Ernest hadn't seen her since she'd set him up, making him walk into the principal's office without knocking. What was it that looked different about her today?

"Unless you're auditioning for the part of the jester? You know I could probably get you onstage at the Renaissance Faire."

Max-Ernest felt himself blush. "Very funny."

How much had she heard? He hoped desperately that he hadn't said anything aloud about the Terces Society or the Secret.

"Oops — what's that I hear?"

The bell was ringing. The second bell. The one that meant first period was starting.

Opal looked at her watch in that exaggerated way people sometimes do. "Tsk-tsk. Looks like you're going to be a little late. I hope you have a note from home."

"Um...not really."

"Well, you better come to the office after next period. We'll see what the principal, that is, Her Majesty, has to say about this."

Max-Ernest stared. It was so unfair. Had the secretary not stopped to talk to him, he might very well have made it to class in time.

He was about to protest when his attention was diverted by an unexpected sight: Benjamin Blake talking to Amber.

Just the two of them. Alone.

They were standing between the administration building and the cafeteria. The space was very narrow and usually only populated by ants and the occasional rodent. Obviously, they had chosen it for the privacy. Only good luck had made Max-Ernest glance in their direction at the right time, and he was determined to take full advantage.

He had to get rid of the secretary quickly. That much was clear. But how was he going to spy on his schoolmates without being seen himself?

"OK, I'll come by after class," he said, edging out of their sight line.

"Good. I'll see you then," said Opal, studying him. She seemed to have noticed his change in attitude.

"Yeah, see you." He started turning, as if he were going to head for class, when she stopped him.

"Oh, Max-Ernest, I'm sorry, can you do me a favor? I just did my nails and they take *forever* to dry. Would you just reach into my bag and get a tissue out for me?" She opened her large black patent-leather purse for him, her fingers spread wide so that her newly applied fingernail polish wouldn't smear on anything.

Impatient, Max-Ernest felt around for the tissues.

"It's right there under my compact—that's that little mirror there," said the secretary helpfully.

The mirror in question was hinged and would, Max-Ernest recognized immediately, make a perfect spy tool.

He closed his right hand around the mirror while at the same time picking up the package of tissues with his left. (Every once in a while, when he was doing a magic trick or was engaged in a spy operation, the experience of having to do two things simultaneously for his parents so many times came in handy.) With any luck, the secretary wouldn't notice the compact was gone. And he could slip it back into her purse when he went to the office later.

It's just borrowing, he heard Cass's voice conveniently reassuring him. *Not stealing*. Besides, this was the woman who pulled a prank on him for no reason the day they first met!

The secretary smirked, delicately pulling a tissue from the package without letting her nails touch anything. "Thank you, Max-Ernest. And tie your shoelace, please!"

Max-Ernest nodded in acknowledgment, then headed in the direction of his class, not bothering to fix his shoelace. When he was satisfied that the secretary would be safely behind her desk, he reversed course and crept back toward the administration building.

Sidling up to the building and keeping as much of himself hidden as possible, he held out the compact and moved the mirror around until he could see Benjamin and Amber. They were still deep in conversation.

The last time he'd seen them together had been when Amber had told Max-Ernest's fortune. It hadn't seemed then that they'd remembered each other. But looking at them now, Max-Ernest had the sense that they knew each other very well after all.

There was just enough of an echo reverberating between the stucco walls for Max-Ernest to hear their whispering:

"You were trying to look into her mind, right?" Amber was asking. "Why? What did they want you to find?"

Benjamin shrugged. "It doesn't matter because I didn't find it."

"Come on—they never tell me anything," complained Amber.

"Well, then, why would you think I could tell you?"

"Please."

"Why do you want to know so badly?"

"'Cause I hate not knowing a secret."

"Then you're very close."

"What does that mean?"

"Oh, nothing," said Benjamin smugly.

"Ugh—I hate you!" cried Amber. "After that whole fortune-telling thing nobody likes me anymore—I totally ruined my reputation for this. I should at least get to look into the monocle!"

Amber reached for the monocle, but Benjamin turned away, preventing her from taking it.

"I'm not allowed."

"So what? Like Dr. L is ever gonna know."

"Something tells me he'll know. Especially when he gets the monocle back."

"Please please."

"Why do you want to see it so badly?"

"So I can see what's in your mind and know what you were looking for in Cass's. Why do you think?"

The monocle, all along it was the monocle! Max-Ernest thought excitedly. He had assumed Benjamin's telepathic power was internal, that it was Benjamin's own unique talent at work, that Benjamin alone could see into Cass's mind. But if his power resided in the monocle, then anybody could be a mind reader—anybody who got hold of the monocle, that is.

Even him.*

While Max-Ernest was speculating about how to get the monocle out of Benjamin's hands, Amber lunged for it. In less than a second, she was holding it up to her eye.

Resigned, Benjamin folded his arms and looked at her. "Well, what do you see?"

"Nothing. It's just like looking through plain glass. If you were just tricking me, I'll be so mad.... No, wait. I see...I see...everybody. Everybody in school! Teachers. Students. Everybody. How cool is that? It's like I can see through walls....Wow, with this thing I could control the whole school—I mean, not that I don't already...."

Suddenly Amber's grin turned into a frown. "Why is Veronica talking to Naomi? I didn't say she could. I hate Naomi, not that I'm a hater, I'm not.... Wait, never mind about Veronica...." Amber pointed in Max-Ernest's direction. "I think there's somebody behind that corner spying on us," she said, lowering her voice, but still audible to Max-Ernest.

"Who?"

"I can't see his face—"

"Give me the monocle back."

"No, never—"

"You have to!"

---

*Lest I be accused of encouraging bad grammar, I feel I must point out that, strictly speaking, those last two words should not have read *Even him* but rather *Even he*. As in *Even he, Max-*

They wrestled, Benjamin straining to keep the monocle away from Amber, until it fell to the ground, skidding in Max-Ernest's direction.

Without thought to the consequences, he seized his chance and scrambled to get it. Benjamin and Amber stopped fighting when they saw him.

"Max-Ernest, old chum! Thank goodness it's you. Somebody I can reason with," said Benjamin calmly. "That monocle is very valuable to me. For purely sentimental reasons, you understand. It wouldn't mean anything to anybody else. I appreciate your picking it up for me. Very kind of you."

"Um, you're welcome...?" said Max-Ernest, clutching tight to the monocle.

"Wonderful. You can give it back to me now," said Benjamin in the tone one uses with a little child.

Max-Ernest took a step backward. "No, I think I'll keep it for the moment because... because..." He stammered, unable to think of a reason that wouldn't give away what he knew about Benjamin and about the monocle.

"Forget him, Max-Ernest," said Amber in her sweetest, most insinuating voice. "Give it to me and I'll be your friend for real."

"When are you going to get it through your head

ERNEST, COULD BE A MIND READER. BUT *EVEN HE* SOUNDS TOO STILTED, TOO UNNATURAL. EVEN FOR A STILTED AND UNNATURAL PERSON SUCH AS ME (I MEAN I!)

that I don't want to be your friend?" asked Max-Ernest.

He wanted to run, but he hesitated. If he ran toward the exit, there was a very good chance Opal, the secretary, would see him through the office window.

"Just give it to me; it's mine," said Benjamin. "This isn't the time for games."

"Sorry—"

Both Benjamin and Amber reached for the monocle at the same time. Trying to evade them, Max-Ernest stepped on his shoelace. He fell backward and wound up sitting on the ground, still holding the monocle tight.

"I'll take that," said Opal, stepping up to them. Apparently she hadn't gone back to the office after all. Before Max-Ernest could think to resist, she took the monocle out of his hand and stowed it away in her big shiny purse.

"The principal will deal with you two later!" said Opal, addressing Benjamin and Amber.

She offered Max-Ernest her hand and pulled him up with surprising strength. "*You* are going to the nurse's office right now. That's going to be a nasty bruise on your elbow."

*   *   *

The nurse's office was empty. The blinds were closed and the computer screen was dark. It looked as though nobody had been in there all day.

"You sit here," said Opal, patting the pillow on the single cot in the room. Max-Ernest noticed her fingernails grazed the sheets without smearing. Funny, he thought, she said they took "forever" to dry....

It was then that he realized what looked different about her today: her mole. He could have sworn that when they first met it was on her right cheek—the right side of her face being the side you saw when you walked into the administration office—and yet now the mole was on her left cheek.

"I'm going to see if I can't scare up that nurse. I must say, I didn't take you for the wrestling type."

Casually dropping her purse on the nurse's desk, Opal gave a shake to her mass of blond curls and walked out of the room on her vertiginously high platform heels.

Not quite believing his luck, Max-Ernest waited until the secretary closed the door, then, as quickly as he could, he opened her purse. He removed the monocle and left her compact in its place.

As soon as he sat back down on the cot, Opal breezed back into the room. "Silly me. I forgot—

Nursie is out for the day. Sick—wouldn't you know it? Guess you'll just have to muscle through."

"Um, shouldn't I at least put ice on my elbow or something?" asked Max-Ernest. Ever since the secretary had mentioned the likelihood of his elbow bruising, he'd been imagining the worst. "I think I could have a fracture. Or maybe a sprain. You know, they say a bad sprain is worse than a break—"

Opal waved her hand dismissively. "Oh, you'll be fine," she said, seeming to forget she was the one who'd brought him into the nurse's office in the first place. "Can you not be such a hypochondriac for once, Max-Ernest?"

As Opal shooed him out, Max-Ernest tried to follow her suggestion; he had more important things to think about than his elbow, after all. Hopefully now that he had the monocle in his possession, he would be able to see what Benjamin had almost seen: into Cass's mind. And, hopefully, he would be able to bring her back home.

And yet, even as he was opening his locker, gathering his things to take to the hospital, he couldn't help wondering: who told the secretary about his hypochondria? It was most definitely odd: a woman he barely knew knowing him so well.

Almost as odd as a mole moving from her right cheek to her left.

Was it possible that the Midnight Sun had another spy — another mole — in his school? She certainly seemed more than capable of putting a KICK ME sign on his back.

ass did not have much of a plan yet; she was hoping inspiration would strike.

She figured if she could make the soldiers turn around, she could slip behind them and untie the bandits, but that was as far as she'd gotten in her thinking. Unfortunately, she couldn't find a stick long enough to poke a soldier at a safe distance. All the available wood in the area had been burned in the campfire. She looked for low-hanging branches she might break off, but these, too, were missing.

"Are you sure you want to make these people your prisoners?" she heard the Jester asking the soldiers. "Will you not then be as bad as bandits yourselves? No, you will be worse! 'Tis true they steal from the rich. But do not the rich first steal from the poor?"

For some reason, Cass didn't have much faith that the Jester's logic would convince the soldiers. Or even that if his logic convinced them, they would necessarily follow his suggestions. A more practical solution was required.

"How much gold have you? Or you? Or you?" the Jester continued. "Has not the King taken from your parents what should be theirs and yours? It is he who is the master thief. The royal band on his head does not make him any less a royal bandit....Aye, that's it, be gone, beasts! Thank you for allowing me to keep my feet!"

The regal beagles, it seemed, had decided to release the Jester from canine captivity. However, from the sound of their barking/bow-wowing/yapping, Cass feared that the reason they were moving on was that they'd picked up another scent — hers.

Sure enough, the yapping got louder and louder, and within less than a minute Cass saw the dogs heading toward her. The soldiers, she knew, would be close behind.

She had the advantage of invisibility, but that went only so far with creatures whose olfactory organs were forty times more sensitive than a human's.

Thinking quickly, she pulled off her sweatshirt and threw it to her left in the direction of a boulder. Meanwhile, she stepped quietly in the opposite direction.

The ruse worked. The beagles piled onto her sweatshirt, pawing furiously at the mysterious garment, looking for Cass. When she didn't appear, they growled in frustration and ran circles around the boulder.

Afraid to break into a run, lest she attract their attention, Cass edged slowly away from the dogs. She was on the verge of escape when the dogs suddenly lost interest in the boulder and started sniffing around again.

Quickly, she unbuckled her belt and tossed it under a bush.

Again, the beagles dove after their quarry, scrambling to get her belt. Again, they were frustrated to find Cass gone, the belt no longer attached to her waist. Again, they sniffed.

Cass, meanwhile, wet her finger to see which way the wind was blowing. Stealthily, she crept in the upwind direction, hoping that way would hide her scent. Alas, she miscalculated; beagles follow not airborne but ground-borne scents, and they started running toward her anyway.

Increasingly nervous, Cass bent down to untie her shoes.

The game continued—although to Cass, obviously, it wasn't a game—Cass tossing her left shoe to the right and her right shoe to the left, then her right sock to the left and her left sock to the right, until she was standing barefoot and shivering behind a tree.

What to do next? She'd succeeded in confusing the dogs enough that they were now fighting over her socks about thirty feet away from her. But they would be diverted for only so long. And the soldiers, no doubt, would be fast behind.

Cass hesitated. She might be invisible, but she certainly didn't relish the idea of undressing any further.

"Heh heh heh."

A peculiar snorting, wheezing, laughing sound startled her. Like a pig imitating a hyena. Or maybe vice versa.

"Heh heh heh."

Cass reeled around to find the homunculus watching her from on top of a rock.

"Mr. Cabbage Face!" she whispered, excited.

"Why do you keep calling me that? My master's housekeeper sometimes called me her 'little cabbage face,' but I thought it was because she was always giving me her leftover cabbage...."

"No, it's because — there's no time to explain. How long have you been here?"

The homunculus shrugged his little shoulders. "Awhile."

"Why didn't you say anything?"

"Too fun to watch you hopping around," said the homunculus, smirking.

Cass noticed that his speaking had improved remarkably now that he was no longer the one being teased but was rather the one doing the teasing.

"Funny. What are you doing here?"

"Right now? Looking for food. But those cheap bandits don't have any meat. Only this rotting potato—" He held up a moldy potato. A worm peeked out the side.

"Gross," said Cass, stepping away.

"They eat like peasants," said the homunculus, throwing the potato to the ground in disgust. The worm he kept—and popped into his mouth. "Mm, not bad..."

"I think that's so they can afford to feed the real peasants," said Cass, trying to ignore the end of the worm wiggling between his lips.

"I came here to warn you. Lord Pharaoh is looking for you."

"Why?"

The homunculus furrowed his brow. "Something about a secret that will make him live forever. You are the only person who can show it to him, or the only person who can keep him from it. One or the other, I forget. He saw it all through that eyeglass of yours."

"You mean he knows about the Secret?" Cass asked excitedly. Although the warning about Lord Pharaoh was ominous, it was also the first clue to uncovering the Secret she'd encountered since entering the Jester's world.

"I don't know about any secrets. All I know is he is a very scary man. If he finds you, I offer you this advice. His weakness is vanity. Show him a mirror and you will gain a minute."

"A mirror? Uh-oh—!"

Whether it was owing to Cass or the potato or Cabbage Face himself, the dogs were back on Cass's trail, yapping wildly.

"Oh, don't worry about those blasted beagles," said the homunculus dismissively. "I can get rid of them."

Cass looked at him suspiciously. "You're not planning on eating them, are you?"

The homunculus grinned. "Now there's an idea...."

"Mr. Cabbage Face!"

"Actually, beagles taste terrible. Very gamey. Come here, I want to show you something before I go."

"There's no time!"

"Look—"

The homunculus hopped off the rock and onto a bed of leaves and pine needles. Brushing them aside, he revealed a large burlap tarp. He lifted a corner—and a silver candlestick poked out. Then he pulled the tarp off altogether. Underneath was the wooden chest the bandits had stolen from the procession. Cass recognized the big brass lock. Half open and filled to the brim with coins and jewels, the chest was a veritable treasure trove. It glistened, glittered, and gleamed, beckoning as only treasure can.

"For you..." He hesitated, not being very experienced with gift-giving. "Nobody ever did anything nice for me before."

"Wow. Thanks. But all this treasure isn't really yours to give, Mr. Cabbage Face," Cass scolded. "Besides, my job now is to free those bandits. And if I offer this stuff to the soldiers, they'll just take it — they won't free anybody."

The homunculus didn't have time to respond. The beagles were fast descending on them.

"Quick — hide under the tarp," he whispered. "I'll get them out of here."

"But you can't run fast enough. They'll catch you."

"Who said anything about running?"

As Cass dove onto the pile of treasure, the homunculus threw the tarp over her. After recovering the tarp with leaves, he headed toward the dogs and let out a shrill whistle. "Beagles, you greedy dogs — you're no better than hogs! Catch me if you can!"

The homunculus made a gesture with his hand that Cass, watching through a hole in the tarp, didn't recognize but assumed was very rude. Then he scrambled up the nearest tree.

Barking angrily, the dogs pawed and scratched the base of the tree trunk until the homunculus climbed out onto a long branch and dropped over the edge, catching the branch with one hand.

"Watch this!" he shouted. And then he...

Swung himself through the air, catching onto the next tree like a monkey. "Ha ha—"

As he swung from one tree to the next, the furious beagles gave chase.

When a group of soldiers appeared over a rise, Cass briefly panicked. But then they, too, started running after the homunculus. She was alone once more.

"Bye, bye, Mr. Cabbage Face," she said softly. She doubted she would ever see him again—whether in the past or the future or some other time zone as yet unknown.

Cass waited about five minutes before peeling the tarp off her head and examining the bandits' hoard.

Never one to be overly interested in jewels, she couldn't help but be impressed and wonder what would happen if she were to take a piece or two back with her to her own time. Everything here must be worth a fortune, she thought. Then again, she didn't know how to get herself back to her own time, let alone how to bring a tiara along for the ride. Oh well, even if she *were* the tiara type, which she most decidedly wasn't (she'd never gone through that princess phase that so many girls go through), she had a feeling her pointy ears would prevent her from wearing any tiaras anyway.

Just as she was about to tear herself away from the glittering mound, she noticed the black rock on which had gathered so many coins and rings and even the blade of a sword. The lodestone, she guessed. The same rock she'd seen during the bandits' raid on the Duke's procession. Although without the Double Monocle it looked leaden and had no bluish glow.

The sword, she thought, was a bit fancy for cutting ropes — it had a bejeweled gold handle and elaborate engravings on both sides of the blade — but it would be serviceable, nonetheless. It took all her strength to pull the sword from the stone. Just like King Arthur, she thought, holding the sword aloft.

She laughed at herself and started lowering the sword, then stopped with it still in midair. An idea had struck her. A crazy, far-fetched idea. An idea that had little chance of success.

But it had one thing going for it: it was the only idea she had.

How to communicate it to the Jester — that was the question.

Using the blade of the sword, she pried as many bits of metal off the lodestone as she could. Then she started retracing her steps back to the campsite.

When she got close, she proceeded more cautiously. Careful not to break any twigs or send any rocks tumbling into the campsite, she hid the sword behind a tree. The lodestone she continued to hold in her hand like the precious object it was.

By now, the Jester's feet were bound together to prevent him from running, but remarkably his hands and his mouth had been left alone. It seemed the soldiers enjoyed his stories; they were demanding that he tell another.

"But I know no more," protested the Jester. "You have heard them all!"

"Then we shall gag you like the others," threatened the Commander, ripping a long strip off a piece of fabric in preparation.

"Wait! Wait! I will think of something! Let me see, have I told you the one about the sea serpent and the maiden?"

"Yes!" shouted the sailors in chorus.

Nobody saw the lodestone rolling on the ground, seemingly of its own volition — or they didn't believe their eyes if they did — and Cass, kicking the rock along like a soccer ball, was able to reach the Jester without difficulty.

When she tapped him on the shoulder, however, he jumped — and everybody noticed.

"You are a squeamish fellow, aren't you?" teased the Commander. "Are there ants in your pants? Or did a mouse follow you from the dungeon?"

"How did you know? A most annoying mouse, indeed!" said the Jester through gritted teeth. He was trying valiantly not to squirm despite the fact that Cass was pressing the lodestone into his back, where it wouldn't be visible to the soldiers.

She waited a moment, then whispered her instructions.

When she'd finished, the Jester bowed formally to the Commander. "Sir, I have thought of another story after all. And it is a most important one befitting this glorious occasion. Indeed, it may change your mind about the very situation in which we find ourselves. You may even find yourself moved to free us all."

"I seriously doubt that," said the Commander.

"Wait and see.... There is a legend I am sure you know about a sword in a stone. He who pulls the sword from the stone is the One True King...?"

"We have all heard this legend, yes. What is your point?"

"My point? Ah, like the point of a sword! You are a punning soldier as well as a cunning one!"

"A pun? Oh yes! You see you are not the only one who is clever with his tongue," said the Commander, puffing himself up. It was obvious that he had not intended the pun, but because he was the Commander, nobody argued with him.

"My point is that there is more to the legend than you might think — a second point to the sword, so to speak," said the Jester. "If the sword is called back to the stone, then he who calls himself King is not the true King, but a false one. We owe him no allegiance."

"What has this to do with us? I see no sword here, nor any stone."

The Jester reached behind his back and presented the black-and-gold lodestone with a dramatic flourish. "Here is the fabled stone to which I allude," he said, lowering it to the ground. "If, when I raise my arm, a sword flies through the air and sticks to the stone, will you renounce your false King and let these bandits go?"

The Commander laughed. "Very well. There is little risk of that. But know that your head will join with Anastasia's on the platter if no flying sword appears."

"Consider me warned." The Jester looked up at the sky, closed his eyes, and solemnly pronounced, "Excalibur, Sword of Swords, if the King be a false one, fly to this rock now!"

The Commander tapped his toes impatiently until one of the soldiers pointed—

The bejeweled sword had emerged from behind a tree and was sailing through the air. Everybody, the gagged bandits included, watched in astonishment as the sword slowed briefly, hovering like a falcon searching for its prey. Then, flashing in the sunlight, it lurched forward and flew straight toward the Jester as if answering his silent call. The lodestone sparkled at his feet.

When the sword reached the stone, it paused in midair, then dove point-first. It landed in the middle of the stone and stood straight, perfectly balanced, seemingly weightless. A miraculous sight.

A surprised murmur rippled through the crowd. Even the bandits opened their eyes wide, seeming to forget for a moment their captive condition.

One by one, the soldiers dropped to the ground, kneeling before the sword as if the sword itself were king. Eventually, only the Commander was left standing. Then he, too, was overcome.

"The Sword knows all," he said to the Jester, eyes glistening. "I renounce the King. You are all free."

"Oh now, now," said the Jester, grinning with delight. "There is no need for such drama. It is I who am supposed to put on the show here!"

He looked over at Anastasia and winked.

Cass, now standing beside the Jester, thought she saw Anastasia offer a reluctant smile in return.

"I'm going to get out of the way," Cass whispered in the Jester's ear. "After the soldiers are gone, come find me over there where we slept. I have to tell you something. It's really important."

As she walked away, she tried to ignore the tired, faint-headed feeling that had been slowly overtaking her all morning.

oe, the janitor, was just starting his one afternoon shift of the week when the short spiky-haired boy flew past him and ran into that poor girl's room.

Or what *had been* that poor girl's room.

He found the boy staring at the empty bed.

"Where is she? What happened?" asked the boy in a whisper. You didn't have to be psychic to tell what he was thinking.

"Don't worry; it's not quite as bad as that," said the janitor. "They took her home is all."

A spark of hope lit up the boy's eyes. "So did she wake up, then?"

"No, not that, either, I'm afraid. The doctor thought it was time for her to be in her own bed. Nothing they can do for her here anymore."

"You mean they're just giving up?" the boy asked indignantly.

"Well, they don't put it like that...."

The boy slumped against the hospital bed, color draining from his face.

"You need a second?"

The boy nodded. Tears in his eyes, he put his hand on the sheet on which the girl had so recently been lying.

"Don't be too long, son. I've got to mop the floor

in there and get the room ready for the next customer."

The janitor hesitated, trying to think of something more reassuring to say. Then he gave up and left the boy alone.

When, several minutes later, Max-Ernest made himself stand up, he noticed that the monocle had rolled out of his jacket pocket onto the bed.

Too late, he thought bitterly. I got the monocle too late.

He picked up the monocle and found that he wanted nothing more than to throw it at the mirror that hung above the sink. A year ago, he remembered, he'd had to force himself to throw things — a magic wand, most notably — in an attempt to express his anger. Now he had to restrain himself from shattering a hospital mirror into a thousand pieces. Perhaps this was progress of a sort.

Rather than throwing the monocle, however, he peered into it, doing a brief survey of the room.

When he came back to the mirror, he stopped cold.

There was a man in the mirror. An old or not-so-old man (it was hard to tell). He had messy hair that stuck out in all directions and a scruffy beard the mixed black-and-white color people describe as salt-and-pepper. He looked slightly insane.

Nervous, Max-Ernest lowered the monocle and turned around, but there was nobody in the room with him.

He looked into the monocle again. The man in the mirror was still there. As clear as day. But as mysterious as the man in the moon.

Was it a ghost? Max-Ernest couldn't help asking the question. All his skepticism about the supernatural, all his logic and reason, seemed to disappear in the face of this apparition.

Whatever it was, was looking in Max-Ernest's direction but seemed not to see him. His brow was furrowed and he looked frustrated, conflicted. He was muttering something to himself.

"Are you trying to tell me something?" Max-Ernest whispered, stepping closer. "Do you have a message from Cass?"

The man didn't respond, just kept muttering.

The mirror looked foggy around the edges, but when Max-Ernest wiped it with his hand, the image didn't change. The fog was behind the mirror.

I must be going crazy, Max-Ernest thought. This is all in my head. It must be.

He peered closer and saw that the man was hunched over a desk. Papers spilled out in front of him, covered with an almost-unreadable scrawl.

Max-Ernest had the odd sensation that he knew the man — something about the man's nose reminded Max-Ernest of his father — and yet Max-Ernest was certain he'd never seen him before.

Could this be one of his ancestors? A great-grandfather, perhaps?

Meanwhile, the man kept muttering. Something was troubling him.

Straining, Max-Ernest could barely make out the words: "Just...one...more...Just...one...more...," the man repeated over and over.

What? Just one more what?

The man's hand inched toward a shiny object lying on his desk. A pair of spectacles? A knife? A bar of gold? What all-important moment in history was Max-Ernest witnessing through the monocle?

"Just...one...more...Just...one...more..."

The man picked up the object — it was indeed a bar of gold, more specifically a bar covered in gold foil — and greedily unwrapped it. He gazed at the bar as if it were a long-lost friend. Then, unable to resist a second longer —

"Hmmgh...."

Oh, thought Max-Ernest. Just one more *bite*.

Chocolate. A man eating chocolate. That was the momentous event Max-Ernest was watching in the mirror. He would have laughed had he been in a better mood — and had he not taken the subject of chocolate so very seriously himself.

The man put the bar down and smiled contentedly, momentarily at peace. Until —

"Well, maybe just one more..."

— he picked up the bar again.

"Hmmgh..."

What's that noise he's making? Max-Ernest wondered.

"Hmmgh...Hmmmgh..."

The noise was very peculiar: part hum, part groan. Max-Ernest found it irritating and yet at the same time irritatingly familiar. It was like an itch he couldn't locate. Like a word that he couldn't remember but that was on the tip of his tongue.

Suddenly, as if somebody had tapped him on the shoulder, the man turned and looked directly at Max-Ernest.

"You know, it wouldn't hurt to try talking once," he said.

"You mean...to Cass?" Max-Ernest stammered.

But the man didn't respond. He just picked up a pen and started writing.

Then the image fogged over entirely. When the fog cleared, the man in the mirror was gone. In his place, Max-Ernest saw only himself.

Frustrated and a little bit frightened, Max-Ernest lowered the monocle and walked out into the hallway.

Instinctively, he headed for the vending machine. There was only one chocolate bar left, and for a second he considered leaving it for later. Then he remembered there would be no later; he had no reason to return to the hospital.

"Hmmgh..."

As he bit into the chocolate bar, Max-Ernest had a startling realization: the reason he recognized the noise the man had been making was that it was the very noise that he, Max-Ernest, made whenever he ate chocolate.

It wasn't a ghost that he'd been looking at in the mirror.

It wasn't an ancestor. It wasn't anybody from the past.

The man in the mirror was his future self.

he Jester didn't find Cass until he almost tripped over her. She was lying on a bed of pine needles, half awake.

"Oh, there you are!"

The Jester hovered above her, his orange curls blocking the sun.

"Are you all right? I've been looking all over."

Cass forced herself to sit up. "I'm fine. I just had to lie down for a second."

"It has been more like twenty minutes....Here, drink." He offered a cup of water, which she sipped gratefully.

"I'm very glad I found you. You never know how useful an invisible friend is going to be until you've had one. I don't think I could possibly survive without one now!" The Jester patted Cass's head. "Braids, am I right?"

"You are very solicitous of this invisible friend of yours."

Cass and the Jester both looked up, startled.

Anastasia smiled mischievously. "I suppose you can't be too careful with invisible creatures. Without proper care, they're liable to vanish altogether."

"Invisible creatures?" the Jester sputtered. "What invisible creatures?"

He stood up and took a step away from Cass, studiously avoiding looking in her direction.

"My question exactly. I would simply have dismissed you as crazy had I not seen that sword fly through the air a little while ago."

"You did not believe the legend, then?" queried the Jester, recovering.

"I know nothing of legends. I know what I see."

"Very well. I'll admit, I invented the legend. But did you not know that I myself am virtually a legend? — a legendary magician, that is. A master illusionist who can make inanimate objects appear to fly."

"What you are is a man who talks to invisible creatures and pats their heads."

"Oh, all right, I confess. I talk to my hand. See — hello, Sir Hand." He held up his left hand and spoke to it in demonstration. "It's a habit I formed when I was a boy. And now if I don't talk to him, my hand refuses to obey. He won't juggle or perform tricks of any kind. Watch — he just sits there...."

He was silent a moment, his hand still.

"Now, if I coax him a little...Oh, go on, Sir Hand. Do a trick for Anastasia. Just a little one —"

His hand quivered in the air for a moment, as if trying to decide what to do. Then in one long, fluid motion, it picked a flower off a shrub, made the flower disappear and reappear again, and finally presented the flower to Anastasia.

Anastasia laughed. "Good try, but I will not be diverted by flowers." She tossed the flower over her shoulder. "Earlier you were speaking to your right side, not to your left hand."

"It's OK," said Cass loudly. "You can tell her. You're not fooling her, anyway."

"So the creature exists!" exclaimed Anastasia, spinning around. "It's one thing to imagine, another to hear...."

"Yes, I exist."

"And you are a young girl, if I'm not mistaken?"

Cass bristled, standing. "Not that young—"

"Of course not—I did not mean to offend. It's just that I imagined some sort of invisible beast. But I am delighted to find that my savior is human instead. Or are you a fairy or some other? Truth to tell, I did not believe in fairies an hour ago, but I did not believe in invisible girls, either."

"Oh, I'm human...er, I think. At least back home I am."

Not that I'll ever get *there* again, she thought.

"I am very glad to hear it," said Anastasia. "Where are you? I should like to shake the hand of the person who saved my life and the lives of my men."

"You didn't shake *my* hand," grumbled the Jester. "Didn't *I* save you, too?"

Embarrassed but pleased, Cass reached out to shake Anastasia's hand. "Here. I'm Cass. Well, Cassandra is my full name. Nice to meet you—"

Anastasia grasped Cass's invisible hand between her two larger ones. "Ah, long fingers. Like mine. Good for handling horses and weapons..."

"And she has ears like mine!" the Jester interjected. "Good for...good for...Must they be good for something?"

"I hear pretty well sometimes," Cass offered. "But I don't think it's 'cause my ears are big and pointy. I think it's 'cause I have strong inner ears or something like that."

"Good hearing does run in the family," boasted the Jester.

For the second time, Anastasia looked astonished. "You and the invisible girl are family?"

"Why are you surprised?" asked the Jester. "To you I am practically invisible myself."

"That hardly explains it."

"Cassandra is my great-great—oh wait. Should I not say...?"

"Oh, I think it's OK to tell her," said Cass. "I mean, just a little bit."

As it turned out, Cass told the story herself, and at great length, filling in details that she had not yet mentioned even to the Jester. Naturally, Cass worried that she was betraying her vows of secrecy by revealing so much about the Secret and about the Terces Society, but she figured telling people in the past wasn't the same as telling people in the present. Besides, the Jester was the founder of the Terces Society, or would be. If anybody should be allowed to hear mention of the Secret, it was he. As for Anastasia, Cass felt a kinship with her she couldn't quite explain.

"I wish I could see what you look like, Cassandra," said Anastasia. "You are a brave girl to undertake a journey across time."

"Uh...thanks. But I just look normal, really. Except for the big ears, like the Jester said."

"Here—" The Jester presented Cass with a scroll.

"What's this?" asked Cass, unrolling the scroll to reveal a piece of blank parchment.

"I was going to write my letter of resignation to the King on it, but I never got the chance. You may have it."

"Uh, what for?"

"To draw yourself, of course. This clay should work perfectly." He handed her a lump of red clay from the ground.

"Yes, please draw, Cassandra," said Anastasia.

"I don't know. I'm really bad at drawing. I don't think I could make it look like me."

"Well, if it doesn't, we'll never know, will we?" the Jester pointed out.

Under pressure, Cass sketched for a few minutes. When she finished, she was distinctly unhappy with the product. Between the stiff braids and exaggeratedly pointy ears, her drawing had the cartoonish quality of something a cruel classmate might have scribbled in a notebook and pasted on Cass's locker. But the adults seemed to like it. At the very least, they were fascinated by the sight of a drawing that appeared to draw itself.

"Ah, I see you do have the Jester's ears — but, trust me, they are far more charming on you," said Anastasia with a sideways glance at the Jester. "May I keep the drawing?"

"Sure. I mean, if you really want to," said Cass shyly. "Hey, did you guys hear that?"

"What?"

"That voice."

"The soldiers must be coming back," said Anastasia. "I expected this. Now that they are away, they are questioning what they saw. And they are worrying what will happen to them if they fail to bring my head to the King. We must go. My men are waiting."

The Jester smiled. There was no more talk of his being exiled from the group.

"No, don't worry, it's not a soldier, it's—" Cass stopped herself before she said Max-Ernest's name. Most likely they wouldn't recognize it, and if they remembered her mentioning her future-residing friend, they would think she was losing her mind. And perhaps she was.

But Anastasia had already strode away and was starting to saddle her horse.

"You can go—I'll catch up," said Cass to the Jester, feeling faint again.

She leaned against a rock and found herself nodding off. In the distance, she kept hearing Max-Ernest saying her name. Or was she just imagining it?

"Cass, where did you go?" The Jester patted the air, trying to find her. "I shall not leave without you."

Max-Ernest would be so disappointed when she came back without the Secret, she thought. *If* she came back.

Cass struggled to keep her eyes open. "I'm right here, but I don't know for how long. I know this sounds weird, but I think someone is calling me away. Or maybe I'm just fading out of this world."

"Nonsense. You look as good as ever—your skin is so clear you are without a blemish."

"Ha ha." Cass tried to laugh but couldn't quite manage it.

The Jester turned serious. "What was it you wanted to tell me earlier? You said it was important."

"Oh, oh! It was about Lord Pharaoh. And it *is* important. Really important." Cass sat up straight, summoning all her energy. "He knows about the Secret."

"*Your* secret?"

"Well, it's not mine yet. That's why, after I'm gone, you have to go after him for me."

"Lord Pharaoh? That awful alchemist? Why would I want to go near him?"

"To find the Secret yourself, of course. And to keep him from learning it. Or from using it if he already knows it. So you can start the Terces Society like you're supposed to."

The Jester looked distressed. "I don't know. Lord Pharaoh is a very powerful man. I'm just a jester, and not even a proper jester anymore...."

"Well, I'm sure Anastasia will help. Anyway, you don't have a choice. History depends on it. Otherwise, the Midnight Sun will have the Secret instead of you."

"You are very bossy for an invisible girl, do you know that?"

"Promise me."

"Very well, I promise."

"And then when you find the Secret, you have to leave it for me."

"How do you leave a secret? Do you assume that it has physical properties?"

"You know what I mean. A clue. A message. Just write something and leave it for me so I can find it... in the future."

"Where? I do not even know where you live. Or rather where you will live."

Cass thought quickly. The name of her hometown would mean little to him. Even the name of her home country would mean little.

She did her best to identify where she lived using names he would recognize. It was a bit like playing Twenty Questions. Then she had an inspiration.

"Forget about my house. It's too iffy. My grandfathers have a fire station. You should leave the message there."

The Jester looked confused. "A fire station? Is that like a signal fire?"

"No, it's not actually a fire—it's for people who put out fires. But that's beside the point. The fire station isn't even a real fire station anymore. My grandfathers have a store in it called The Fire Sale. The problem is, it doesn't exist yet...."

Cass thought for a second. "What if you made some kind of time capsule or something? You know, like people put under cornerstones?"

"Hm, maybe..." The Jester, it appeared, was not exactly following every word. "What if I left a message under the lodestone? You would recognize the lodestone if you saw it...."

"OK," said Cass eagerly. "Where will you leave the lodestone?"

She tried to push herself up farther, but she was too weak and she fell backward. Above her, the Jester was answering her question, but she couldn't make out the words.

Again, she heard the voice saying her name.

"Max-Ernest?" she called out impulsively.

And soon, though she tried as hard as she could to keep her eyes open, darkness overcame her.

Will I ever wake up again? she wondered as she fell asleep.

And if I do, when will it be?

ax-Ernest had never seen Cass's house looking like this.

Her mom, Melanie, was one of the neatest people Max-Ernest knew. It had been strange enough to find the front door unlocked with unread newspapers strewn around it, but to see dishes piled in the sink and even on the counter and on the table? The house looked almost as cluttered as Cass's grandfathers' store.

The one spot in the kitchen that wasn't in complete disarray was the refrigerator. Max-Ernest and Cass had long ago devised a special, random-looking way of arranging the magnetic letters on the fridge that made it easier to leave coded messages for each other. In normal times, Cass had to reorganize the letters on an almost nightly basis because her mother compulsively alphabetized them during the day. And yet there they were, just as Cass had left them; two weeks had gone by without Cass's mother touching the letters. Clearly, Melanie was not herself.

On the stove, a teapot was whistling. Max-Ernest got the sense the water inside had been boiling for a while.

He turned off the flame.

"Tea...tea is just the ticket...." Cass's Grandpa Larry entered the kitchen, muttering to himself. He looked at the teakettle, perturbed. "Why did I think I heard it whistling?"

Max-Ernest coughed. "Hi, Grandpa Larry."*

Larry's eyes lit up. "Well, if it isn't young Master Max—what a stroke of luck!" Larry offered his hand with forced joviality.

"Wayne. Melanie. Get down here and see who that sneaky old cat dragged in! Looks like we can go out, after all," he called up the stairs behind him.

"I was going to see about getting a nurse to sit with Cass while we took her mother to dinner, but I feel much better with you here," he explained to Max-Ernest. "What that girl needs right now is to be surrounded by people who love her, not more so-called medical professionals."

Max-Ernest was shocked by the sight of Cass's mother. There were dark, raccoon-like circles around her eyes. Her clothes hung loosely on her shoulders. Her hair was stringy. If you didn't know any better, you'd think she, not her daughter, was the patient.

Larry and Wayne, in contrast, had trimmed their long unruly beards and looked much more cleaned and pressed than usual. If grief and anxiety had made Cass's mother fall to pieces, it had had almost the reverse effect on them. They were rising to the

*CASS'S GRANDFATHERS ALWAYS INSISTED ON THE *GRANDPA* TITLE. IF CASS WAS THEIR SUBSTITUTE GRANDCHILD, THEN MAX-ERNEST, THEY SAID, WAS THEIR *SUBSTITUTE* SUBSTITUTE GRANDCHILD. OBVIOUSLY, THEY DEFINED FAMILY A BIT DIFFERENTLY THAN THE HOSPITAL DID.

occasion, it seemed, taking care of Melanie, not just Cass.

It took Cass's grandfathers over an hour to convince Cass's mother to leave the house for under an hour.

"We need to put some meat back on your bones," said Wayne. "You look like you haven't eaten in weeks."

"That's because I haven't. How could I? Especially now..." She broke off.

"Do you think that's what Cass would want—for you to waste away?" asked Larry heatedly.

"You know how conscious she is of keeping everybody's blood sugar levels up," said Wayne. "Just in case you have to deal with a sudden electrical fire or earthquake or nuclear attack. Right, Max-Ernest?"

Max-Ernest nodded. This was absolutely true. Cass was always trying to keep everybody's energy supply high.

"We're taking you out for a burger right now, and when we get back I'm cleaning up this kitchen," said Larry. "This place looks worse than the galley onboard the *The Warren Harding*.* I remember once when I was in the navy and I had to cook for six hundred seamen, a sudden storm rocked the ship, and

---

*WARREN HARDING WAS THE TWENTY-NINTH PRESIDENT OF THE UNITED STATES AND IS WIDELY REGARDED AS THE WORST. TO THE BEST OF MY KNOWLEDGE, THERE IS NO NAVY SHIP NAMED AFTER HIM. NONETHELESS, I THINK WE SHOULD GIVE GRANDPA LARRY'S STORY THE BENEFIT OF THE DOUBT.

my giant vat of chili spilled out onto the deck. It took me three days to clean, but I—"

Max-Ernest looked confusedly at Larry. "Navy? I thought you were in the army."

"Details. Details. When, young man, are you going to learn to enjoy a good story?"

Eventually, Melanie succumbed to the pressure.

She agreed to go to dinner, but not without grilling Max-Ernest first:

"You really know how to read the heart monitor?"

"Yes, I swear. Remember how many times I've been to the hospital? I'm an expert."

"I don't want you to be an expert. Just make sure her heart isn't beating too fast or too slow."

"OK."

"Or too unevenly."

"Has to be even. Got it."

"And don't touch the IV, whatever you do. You may think you're a medical expert, but you're not a nurse."

"I know I'm not, I mean, I won't."

"If there's any irregularity at all, anything, call me right away."

"OK."

PERHAPS, FOR EXAMPLE, *THE WARREN HARDING* WAS A NICKNAME FOR A DIFFERENTLY NAMED SHIP THAT HAPPENED TO HAVE PARTICULARLY BAD LUCK AT SEA.

"Even if you don't think it's important."

"Even if."

"If she blinks, call me."

"Definitely."

"If she even twitches…"

"Absolutely."

"And if she mumbles anything…?"

"I'll call you."

"Yes, immediately! And write down what she says, too."

"OK, I'll write it down."

"I'm very serious, Max-Ernest."

"I know you are."

"Even if you don't recognize the word. Write the sounds."

"OK."

"Even if it doesn't sound like a word, just a breath or a sigh."

"OK."

"And you have Larry's number in case you don't get me for some reason?"

"Yeah."

"And Wayne's?"

"Uh-huh. But they never leave their phones on."

"What?"

"Nothing."

"If you can't get any of us, the phone number of every neighbor on the street is next to the refrigerator. Also the number of the police and the nearest hospital and the city council office and school. And poison control."

"OK."

"But don't poison her!"

"No poison. Got it."

"Of course, if there's a real emergency, you should call 9-1-1 first. Do you have that number?"

"Um, it's 9-1-1, isn't it?"

"Please don't get smart with me right now, Max-Ernest. . . ."

"Sorry, I wasn't trying to be smart. You confused me, that's all."

"I *knew* this was a bad idea."

"Come *on*, Melanie," said Larry. "We're only going to be three minutes away."

Before she could say another word, he and Wayne each took her by an arm and escorted her out the door.

"Well, here goes nothing," said Max-Ernest to the empty room, bracing himself for his visit with the silent girl upstairs.

The author of this book has requested a fifteen-minute break to restore his energy before writing what promises to be a very intense and emotional chapter. Please take this opportunity to have a snack or use the restroom. If you choose to stay with the book during this time, we offer the following items for your consideration and/or consumption.*

IF YOU LIKE THE SECRET SERIES BY
PSEUDONYMOUS BOSCH, YOU MIGHT ALSO LIKE:

 **a pie in the face**

 **eating dirt**

 **smelling your own farts**

*THESE ITEMS HAVE BEEN SELECTED BASED UPON YOUR CHOICE OF THE BOOK *THIS ISN'T WHAT IT LOOKS LIKE* BY PSEUDONYMOUS BOSCH. IF YOU FEEL THE ITEMS HAVE BEEN SELECTED IN ERROR, OR YOU WOULD PREFER NOT TO HAVE YOUR PERSONAL TASTES PIGEONHOLED BY AN ANONYMOUS CORPORATE MACHINE, WELL, FRANKLY, THERE IS LITTLE YOU CAN DO ABOUT IT.

PEOPLE WHO HAVE PURCHASED *THIS ISN'T WHAT IT LOOKS LIKE* HAVE ALSO PURCHASED:

a bullwhip

an egg timer

a wig

TREAT YOURSELF:

**a melted
ice-cream cone**

**a sat-upon
sandwich**

a ton of bricks

Max-Ernest had run all the way from the hospital, but he walked upstairs to Cass's room as if his feet were dipped in concrete, not even bothering to count the steps.*

Somewhere between the hospital and Cass's house he had begun to lose faith. Perhaps he should have been excited—now that he finally had in his possession the means of reading Cass's mind. But that was the problem. He was afraid he didn't have the means, after all.

The monocle, which he'd looked through again and again, hadn't helped him see into the minds of the healthy, walking, talking people he'd passed on the street. How could he expect it to help him look inside the mind of someone in a coma?

The one clear image he'd seen through the monocle was one that, on balance, he'd rather not have seen: the image of his adult self, chocolate-addicted and seemingly half mad.

It wouldn't hurt to try talking once, the older Max-Ernest had said.

The younger Max-Ernest assumed this meant he should talk to Cass. But was talking to her supposed to wake her up? That sounded like exactly the sort of superstitious nonsense he couldn't abide. He

---

*He knew from the one hundred seventy-seven times he had climbed the stairs that there were twenty-four, but he almost always counted nonetheless.

was embarrassed that his adult self would recommend it.*

The door to Cass's bedroom was wide open, but Max-Ernest stopped and stood in front of it for a full minute. It took all his self-control not to turn around and flee.

The last time Max-Ernest had been in her bedroom was the day Cass had fallen into the coma. With the exception of the hospital bed in the middle (and Max-Ernest couldn't quite get himself to look at that yet), much of the room looked exactly the same as it had looked then. Only sadder. In the past, Cass's sock monsters — there were now quite a few of them — had always provided a little levity.** Cass had never been one to play much with dolls or stuffed animals, but she used to give each sock monster its own voice and character; and the sock monsters would lecture Max-Ernest on the finer points of emergency communication and first aid. Now the monsters just stood lifelessly on their shelf, a Greek chorus gone silent. Even Cass's "Wall of Horrors" (as her mother called it) wasn't as entertaining as it had once been. All the pictures and articles that Cass had clipped and taped above her bed — the imploding

---

*I HAPPEN TO KNOW THE OLDER MAX-ERNEST WASN'T RECOMMENDING ANY SUCH THING. IN FACT, HE WASN'T SPEAKING TO THE YOUNGER MAX-ERNEST AT ALL; HE WAS SPEAKING TO HIS CAT.

**IF YOU AREN'T FAMILIAR WITH SOCK MONSTERS, THEY ARE EXACTLY WHAT THEY SOUND LIKE: MONSTERS MADE OF OLD SOCKS (AND ASSORTED SCRAPS). CASS HAD A HABIT OF MAKING THEM IN MOMENTS OF STRESS.

mines and exploding volcanoes, the forest fires and the flooded towns — were grim reminders not only of disaster and destruction but of the pointy-eared survivalist herself.

Given that they have to die (and despite what the Masters of the Midnight Sun would wish, everybody has to die sometime), most people would prefer to die in bed at home, surrounded by loved ones. Yet Cass, Max-Ernest reflected morbidly, would have preferred a much more dramatic demise — if not a shark attack or an avalanche, then at least a collapsed building or a plane crash.

If he couldn't save her life, could he at least improve her death? Would a real friend make sure she died not in her boring old bed but in some spectacular disaster?

Briefly, he considered ways of ensuring a more exciting end to the story of Cass's life. It was hard to think of one that wouldn't cause collateral damage. Years of friendship with Cass had trained Max-Ernest to think of worst-case scenarios:

- If he left Cass on the road, he was likely to cause a multi-car collision. The result might be even worse if he left her on a train track.

- If he threw Cass off a bridge, her body might never be recovered. He knew from watching television that an unrecovered body was never a good thing.
- If he set Cass's house on fire, the house next door would very likely catch on fire as well. And where would Cass's mother live afterward?
- As for natural disasters—earthquakes, hurricanes, killer viruses—you couldn't exactly snap your fingers and make them appear. And even if you could, the rule of unintended consequences was certain to go into effect.

No, there didn't seem to be a way to make Cass's dying any more tolerable. He would just have to try again to bring her back to life. No matter how long the odds.

Max-Ernest sat down on the corner of the hospital bed and, without fully intending to, started talking aloud to Cass. Fast. And at great length. The way he used to.

"Hi. I don't know if you can hear me. Actually, I'm pretty sure you can't. I know people always talk to plants and babies and stuff, but it's pretty silly, if you ask me. You may as well just talk to yourself. Anyways, I'm talking to you now because, well, because I want to, I guess, even though it doesn't make any sense. And because, well, you never know, right? Maybe it *is* what will wake you up. I mean, just to get me to *stop* talking or something... By the way, speaking of babies, I'm going to have a baby brother. How 'bout that? My parents are being pretty weird about it, well, not *weird* weird, more like just terrible, but I'm kind of excited anyway. I always wanted a brother. Just to get my parents off my back. But now they're off my back and I still want a brother. Kind of weird, huh? Why do I keep saying *weird*? I hate it when people use that word! I guess I want to have somebody to talk to and stuff. Not that I don't have you, or that you're not going to be around to talk to anymore... Forget that — what I wanted to tell you was, no matter what happens, you'll... I'll always think of you as my friend. My first friend. My best friend. But more than a friend. Not *more than a friend* more than a friend! More like a sister, I guess... Anyways, I keep thinking about all those times you pushed me in the water even though I can't swim. Like at the Midnight Sun Spa — remember when we had to get through that moat to save Benjamin Blake and I didn't want to go in the water? Or that time you pushed me into the ocean off Dr. L's boat? Sure, I might have drowned, and you should probably be arrested for attempted murder, and at the time I totally wanted to kill you, but now that I think about it, I think you actually meant well. It was probably good for me to jump in the water and to have to swim. Besides the fact that the Midnight Sun would have fed me to sharks otherwise. I mean good like I learned a lesson. Not to be afraid of water or whatever. Yeah, yeah, I know, I'm still afraid of water, but you know what I mean. And there was that time with the waterfall at Wild World...Anyways, I want you to know, no matter what happens to you, I won't stop doing the kind of stuff you make me do. Even if I wanted to stop I couldn't because whenever I want to run away from something, your voice is in my head telling me to turn around and jump in the water. Like just now, when I wanted to run away from here...from you. No offense...Well, that's what I wanted to say. Just in case you were worried about me or anything...OK, I guess it's time to try the monocle. All this talking is just stalling, isn't it...?"

Wiping his tears, Max-Ernest took the Double Monocle out of his pocket—then immediately put it back.

"Oh, I almost forgot, Yo-Yoji sent me something to play for you first. He thought maybe it would activate some part of your brain or something. He says hi, by the way...."

Max-Ernest pulled his laptop computer from his backpack. He opened it on the bed next to Cass and then clicked on a sound file on his desktop. A loud guitar chord suddenly issued forth from his computer. Followed by an extended riff in Yo-Yoji's unmistakable junior–Jimi Hendrix style.

"Cool, huh? And don't tell me not to use the word *cool*—I know I'm using it right this time!"

After the guitar solo wound down, Max-Ernest closed the computer and put it back in his backpack.

At first he didn't notice that the sounds persisted after they should have stopped—the reverberating guitar chords might almost have been a lingering echo—but when the music started to grow louder again, he turned around in amazement.

Yo-Yoji was standing in the doorway of Cass's room. In his hand was the guitar Max-Ernest remembered so well, the blue guitar with the bright orange sticker for Yo-Yoji's band, Alien Earache. Between his hair, which was now bright green, and his sneakers, which were an even brighter yellow, Yo-Yoji looked like he had flown in from some psychedelic alien planet.

"Most definitely cool! I think you were using the word just right, yo," said Yo-Yoji, grinning. "So. Aren't you going to say hey?"

"Hey," said Max-Ernest, managing a small grin back—barely. "I thought you weren't coming for another month."

"I got my parents to send me back early. I'm staying with you, duh. My mom talked to your mom—didn't she tell you?"

Max-Ernest shook his head. "I don't know if she even remembers I exist these days."

Yo-Yoji plugged his portable amplifier into an electrical socket, played one last deafeningly loud chord, then leaned his guitar against Cass's Wall of Horrors.

His face turned somber as he took in the scene in front of him. "Whoa. It's like a full-on hospital in here. How's she doing?"

"Um, she's doing...," Max-Ernest stammered, unable to finish the sentence.

"Not good, huh?"

Max-Ernest shook his head. "I was supposed to bring her back," he said, his voice cracking. "It was my job."

Yo-Yoji took a step toward Cass, then stepped back, visibly shaken. "Well, I know you're doing your best. I know she knows it, too. OK?"

"She doesn't know anything," said Max-Ernest, hiding his face in his shirtsleeve so Yo-Yoji wouldn't see him crying. "She's in a coma."

"You don't know for sure. She might be listening to everything we're saying right now, and thinking what a dork you are," said Yo-Yoji, trying hard to remain upbeat. "Hey, is that supposed to be doing that—?"

Max-Ernest looked over at the heart monitor and thought he felt his own heart stopping. The green line on the screen had gone flat and the monitor was buzzing loudly.

A second later, the monitor turned off altogether. And so did all the lights in the room and in the hallway. Only a sliver of moonlight, passing through the tree outside Cass's window, still illuminated the room.

Max-Ernest and Yo-Yoji both rushed to Cass's side. Max-Ernest felt her wrist.

"She still has a pulse! There must have been a power surge or something," said Max-Ernest quickly. "You go down and see if you can turn the electricity back on—the fuse box is right outside the kitchen. I'll call 9-1-1 just in case."

By the time Max-Ernest picked up the cordless phone Melanie had left for him, Yo-Yoji was out of the room. His hand shaking, Max-Ernest started to dial the number, then realized he had no dial tone.

That was when he felt the hard, cold object sticking into his back.

"Put that down, old chum. I think I cut all the telephone wires, but I'm not taking any chances."

Benjamin Blake.

Of course it was Benjamin, Max-Ernest thought. They had discussed turning off the power in the hospital in order to get access to Cass. How much easier to do it here in Cass's house!

"Hi, Benjamin," he said, letting the dead phone drop to the floor. He was surprised that he was able to make himself sound so calm. "That was a really terrible thing to do, you know. What if Cass had been on a respirator or something?"

"Well, lucky for her, she wasn't. Now give me the Double Monocle. Or I won't hesitate to use this."

"Use what?"

"What do you think I'm holding in my hand, my dear fellow?"

"You don't have a gun. I may not be able to read your mind, but I know that."

"How can you be sure? Maybe I got it from our mutual friends at New Promethean."

"The Midnight Sun don't have guns. They don't need them."

"You really want to risk it, old chum?"

A good question. True, he didn't remember ever seeing a Midnight Sun member hold a gun, Max-Ernest reflected. But they were so ruthless, they wouldn't hesitate to give one to Benjamin if they thought it would further their aims.

"How does the monocle work, anyway?" Max-Ernest asked, stalling. "I couldn't see into anybody's mind with it. I saw...something else."

"It's the second lens—it gives you second sight. That means something different for everyone," said Benjamin impatiently. "Some people see ghosts, some people see into people's minds, some people see the future. It depends on who you are and what you need to know. Except *you* always need to know everything, so I can't begin to imagine what you saw," he sneered. "Now give it back to me. It's mine."

"Is it yours, really? Where did the Midnight Sun get it? Knowing them, I'll bet it's stolen."

"Not at all! It's one of their oldest treasures, dating back to Lord Pharaoh himself. And I have been entrusted with it," said Benjamin proudly. "I think you know Ms. Mauvais well enough to know we will all regret it if it gets lost."

While Max-Ernest was considering his options, he caught a glimpse of blue — Yo-Yoji's guitar flashing in the moonlight — and just managed to step out of the way as the guitar came crashing down on Benjamin's head.*

He turned to see Benjamin slumped at his feet, unconscious.

A flashlight rolled onto the floor. Clearly, the flashlight, not a gun, had been the object sticking into Max-Ernest's back.

"Thanks, Yo-Yo —," Max-Ernest started to say.

But it wasn't Yo-Yoji standing over Benjamin, holding the guitar. It was —

"Cass?!"

---

*In case you're worried about it, I hasten to inform you that Yo-Yoji's guitar was a very lightweight model, unlikely to do serious lasting damage.

know, you're a bundle of conflicting emotions right now, aren't you? Like Max-Ernest at his worst, you have no idea how you should feel.

On the one hand, you're relieved that Cass is OK. You know her so well by now. She's like a friend, and you wouldn't want anything bad to happen to her. Nothing truly bad, anyway. Sure, she's stubborn and willful. She makes mistakes that imperil herself and her friends. She's sometimes not very nice to her mom. Her ears are too pointy. But she doesn't deserve to be punished so severely. Certainly, she doesn't deserve to perish on some long mental journey into her ancestral past.

You're glad, in short, that she is still alive.

On the other hand, you're absolutely furious with me, your not-so-humble narrator, for putting you through this arduous ordeal. Go on, admit it. You hate me. Why couldn't I have told you at the outset that Cass was going to survive? Why couldn't I have skipped the coma altogether? Why put you through every blip and beep and zig and zag of her heart monitor? Do I have no heart myself?

In my defense, I could say that it is my duty to report the truth, whatever it is, wherever I find it. But you know better than that. You know *me* better than that.

So I will respond by stating the obvious: you could have put the book down.

And yet you kept reading, didn't you? You have kept reading about Cass and Max-Ernest book after book, if I am not mistaken, almost as if you enjoyed seeing these two innocent young people put in harm's way. As if their trials and tribulations existed purely for your entertainment. As if they had no feelings of their own.

Please, therefore, spare me your criticisms and accusations, your pleas and complaints. At the end of the day, you, dear reader, are nearly as guilty as I. We're in this mud pit together. And don't you ever forget it.

There. I don't know about you, but I feel much better getting that off my chest. Now can we please get back to the story?

Thank you.

Let us begin this chapter anew by asking the most basic question:

What awakened Cass?

If you're the sentimental sort, you might be inclined to believe it was Max-Ernest's long and heartfelt bedside speech that roused her. All Max-

Ernest's memories stirred Cass's own memories and brought her back to the present. Combined with the familiar yet always jarring sounds of Yo-Yoji's guitar, they were too powerful an antidote to resist. That's probably what Cass's grandfathers or even Pietro would say.

Personally, I think it more likely that the power surge Benjamin created was responsible and that an electrical charge jolted Cass awake. Just think of Frankenstein's monster or a frog on a dissection table.

Of course, it's also possible that she would have awakened on her own, regardless. As the all-powerful author of this book, I give you permission to choose whichever explanation you like best. The happy fact remains that Cass was back, returned from wherever and whenever it was that she had gone.

As for Cass, not only was she unsure what had woken her, she didn't even remember what had put her to sleep.

After Yo-Yoji returned to her room, he and Max-Ernest filled her in on a few vital details (for example: that she'd been in a coma for two weeks; that, yes, that was Benjamin Blake lying unconscious at their feet; and that, no, the lights were not out because of a nuclear attack or even an earthquake but rather because their old classmate had cut the power). Then Max-Ernest tied Benjamin's hands together. "This is the Handcuff Knot," he explained to his friends. "The Spanish Bowline might also work, but I think it's better for ankles."

Meanwhile, Cass lit a couple of her emergency glow sticks, adjusted her IV to a more comfortable position, and settled back into bed. "OK," she said. "You guys have been holding out on me long enough. What happened?"

"What do you mean?" asked Yo-Yoji.

"I mean, what happened to me? What else would I mean? I was in a coma, right? People don't just fall into comas for no reason. Was I in a car accident? Did I almost drown? Do I have a rare infectious disease? Is there an alien virus in my brain? Tell me. I can take it...."

"You mean you don't remember?" asked Max-Ernest. "For real?"

"Remember what?"

"Eating the chocolate..."

"Señor Hugo's chocolate? That's what did this?" asked Cass, completely surprised. "Who gave it to me?"

"You did," said Max-Ernest, confused. How could she not remember?

"Why would I do that? It nearly killed me and Yo-Yoji the first time! Right, Yo-Yoji?"

Yo-Yoji nodded, grimacing. "No doubt. It was insane. Fun. But insane."

"So, then, all that time, you were just...unconscious...you weren't...traveling back in time?" asked Max-Ernest slowly.

"Was I supposed to be?"

They didn't have a chance to discuss the issue further because Cass's mother had gotten home. She and Cass's grandfathers could be heard downstairs at that very moment worrying about the lack of electricity.

"Max-Ernest, are you up there? Is Cass OK?"

"Quick, you guys, untie Benjamin. Just pretend he came to visit with Yo-Yoji," whispered Cass. "It's going to be hard enough to explain why the lights are out."

"Actually, it might make it easier. We could tell her there was a break-in and the burglars tied him up," said Max-Ernest. "How 'bout that?"

Cass shook her head. "No, then she would call the police. Too complicated."

"Wake up, dude—this is your lucky day," said

Yo-Yoji, tugging on Benjamin's ear while Max-Ernest bent down to untie the knots he'd made only minutes earlier.

Was it really possible the chocolate didn't work? Max-Ernest wondered. As happy and relieved as he was about Cass's recovery, happier and more relieved than he'd ever been about anything before, he couldn't help feeling a little disappointed.

And more than a little worried about what this meant for the future of the Secret.

1. Cass and the Secret

Cass's first flash of memory came late that night, when she slipped under the covers of the hospital bed. (Her mother refused to let her sleep in her own bed until she'd been evaluated by a doctor.) Caught between the sheets was an odd gold monocle with two lenses. Cass didn't know where it came from (later, of course, she would learn the story from Max-Ernest), but she knew that she'd seen it before. And when she looked through it, the sensation was familiar — so familiar that it didn't even surprise her when she noticed the monocle gave her X-ray vision. She held on to the monocle and studied it for the better part of an hour, but she couldn't remember whether she'd seen it five hundred years earlier or merely five *weeks* earlier.

She didn't need a monocle. She needed a crystal ball.

Still, she clutched it like a baby clutching a blankie. It was, she hoped, her key to unlocking the secrets of the past, and to learning the Secret that it was her mission to guard in the future.

When she woke up in the morning, she remembered a bit of more of her journey, but only the way you remember a dream: in little fragments that make no sense when you try to put them together.

"There was a bright light, a ghost, a flying sword, a Renaissance Faire...or was that last year's field trip? It's all so confusing!" she told Max-Ernest on the phone.

As for the big questions, she couldn't even remember whether she'd found the Jester, let alone whether she'd learned the Secret.

At this point, dear Reader, you know more about her life than she did.

Over the next few weeks, her mother celebrated Cass's miraculous recovery, squeezing Cass every other minute and rarely letting her out of her sight (which was annoying but at the same time kind of nice), and Cass's doctors kept calling her in for checkups and exams, desperately trying to explain what happened to her (which was funny but mostly aggravating). Cass, meanwhile, grew increasingly despondent — and increasingly certain that her epic journey had never taken place. She'd merely experienced a few chocolate-induced hallucinations and caused everyone a lot of anguish for nothing.

The worst was when Pietro visited, posing as a hospital social worker who wanted to help Cass "reintegrate into the society of the outside world." (A funny role for a hermit like Pietro to choose; Cass couldn't think of anyone less integrated into society.) Cass was pleased to see him, of course, and couldn't help welling up when he told her how proud he was of her for having embarked on such a perilous expedition, but the words that followed were hardly reassuring.

"Please try and remember as much as you can, *cara*," he said. "I do not want to put any more of the pressure on you, but I am afraid if too much of the time passes, you will never remember this thing that you alone can know. That you alone *must* know."

"Can you help? Like hypnotize me or something?"

Pietro shook his head. "I'm sorry, I cannot. Nobody can. It is too dangerous. The temptation to learn the Secret for myself, it would be too great."

Cass sank further into despair. What kind of Secret Keeper was she? She didn't even know if she knew the Secret.

2. Max-Ernest and PC

Once Cass was safely returned to the present, Max-Ernest, naturally, was very curious to hear about her trip to the past—if indeed it was a trip she had made. Unfortunately, as much as he would have liked to spend all his time devising games and tests to jog Cass's memory, Pietro had given him strict instructions *not* to do precisely that.

"She must remember this on her own—for two reasons," said the old magician. "First, there is the danger you would learn the Secret. I do not say you would do so on purpose, but…it is a danger. Second, if she is pushed too hard, we do not know, her brain, it is fragile. The coma, it might return. We could lose her again to the past."

Even if he'd wanted to disobey Pietro, Max-Ernest

immediately became far too busy to spend much time with Cass. The very night that she recovered from her coma, Max-Ernest found himself returning to the hospital to visit another patient. This time, he didn't have to sneak in; the patient was an official family member. His baby brother. Born several weeks prematurely. And very small. But nonetheless thriving.

"He looks like a peanut, a really old peanut," he told Cass the next day. "Why do newborns always look so old?"

His parents, alas, did not fare quite as well as their new son. It seems they'd been avoiding the subject of names up until now, knowing how problematic it had been in the past (when their inability to settle on a name for Max-Ernest had resulted in his having two names and in their having two households). Sadly, avoidance had not healed old wounds. No sooner had their baby arrived than they started fighting about what to name him.

"We have to name him after my Uncle Clay," declared Max-Ernest's mother.

"No, we must give him the name of my Uncle Paul," countered Max-Ernest's father.

In the end, when neither parent would give in, their second son was given two names like their first: Max-Ernest's brother became Paul-Clay.

Max-Ernest was not surprised and was only somewhat disappointed to see their argument escalate so quickly. He had been expecting them to fall out of love and re-divorce sooner or later — although perhaps not in the space of a single hour with a newborn baby crying one foot away.

Needless to say, once they were again living on opposite sides of their house, Max-Ernest's father was not about to let Max-Ernest's mother take care of *his* baby. And Max-Ernest's mother refused to let Max-Ernest's father take care of *her* baby. The situation called for a Solomonic solution.* Yet Max-Ernest feared if he offered to split Paul-Clay in half, they would take him up on it. After all, they had split their house in half more than once. The only way Max-Ernest could make peace, and also ensure Paul-Clay remained in one piece, was to offer to feed and care for the baby himself. They gratefully agreed.

Knowing how much he'd always disliked having two names, Max-Ernest shortened the tiny baby's name to PC and proceeded to take charge of his little life.

For Max-Ernest, the next month was a nonstop series of diapers and bottles and burp cloths and sponge baths. I won't go into detail about the first diaper change. Or even the second. Or third. Or

---

*I REFER, OF COURSE, TO KING SOLOMON'S FAMOUS OFFER TO SPLIT IN HALF A BABY THAT WAS CLAIMED BY TWO SEPARATE WOMEN. HE ASSUMED THAT A REAL MOTHER WOULD RATHER GIVE UP HER BABY THAN SEE IT IN PIECES. OBVIOUSLY, HE'D NEVER MET MAX-ERNEST'S PARENTS.

fourth. Or fifth. But I will tell you that the sixth went smoothly, as did *most* diaper changes thereafter. Perhaps Max-Ernest was not the most natural caregiver in the world, but what he lacked in instinct he made up for in determination. When the baby was asleep, Max-Ernest read baby how-to books and watched videos and consulted medical professionals (the receptionist at the hospital was particularly helpful). During school hours, he arranged for his parents to "babysit" their own child according to a schedule so evenly divided and so strictly enforced that neither parent could complain of unfairness. Max-Ernest was such an efficient and unbending taskmaster that his parents, each of whom had previously been desperate to hold on to the baby, began to rebel and started to skip out on their babysitting sessions. In order to keep them in line, he had to start paying them to babysit with the allowance money they gave him.

By the end of the month, I am proud to say, Max-Ernest may well have been the most expert baby wrangler in middle school.

3. Yo-Yoji and the Nuts Table
Of our three young heroes, only Yo-Yoji had much contact with the older Terces members during the ensuing weeks. Violin master and Terces chief of

physical defense Lily Wei had finally deemed his violin playing sufficiently advanced that he might forgo one hour of violin practice a day and devote it to martial-arts training. Yo-Yoji was ecstatic and spent as much time as he could under her martial/musical-arts tutelage. As Cass mentioned, Yo-Yoji had once eaten Señor Hugo's chocolate and had visited his ancestral past himself; it seemed now that whatever samurai spirit had then possessed him had left Yo-Yoji with a residue of samurai skills.

When, three weeks after her recovery, Cass's mother at last allowed Cass to return to school, and the three friends were reunited once more at the Nuts Table, Yo-Yoji gave a whispered update on the doings of the Terces Society. The report was not long. Owen, as usual, was away on assignment. Mr. Wallace, the certified public accountant who was secretly the Terces Society archivist, was spending every waking hour buried in files, searching for documents for Pietro. Pietro, meanwhile, was obsessively playing *Tarocchino* day and night.

"He says he's trying to figure something out about the Midnight Sun, but I think that old dude just likes to gamble."

"He wouldn't tell you what he's worried about?" asked Cass, hoping that she, Cass, wasn't the subject that Pietro was losing sleep over.

Yo-Yoji shook his head. "I guess it's really top secret. He said he sent Max-Ernest a warning about it."

Max-Ernest frowned. "Me? What warning?"

Yo-Yoji shrugged. "No idea. All I know is, he's really hoping Cass remembers more stuff. It's almost like he thinks she's the only one who can stop whatever it is — Oh wait. I wasn't supposed to say that. He doesn't want to—"

"He doesn't want to put any more pressure on me, I know," said Cass, miserable. "Thanks for telling me anyway."

"Sorry—"

The conversation got cut short by the arrival of Glob and Daniel-not-Danielle at the Nuts Table.

"OK, who wants a free dinner at Medieval Days after Ren-Faire next week?" asked Glob, laying a couple of restaurant coupons in front of Max-Ernest. "Oh, I forgot—" He picked up the coupons before Max-Ernest could grab one. "You're not interested in Medieval Days, are you, Max-Ernest?"

"C'mon, Glob, give it a break," said Daniel-not-Danielle from behind his dreadlocks. "Either give him the coupons or don't. It's not that big a deal."

"Free dinner? I don't know about Max-Ernest, but I'm all over it," said Yo-Yoji.

"Me, too," said Cass.

Cass wasn't sure how she felt about Max-Ernest's new non-friends at the Nuts Table. She couldn't help resenting a little their intrusion on her life, and she didn't relish the prospect of dinner with Glob. But, she thought, if the Renaissance Faire doesn't help my memory, maybe Medieval Days will. Who cares if Renaissance and medieval aren't the same thing?

"Oh well, guess you're out of luck, Max-Ernest," said Glob. "Only had two."

"Actually, if he wants, he can have mine... I can't go," said Daniel-not-Danielle.

"You're not going to Ren-Faire?" Glob looked horrified.

"Sorry, man. There's that comic book convention, remember? My dad is so desperate for me to read anything with the word *book* in it, he said I could go even if I had to skip school."

"I-I don't know what to say," Glob sputtered. "That's... that's betrayal!" Reeling from the shock, he sat down at the table.

Rolling his dreadlock-covered eyes, Daniel-not-Danielle sat down across from him.

There was no way for the others to continue talking without the newcomers hearing. The question of Pietro's warning would have to wait.

The Nuts Table had rarely been so silent.

But that night, Cass dreamed about an eye, dark green and almost reptilian, staring at her through the Double Monocle. She awoke with a sense of foreboding, wondering just what Pietro's warning might have been.

THE GLOB BLOG
a Food Blog by, duh, Glob

ABOUT GLOB

Wassup, Munchers? If you're reading this you probably know who I am, and if you don't, like, where have you been, man? No, seriously, just in case you stumbled on this website by accident or, like, you did a search for "best blog in the universe" and wound up here, lol, I'm that guy you know who will eat anything once. And a lot of things twice. Just nothing that grows in dirt. Veggies suck!!!!! But I will make an exception for potatoes because some total genius figured out how to turn them into French fries. French fries rule! Especially the curly kind. And Cajun seasoning never hurts. Just sayin'. But enough about me—get ready to munch! Oh wait. I'm the one munching. Get ready for ME to munch! Don't be jealous. Or not TOO jealous. Ha ha.

CATEGORIES

Bubble Gum • **BURGERS** • Candy (old school, like Raisinets) **CANDY** (new kinds) • Chips • **CHURROS** • Cookies Corndogs • **COTTON CANDY** • Cupcakes • **DONUTS** (filled) **DONUTS** (normal) • Donut Holes • **DRIED MEATS** • French Fries Hot Dogs • **HOT WINGS** • Nachos • **PIZZA** • Pizza Pockets **POPCORN** • Pretzels (hot) • **PRETZELS** (chocolate or yogurt-covered) • Soda • **TACOS** • Weird-Colored Food • **WRAPS**

SPONSORS

Medieval Days Family Restaurants: "Where every table is the Round Table, and you're a knight every night!"

THE RENAISSANCE FAIRE
LIVE BLOGGING

9:20 AM*

Hear ye! Hear ye!

Ha ha. Did you think I was going to go all Shakespearean on you? Actually, I thought about it but it's too hard to write like that. Anyway, welcome to the Glob Blog's official live blogcast of the Xxxxx School Annual Field Trip to the Renaissance Faire. We're about to get off the bus and me and my handheld computational device are ready for some tasty Ren-Faire eats. Wait, what's that I hear? Methinks it's Ye Olde Bloomin' Onion calling my name!

9:35 AM

OK, right now they're walking us through the "village square" and I just stopped at a place where they're selling bongo drums and bracelets and other hippie stuff 'cause there's a plug where I can charge up. It's supposed to be "market day" but I'm pretty sure in the Renaissance they weren't selling tie-dye T-shirts. Next to the square is a big outdoor stage. "Theater in the round" they call it 'cause it's, duh, round. Onstage now there's some guy juggling and telling jokes but nobody's really listening.

So Mrs. Johnson, our principal, is Queen Elizabeth again and she's walking around making everybody bow and curtsy. Amber

---

*NOTE: AS YOU PROBABLY KNOW, ON MOST BLOGS, NEWER POSTS APPEAR BEFORE OLDER ONES, SO YOU THE SEE MOST RECENT POST FIRST. HERE, FOR YOUR READING CONVENIENCE, I HAVE REARRANGED GLOB'S POSTS SO THEY NOW APPEAR IN CHRONOLOGICAL ORDER, OLDEST FIRST. I HAVE ALSO TAKEN THE LIBERTY OF CORRECTING A FEW TYPOS.

and Veronica (surprise surprise) are her ladies-in-waiting. They keep fanning her with these big feathers and holding her dress. This is what I want to know, why does Mrs. Johnson get to be Queen? Not that I want to be Queen!! King for the day, that would be me. But not King Elizabeth!!! That would be Daniel-not-Danielle. Heh. Just kidding! Or how about King Egbert-not-Elizabeth?? Kidding. Sorry, dude. But you got to admit it was funny. That's what you get for staying home "sick" today!

By the way, kind of off the subject, but did you know that in Shakespeare's time, all the actors playing the girl parts were guys? Our new school secretary, who's kind of our Ren-Faire escort, just told us that. Which is pretty funny considering she's a girl dressed as a guy today — sort of. She's got a jester outfit on and she's calling herself Lady Fool.

Oops. Better unplug. Everybody's moving.

10:53 AM

So what about the chow, you ask? I keep thinking there's going to be some of those big drumsticks you see in those pictures of King Henry the whatever-eth. Or maybe a pig roasting on a spit. But the closest thing I see in Her Majesty's Food Court is a hot-dog stand with one of those old-fashioned British signs calling it the Regal Beagle. Oh, wait — they have corn dogs! My favorite kind of dog. Well them and my cocker spaniel, Munchie, lol. Let's see, what else? There's Sir Lancelot's Chicken on a Stick...the Fishwife's Fish and Chips... Btw, Glob Blog Tip: Malt vinegar = awesome on fries, which is actu-

ally what chips are. (English people sound all smart but they don't
even know the difference between a chip and a fry! Ha ha.)

We're on the way to see a "camera obscura," whatever that is. Some kind of dark room. People are joking that it's a kissing booth. Really mature, huh? After that, it's the big joust. Excuse me, the Medieval Days Royal Tournament and Joust. (Sorry, Medieval Days! Your Belgian waffles rock even if your burgers suck—kidding! No really, the burgers are good, guys. And I'm not just saying that because they're paying me. Or am I? Ha ha.)

Anyways, I think I might have to hang by myself for a minute— let's see, camera obscura or corn dog? No contest, right? If Mrs. Johnson finds out, do you think she'll have me beheaded?

11:09 AM
Hi again. Tell the truth, did you think the Globster would have the huevos rancheros to ditch the field trip? Wrong!

o(^_^o)

(o^_^o)

(o^_^)o

(does victory dance)

So first I wait behind the hot-dog stand while everybody leaves to go to the camera obscura, which is no big deal except this guy from school named Max-Ernest almost blows my cover by saying hi really loud. He's, like, the least cool-acting person I've ever met. Even by Nuts Table standards. (And HE thinks he's too good to put on a pair of tights? Note to self: if you ever need a spy or start a secret society or something, do NOT invite him.) So anyway, after everybody's gone and I don't have to pretend to be super-interested in wind chimes anymore, I go up to the counter of the Regal Beagle. I'm about to order my corn dog, extra mustard, extra relish, when all of a sudden I smell this smoky barbecue smell. Forget hot dogs, that's gotta be my pig on a spit! So like the saying goes, I follow my nose.

I figure I'll find a bbq right behind one of the food stands but actually there's this dried-up riverbed and then woods. That's it. End of Ren-Faire. I was gonna turn around but then I hear this crackling sound on the other side. I don't see anybody but when I look close there's some footprints leading into the woods. And when I look up there's a puff of smoke coming from somewhere deeper in. The bbq!

OK, it makes me a little nervous, but I decided as a fearless chowhound I have to go check it out. I'm telling all of you now — just in case I don't come back alive. Ha ha.

Wish me luck! And don't forget to dine at Medieval Days! "Eat, Drink, and Be Medieval!"

Your official court taster,

—Glob

11:35 AM

EMERGENCY POST—PLEASE READ! HELP NEEDED!

I know this sounds like a prank but right now I'm hiding in a cave and scared for my life. THIS IS NOT A JOKE. If nobody ever hears from me again, somebody please tell my little sister I lied, she wasn't really born with a tail. Daniel-not-Danielle, you can have all my vintage action figures AND my Guinness World Record-breaking snack cake wrapper collection. I know you think this blog is bogus, but I would seriously consider keeping it up if I were you. You could even expand to movie and game reviews. Hello banner ads! That could be some serious bank.

Alright, I better catch you up while I still have some power left. On the other side of the riverbed there wasn't really a trail but you could follow all the crushed leaves and muddy footprints and stuff. I walk for about five minutes and it's like I'm not getting any closer. At first I figured it was a bbq for people who work at Ren-Faire, which seemed cool. You know, like, insider stuff. But now it's seeming kind of far for Ren-Faire people. Is it just people camping? Like tramps or outlaws? I keep going though 'cause I feel like I'm on one of those nature expedition shows and anyway it's something to blog about, right?

Suddenly, the smoky smell gets really strong and I hear all this chanting. Not like at a ball game, more like monk-sounding. You know, like in Latin but probably way older? So I get to this place where the trees have been cut. There's a big fire in the middle with lots of huge logs burning. A dozen or so people are standing around in a circle. They're all wearing these long cloaks and my first thought is, oh, OK, they're from Ren-Faire after all and they're practicing to be monks for a show later.

Something tells me not to go up to them yet though. I look

around expecting to see a table full of barbecue fixings, cole slaw, and whatever. But there's no food at all. And what's really weird is when I look closer at the fire, I see it's not a bbq at all. There's no meat, no grill. Just this big glowing ball. The ball is glass I think, with, like, a white fire inside. It's so bright it's hard to look at, like the sun.

The chanting changes and suddenly I can understand what they're saying. Just the word SECRET over and over. Like if they say it enough times that glowing ball was going to shoot into the sky or something. Then this woman, who looks like the leader, she holds up this big goblet and drinks out of it. She's in a cloak like everybody else but underneath she's wearing some kind of white sparkly dress and she's really pale and maybe the prettiest woman I've ever seen, but she never smiles. Seriously, it's like her face never moves. She's kind of scary but she is definitely H-O-T. I better stop looking at her, I think, or she's going to notice and like turn me into a statue or something. Ha ha. She passes around the goblet and everybody drinks out of it and I notice another weird thing. They're all wearing these white gloves.

OK, now, this is the part you're really, really not going to believe, but I swear on my snack cake wrapper collection it's true. After the goblet goes all the way around the circle, the leader lady holds it up in the air and . . . just leaves it there. In the air. Floating. Then guess what happens! The goblet tips and this white liquid that looks like milk pours out for a second and then disappears in the air. Just vanishes. Gone. I swear there was a ghost drinking from the goblet. Either that or they were the greatest magicians of all time but who was the magic for? There wasn't any audience.

The whole scene is just total spooksville and I finally start backing away. I guess I make a noise or something because that's when they see me. It's hard to describe their expressions, but it was like I was a monster and about to steal their baby.

Somebody goes, "Hey, you, what are you doing there?" And somebody else is all "Get him!" or something like that.

So I start running as fast as I can. I think I hear footsteps following me, but I'm too scared to look back. I'm going so hard my chest hurts and I can't breathe. I look for a place to hide. Right off the trail there's this big boulder shaped kind of like a hamburger with a bite out of it. Underneath where the bite is, there's this hole just big enough to fit through. So I squeeze in. (I know, my stomach isn't so small, yeah yeah, ha ha, so what.) It turns out there's a cave. Like with a dirt floor and stone walls. A *cave* cave. And that's where I am now. Some people have been here before because there are soda bottles and a corn chip bag. I'm starving but the bag's empty, I looked, plus it's not my favorite brand anyway. (I won't name it though, just in case they want to sponsor me someday. Ha ha.) And now—oh wait, this thing is beeping, I better post before it runs out of juice!

ass couldn't get used to seeing so many jester hats.

There were red ones and green ones, velvet ones and felt ones. Some were oversize with long pointed ends stretching out like antlers. Some were small and economical, not much more substantial than skullcaps. Some had brass bells, others silver.

And yet, as wildly varied as the hats were, they all bore a teasing resemblance to a certain hat that was hovering on the edge of her memory. The three pointed ends flapping and flopping this way and that—she'd seen a hat flap and flop in just that way. The bells jingling and jangling at the wearers' every step—she'd heard bells jingle and jangle with just that tone and timbre. She was more and more convinced that she must have found the Jester at some point during her journey—why else would the bells on the hats ring so many bells in her head?—but where? When? What did he say?

Things only got worse when they got to the camera obscura—a small round, windowless structure that stood on a rise near the center of the faire. Their guide, Opal—or Lady Fool, as she insisted upon being called—was wearing not only a jester hat but also a diamond-patterned harlequin outfit not unlike one *the* Jester might have worn. (Although, truth to tell,

Cass couldn't imagine the Jester's outfit being decorated with rhinestones.) As Opal led their group into the dark interior, her hat-bells taunting Cass with their jolly jingles, Cass suddenly remembered hearing the Jester's bells jingling in a similar room. A dungeon, that was it! The royal dungeon. So she was right. She *had* met the Jester. At least once.

Or was her mind playing tricks on her?

The camera obscura was about the same size as the dungeon cell in Cass's memory, but much more crowded—there were about three classrooms' worth of kids—and here one wall was illuminated with an exact image of the world outside. Opal stood in front of the wall, holding a stack of cue cards.

"You are now inside a camera—a big camera," she read, her nasally New York accent in full effect. "In fact, this was the first kind of camera ever invented."

Cass blinked. As she looked at the image on the wall, she had the sense that she was hanging from her feet, looking at the world upside down. The ground was the sky, and the sky the ground. Costumed faire-goers in wizard capes and fairy wings walked around on the dirt sky, apparently weightless.

"Is that picture upside down? Or am I just dizzy or something?" she whispered to her friends.

Yo-Yoji grinned mischievously. "What are you talking about? Looks right-side up to me."

"That's not funny," whispered Max-Ernest, who, although a month had passed, still half-expected Cass to fall back into a coma any second. "What if she really was dizzy? It could be a sign that something was seriously wrong. I think it's supposed to be like that, Cass...."

"Oh," said Cass, only somewhat relieved.

She hadn't wanted to tell her friends, for fear they would make her go home, or worse, go to the hospital, but she really was not feeling like herself. It wasn't just the jester hats. All morning, ever since she'd woken up from the dream about the green eye, she'd had the sensation that she was in two places at once. Or maybe that she was between two places. It was hard to pinpoint the sensation exactly.

"You see that little hole—?" Opal pointed to a quarter-sized hole in the wall opposite her. Light streamed out of it in a cone shape, as if it were the lens of a movie projector. "Light travels in a straight line. So when light rays pass through a small hole like that one, the rays cross, flipping an image upside down."

"I bet you could make one of these yourself," said Yo-Yoji. "It might be helpful in a stakeout."*

---

*YO-YOJI WAS RIGHT. YOU *CAN* MAKE A CAMERA OBSCURA YOURSELF. AND IT JUST SO HAPPENS YOU WILL FIND INSTRUCTIONS FOR DOING SO IN THE BACK OF THIS BOOK.

"Silence! *We* will not tolerate any more noise!" said Mrs. Johnson, who was standing on the side of the room, flanked by Amber and Veronica, her ladies-in-waiting. "Pray continue, Lady Fool."

"Yes, Your Majesty," said Opal. "Such rudeness in your royal presence momentarily shocked me into silence."

The secretary bowed and continued reading. "In the Renaissance and after, artists—even many very famous ones—used camera obscuras in order to paint more naturalistically. They traced the image it projected...."*

Somebody gasped dramatically in the darkness. "They traced it? So you're saying all those famous artists cheated!" she cried out.

It was Amber. She didn't seem outraged so much as gleeful at the thought.

In fact, this was what Max-Ernest had been thinking. But hearing Amber say it made him wonder if it might not be wrong.

What is the cheating? Pietro's words rang in his head. *There is no cheating in magic, only in poker.*

A few feet away, Benjamin Blake coughed and started mumbling. "...yellow...cheating...pencil...orange...oven..."

---

*WITH ALL DUE RESPECT TO THE SECRETARY, I BELIEVE THE PLURAL OF CAMERA OBSCURA SHOULD BE CAMERAE OBSCURAE. IN OTHER RESPECTS, HER ACCOUNT IS CORRECT. NOBODY IS SURE HOW MANY ARTISTS USED CAMERAE OBSCURAE, BUT LEONARDO DA VINCI WROTE ABOUT THEM IN HIS NOTEBOOKS, AND VERMEER IS WIDELY BELIEVED TO HAVE USED ONE.

"What's that, Benjamin? Did you have something to say to your schoolmates?" asked Opal.

He mumbled again, and the crowd of students tittered.

Max-Ernest started pushing his way through to Benjamin. Ever since the night Cass woke up from her coma, Benjamin had been trying to talk to Max-Ernest as well as to Cass and Yo-Yoji, but they all had given him what is known as the cold shoulder. For obvious reasons. As far as Max-Ernest could tell, however, the blow to the head from Yo-Yoji's guitar had "cured" Benjamin. He was no longer the suave and insouciant dandy; he was his old, inarticulate, artistic, synesthetic self.

Hopefully, this meant he was no longer under the Midnight Sun's spell.

"I don't know why I'm doing this for you," Max-Ernest whispered. "You owe me."

Then he started translating for the room at large:* "Ben says the artists didn't cheat. A camera obscura is just a tool. It's like a writer using a computer instead of a pencil. Or a cook using an oven... I guess as opposed to a campfire—?"

Mrs. Johnson wasn't buying it. "Perhaps I am old-fashioned, but I...*we* are with our lady-in-waiting. Cheating is cheating," she said huffily.

*APART FROM BEING AN EXPERT DECODER, MAX-ERNEST WAS A MUMBLER HIMSELF, AND HE'D ALWAYS BEEN VERY GOOD AT INTERPRETING THE SOUNDS BENJAMIN MADE—THAT IS, THE *OLD* BENJAMIN.

She sounded rather as if she were about to march out of the camera obscura in protest. Instead, she walked in front of the illuminated wall. Upside-down images of the outside world flitted across her, making the tiara on her head sparkle and the black pendant around her neck gleam.

With so much else to see, nobody seemed to notice that the pendant was floating ever so slightly in the air.

"Next thing you know, they'll be defending forgery!" she declared, patting down her pendant. "Now students, I . . . I mean, *we* want you to start exiting quietly, and single file, not like a bunch of heathens."

The small room erupted in noise, all the students trying to leave at once. On his way out, Ben tugged on Max-Ernest's sleeve.

"Thank me later," said Max-Ernest, pushing away from him. "Can't talk right now."

"What's that around Mrs. Johnson's neck?" asked Cass when Max-Ernest rejoined her and Yo-Yoji. With all the clamor around them, she could speak almost normally without being overheard.

"Yeah. Why does it look like it's floating?" asked Yo-Yoji.

"Because it is," said Max-Ernest. "It's a lodestone. A naturally occurring magnet."

Cass scratched her head. "I knew that, but how did I know that...?"

"Mrs. Johnson is obsessed with magnets now. You should have heard her talking about them when I went to give her the Tuning Fork."

Cass took the Double Monocle out of her pocket and surreptitiously looked at the lodestone pendant through it. Although there were at least half a dozen arms and shoulders in the way, the monocle gave her a clear view. As she stared at the black stone, it glowed blue and appeared to pulsate. Cass felt a tug on the monocle—the pull of the lodestone—and a matching tug on her memory.

"I've seen that stone before," said Cass, amazed to see another object from her journey into the past appear in the present. "It looked different, bigger, rougher, but it's the same stone."

The sense of being in two places at once intensified. Suddenly, she couldn't bear it a second longer. "I'm feeling totally...claustrophobic. I have to get out of here right now."

Before her friends could stop her, she started pushing through the crowd and rushed out of the room.

Excited whispers followed in her wake:

"That's that girl that was in the coma!"
"Do you think she's OK?"
"Maybe she's having a relapse!"

"She's going to be fine," said Max-Ernest angrily. He then started pushing his way out after her.

Yo-Yoji followed. "Yo, guys, wait up. You know, you might actually need me sometime!"

They caught up with Cass in front of a dusty carnival tent. A sign hung on a chain:

CLARA *The* CLAIRVOYANT
She
sees
All

"I'm going in here," said Cass.

"Then we're going in, too," said Yo-Yoji. "Pietro said we should keep you in sight."

"I'll be fast."

"I thought you were feeling claustrophobic," said Max-Ernest. "That's the kind of condition that gets worse over time. It doesn't just vanish—"

Ignoring her friends, Cass pushed the heavy curtains aside and entered the tent. She wasn't sure why, but she simply had to go inside. It was almost as if she'd been hypnotized and instructed to enter precisely this tent at precisely this time.

"Hello, Cassandra."

It was the Seer. Clara. Sitting at her tree-stump table in front of a deck of tarot cards. As soon as Cass saw her, Cass remembered every detail of her appearance. The long straggly hair. The skin so pale it was translucent. The eyes of unblinking blue.

"Hello, Cassandra," Cass echoed, recalling that hers was one of the names by which the Seer was known.

She'd never been so happy to see someone she barely knew. At last her memories were coming back! Of course, it was odd that the Seer should be here at the Renaissance Faire five hundred years after Cass had last seen her. But Cass felt a renewed sense of confidence; she was certain that the Seer's appearance— and everything else—would now be explained.

"It is good to see you again," said the Seer. "Sit. I will read your cards." She gestured toward the waiting stool.

Her ears tingling with anticipation, Cass obeyed.

As before, the Seer passed a hand over her tarot deck and a card flipped over as if by its own volition. A trick all the more astonishing now, in the present, in the real world.

"Ah. The Ace of Wands returns. But this time, right-side up." The Seer looked quizzically at Cass. "You have come to return something, then?"

"No, not really... like what?"

"Did I not once tell you that something must be returned to its rightful owner?"

Cass struggled to recall their conversation. "Yeah, but... I don't think I ever figured out what it was."

"Oh no? I should think it would be obvious. Do you not have something with you that is mine?"

Cass hesitated, perplexed. Then...

"Oh, you mean the monocle!"

"The Double Monocle, yes. For years it has been out of my hands and away from my eye."

Fumbling, Cass brought the monocle out of her pocket and handed it to the Seer. Cass couldn't help feeling a pang of regret; the monocle had been her primary link to the past. But if giving up the monocle was the price of restoring her memory, she would gladly pay.

The Seer put the monocle up to her right eye and peered out at Cass. Then the Seer looked beyond Cass, seemingly to some distant time or place invisible to the naked eye. She appeared to be testing the focus as one would with binoculars or a zoom lens.

"Ahh. Much better. Thank you," she said, lowering the monocle.

"You're welcome, but I thought you meant

return something that I already took," said Cass, sorting through her still-disjointed memories. "When you read my cards before, I didn't even have the monocle yet... right? How could I return it?"

A hint of a smile crossed the Seer's lips. "Yes, the cards work in mysterious ways, don't they?"

She passed her hand over another card. It flipped over in the air, then settled back down like an autumn leaf.

"Did you ever find your jester?"

"Yeah, I think so.... At least, I'm pretty sure we were in a dungeon together."

The Seer nodded. "He may need finding again. Look, this time it is he who is upside down —"

She pointed to the latest card to turn faceup. It was the Jester, the card that so closely resembled Cass's Jester, *the* Jester. But he was facing Cass instead of the card reader — upside down in tarot terms.

Cass frowned. "You're not saying I'm supposed to go back in time again, are you?"

The Seer shook her head. "I wouldn't advise it. You have spent too much time out of your time already. It has changed you. I could see right away."

"Changed me? How?" asked Cass, alarmed.

"Are you not seeing things yourself now?"

"Like what? What things?"

"Things you didn't see before."

"No, I mean...why? Should I be...seeing things?"

"Only if there are things to see."

"Are there...things to see?" Cass asked, growing nervous.

"There is always something to see...just not always with those two marbles you call your eyes."

"With what, then?"

"Have you heard of the inner eye—the third eye?"

"Yeah, I guess, but I never really believed in it...."

"A tiny housefly has hundreds of eyes. Why should it be so hard to believe you have three?"*

"Are you saying I'm a..."—Cass stumbled over the word—"seer...like you are?"

"Perhaps not so much like me, but we are both called Cassandra, aren't we?"

Cass nodded hesitantly.

"And your Secret? Did you find that?"

"No, at least, I don't think so....No, wait, that's it—that's why I remembered the lodestone!" exclaimed Cass, almost jumping off the stool in her excitement. "The lodestone hanging around Mrs. Johnson's neck—the Jester said he would leave the Secret under it. Or, like, a message about the Secret."

"Oh?" queried the Seer mildly. "The Secret must

---

*I'M SORRY TO SAY THAT THE SEER IS INCORRECT — ABOUT FLIES AT LEAST. STRICTLY SPEAKING, A FLY HAS ONLY TWO EYES. EACH FLY EYE HAS HUNDREDS OF FACETS AND THEREFORE CAN SEE IN HUNDREDS OF DIRECTIONS — ERGO, THE MYTH THAT A FLY HAS EIGHT HUNDRED EYES.

be very short if it can be written under such a small stone."

"So then…you don't know whether I'm right about Mrs. Johnson's necklace?" asked Cass, a little frustrated that her revelation hadn't been greeted with more enthusiasm.

"I can only tell you what the cards tell me—"

The Seer flipped the next card over with a breezy wave. On the face of the card, a robed man held his wand aloft in his right hand while pointing down with his left — the Magician.

"Remember: *as above, so below*."

"I remember — but what does it mean?"

"That depends on what is above and what is below, naturally."

Based on her previous experience with the Seer, Cass had expected the Seer to lay out several more cards, but it appeared from the way the Seer folded her hands that she considered the reading finished.

"OK, then. Thanks, I guess."

Cass stood up, distinctly unsatisfied, but anxious to tell her friends the news.

Max-Ernest and Yo-Yoji were waiting impatiently outside the tent.

Before either could say a word, Cass launched

into a breathless account of her adventures with the Jester, almost all of which she now remembered, ending with the Jester's promise to hide a message about the Secret under the lodestone. "The thing is, I don't know if he ever even found the Secret. He hadn't even heard of it until I told him about it."

The other two Terces members stared at her in disbelief.

"How could he not have heard of it?" asked Yo-Yoji. "He's practically the only one who ever knew it!"

"I know, I couldn't believe it, either. But the worst thing was that Lord Pharaoh already knew about the Secret—that's what the homunculus told me—so I made the Jester promise to find it before Lord Pharaoh did...."

"You...you *made* him?" Max-Ernest stammered.

"Wait...you didn't...*meet* Lord Pharaoh, did you?" asked Yo-Yoji, stammering as well.

Cass nodded, seeing again the dark green, reptilian-looking eye magnified by the Double Monocle. "Yeah, it was pretty scary."

Her friends shook their heads in amazement, unable to hide how impressed they were to hear Cass speak in such a familiar way about the Jester and

Lord Pharaoh—the Terces Society's legendary hero and legendary villain, respectively.

"Well, logically, the Jester must have found the Secret eventually," said Max-Ernest, recovering. "He did start the Terces Society, didn't he?"

"And you think that rock around Mrs. Johnson's neck—that's the Jester's lodestone?" asked Yo-Yoji.

Cass nodded. "Uh-huh. Well, carved up. But from the same rock. I know it sounds crazy. Like how would she get it? But it looked exactly the same when I looked at it through the monocle."

"Maybe it's not so crazy," said Max-Ernest. "Mrs. Johnson said the lodestone came from the same witchy aunt of hers as the Tuning Fork."

"Wait...wasn't her name Clara?" asked Cass, noting silently that the name was the same as the Seer's.

"Yeah. That's the one. How 'bout that?"

"So that means if we want to see the lodestone up close, we have to get it from...oh man!" Yo-Yoji groaned.

The others nodded glumly in agreement. Once again they were going to have to retrieve a precious heirloom from their principal.

"That's it, it's over. This time we won't be

expelled; we'll be sent straight to juvenile hall!" declared Max-Ernest. "I almost wish you never went to talk to that mannequin."

"What mannequin?" asked Cass.

"Uh, the one in the tent you've been in for the last twenty minutes. You must have fed it a lot of quarters."

"What do you mean?" Cass's ears began to tingle with panic. "There's no mann—wait just a sec. I think I forgot something."

She turned and ran back to the tent, throwing aside the striped curtains.

Sure enough, sitting behind a window in a small booth, where a moment ago she'd seen the Seer, or *thought* she'd seen the Seer, there was now a mannequin. More accurately, an automaton. A robot fortune-teller in a red velvet turban. The kind you see at carnivals. The kind that hands out little cards that say things like *You will live a long and prosperous life* or *You will have many children.*

Other than Cass, the only living thing in the tent was a fly buzzing around a dusty shaft of sunlight. Not even the tree stump was there.

Cass stared at the booth, shaken.

It was true: she *was* seeing things. And hearing them, too.

She looked down, expecting to see the monocle lying on the ground. It wasn't there, either. Strange. But by now she was so unsettled, so insecure about her perceptions, that she couldn't be certain she hadn't left the monocle someplace else earlier. Or perhaps she'd never had it at all and she'd just imagined the monocle as she'd imagined the Seer?

Distraught, Cass was about to exit when she noticed the coin slot next to the fortune-teller's hand. It read: 25 CENTS. On impulse, Cass dropped a quarter into the slot.

The carnival-style lights that circled the booth started to flash and the robot fortune-teller nodded jerkily.

"Greetings, traveler. Clara the Clairvoyant sees all," said a recorded voice that sounded nothing like the Seer's. *"Ask your question. Then read your fortune."*

Cass looked over her shoulder to make sure she was still alone, then whispered, "Was what I saw real? Was Cassandra here?"

A bell rang and a small card appeared in the fortune-teller's hand. Gears creaking, the fortune-teller lowered her mechanical arm and dropped the card into the dish at the bottom of the small opening in the booth window.

What am I expecting? Cass asked herself as she

took the card. It's probably just going to tell me what my lucky number is or something.

She turned the card over.

As above, so below, it read.

Cass was so startled she almost dropped the card. That was when she saw what the fortune-teller was wearing. The monocle magnified the automaton's pale blue eye the same way it had the Seer's. Only the automaton's eye was marble.

"So she *was* here....You *are* here...," Cass whispered.

The fortune-teller's bell rang; and as Cass watched, the fortune-teller lowered the monocle and dropped it into the dish reserved for the fortune-telling cards.

"You want me to...take that back?" Cass stammered.

The bell rang. And the fortune-teller dropped another card into the dish next to the monocle.

You have a gift. You will have need of it.

Cass blinked, unsure whether the message was an answer. Did it mean the monocle was a gift? Or was it another reference to second sight?

Again the bell rang. Again the fortune-teller dropped a card.

You are haunted by the past.

"Do you mean *haunted* haunted?" Cass asked nervously. "Or just, like, worried about the past?"

Again the bell. Again a card.

As before, so now.

Thoroughly mystified, Cass waited for another card to drop. But none appeared.

She pulled the first card out of her pocket and placed it on top of the others.

Your lucky number is seven, it now read.

Cass walked out, clutching the monocle tight in her hand and wondering if this was what it was like to be crazy.

Inside the tent, the fly continued to buzz.

When Cass emerged from the fortune-teller's tent for the second time, Max-Ernest was standing alone.

"What happened to Yo-Yoji?" she asked, blinking in the sunlight.

"He went to go sign up for the joust."

"You mean, like, to be in it? That's crazy!"

"How else are we supposed to get close enough to Mrs. Johnson? She's been surrounded by Amber and Veronica all day. Plus that secretary lady—"

"I can't believe they would let Yo-Yoji sign up. I thought kids weren't allowed."

"We're not. That's the beauty of it! If he wins, he

gets knighted by the Queen. If he gets caught, he gets sent to the principal. He sees Mrs. Johnson either way. It's win-win. How 'bout that?"

"How 'bout that...?" Cass didn't like the plan (mostly, I suspect, because it had been concocted in her absence), but she didn't have an alternative plan to offer.

"By the way," said Max-Ernest, lowering his voice. "I figured out what the warning was that Pietro sent me. What you said before about Lord Pharaoh and the Secret, it reminded me."

"Yeah, what?" asked Cass, still focused on the joust.

"Well, I got this note—it was in code but it said LORD PHARAOH LIVES."

Cass snapped to attention. "Did you just say 'Lord Pharaoh lives'?"

"Uh-huh. I thought it was from the Midnight Sun. You know, like kind of a taunt. But now I think Pietro must have written it. I just can't figure out why."

"Well...it could be true," said Cass slowly. "Did you think of that?"

"True that Lord Pharaoh is alive? But he would be five hundred years old," Max-Ernest scoffed.

"Besides, didn't Mr. Cabbage Face say he ate him? We even saw Lord Pharaoh's grave—"

"You're right, it was a crazy idea."

Cass shivered. A horrible, horrible thought had occurred to her, but she pushed it away.

The important thing was to get her hands on the lodestone. To learn the Secret.

our Majesty, dukes and duchesses, counts and countesses, barons and baronesses, lords and ladies, knights and damsels, lads and lasses, yeomen and serfs, peers of the realm, and—whom did I miss?—students from the Xxxxx School, let the games begin!"

Standing in the middle of the stadium and dressed in a suitably bright and ballooning satin outfit, the announcer, or "Master of Arms" as he'd introduced himself, lowered his bullhorn and raised a trumpet to his lips.

"In the real Renaissance, I don't think they would've had Porta-Potties next to the royal stands," complained Max-Ernest, who was sitting in said stands next to Cass. The Porta-Potties were directly behind them, and the smell was distinctly unpleasant.

"Trust me, in the real Renaissance, it was worse," said Cass. "People just went wherever they wanted to."

"Gross.... How do you know where people went in the Renaissance, anyway?" asked Max-Ernest. "—Oh right, I forgot."

"Actually, you're right. How do I know? I don't know anything anymore," said Cass grimly.

"What do you mean? What's wrong?" asked Max-Ernest. He had seen Cass in many moods in the past—but never in a self-doubting one. It was disturbing to his sense of order.

Cass shrugged. "Nothing. I don't mean anything...." She wasn't about to tell Max-Ernest the true reason behind her state of mind. Not today, anyway. If she told him about her experience—or non-experience—with the Seer, he would probably rush her to the hospital.

As they spoke, about twenty knights on horseback (or men and women dressed as knights on horseback, I should say) rode into the ring. Each wore a number over his or her breastplate and each held a flag, some representing nations, others representing local businesses or bowling leagues.

"Ladies and gentlemen, I now present the finest knights in the kingdom," declared the Master of Arms. "They have come from all over the country, indeed from all over the world, to compete in a contest of skill and will. The winner will be honored by the Queen herself."

He proceeded to introduce the contestants, each of whom had adopted a grand title for the occasion: Sir Daniel the Daring, Sir Michael of the Moors, Lord Phillip the Fair, and so on.

Cass and Max-Ernest applauded when they heard Yo-Yoji announced:

"And here, from Feudal Japan, comes Sir Yoji-San, the Samurai Knight!"

Yo-Yoji rode into the ring on a feisty black horse. He was dressed in traditional European-style armor (a couple sizes too big) but holding a samurai sword and carrying a Japanese-style flag (decorated with what I can only describe as some sort of anime alien — or perhaps it was meant to be one of Cass's sock monsters). As his horse pawed the ground and jerked his head this way and that, Yo-Yoji squirmed in his saddle; he looked as if he might fall off before the games even began.

"Since when does Yo-Yoji know how to joust, anyway?" asked Cass.

"He doesn't. I don't even think he knows how to ride a horse," said Max-Ernest. "But he knows all about swords from all those kendo lessons with Lily. Plus he has samurai experience, remember?"

"Oh great. I'm sure this will be a piece of cake, then."

"Quiet! The Queen speaks!"

A hush fell over the crowd. Mrs. Johnson stood up in the royal box.

"Loyal subjects, we thank you from the bottom of our royal heart for being here today on this great occasion," she said, attempting to maintain her

English accent as she shouted into a bullhorn. "Brave knights, who among you will be our champion? To earn our patronage, you must have the courage of a lion and the cunning of a fox, the eyes of an eagle and the ferocity of a wolf, the heart of a bear and the mind of a...well, never mind. May the best man win!"

The crowd clapped and cheered, "Long live the Queen!"

I regret to say Yo-Yoji's first effort was not auspicious. Despite his vaunted samurai experience, he passed by the quintain entirely, got thrown from his horse, and wound up pole vaulting over his lance — a neat trick but hardly a way to earn points in a hastilude.*

Happily, he was able to stand up immediately afterward, a bit bruised but mostly unscathed. The audience's laughter was, as you can imagine, uproarious.

Soon, however, the games turned from military showmanship to direct combat. Now on foot, the knights competed in a round-robin of hand-to-hand matchups featuring a variety of weapons, including not only swords but flails, battle-axes, and spears — all, of course, stage props and not real weapons. (This was, after all, not a real knights' tournament but a

---

*ON THE OFF-CHANCE THAT YOU HAVE NEVER COMPETED IN ANY MEDI-EVAL TOURNAMENTS, I SHOULD TELL YOU THAT THE WORD *QUINTAIN* HERE REFERS TO THE TARGET AT WHICH THE KNIGHTS AIM THEIR LANCES.

staged event at a faux Renaissance Faire.) I am pleased to inform you that Yo-Yoji's performance improved greatly with every matchup. Highly trained by martial-arts master Lily Wei, Yo-Yoji was light on his feet and extremely deft with the sword and flail especially. He had an unerring instinct for when to thrust, when to parry, and when to leap over the heads of his opponents (well, perhaps not literally over their heads, but he did jump quite high considering the weight of his armor).

By the time the knights were supposed to remount their horses, Yo-Yoji's score, previously the lowest, qualified him for the final round of jousting—the result of which would determine who would become the Queen's champion.

The competition had come down to four contestants.

Compared to the first round of quintains, the targets were smaller, the stakes higher. But luck was on Yo-Yoji's side. The first of the four contestants seemed to lose his grip on his lance at the last moment, so that he barely grazed his quintain and earned a low score of four. The second contestant, fighting a gust of wind, missed his target entirely.

Yo-Yoji was next. When the Master of Arms' whistle sounded, Yo-Yoji spurred his horse. This time,

---

A *HASTILUDE*, MEANWHILE, IS ANY KIND OF MILITARY-STYLE GAME THAT WAS UNDERTAKEN IN THE MIDDLE AGES, BUT MOST ESPECIALLY A JOUST.

he sat firmly in his saddle—it was clear he intended not to be thrown off again—and he held his lance straight, connecting near the center of his quintain and earning a more-than-respectable nine out of ten points.

A moment later, the whistle sounded once more. The fourth contestant was about to make his move when suddenly his horse bucked as if spooked by something. The unfortunate knight was thrown to the ground. While he shouted for his horse to stop, the horse tore off in the direction of the stables, kicking up a cloud of dust in its wake.

"Is it possible Yo-Yoji just won by default?" asked Cass.

Before Max-Ernest could answer, there were shouts and cries from the other end of the stadium. Like everyone else in the audience, Cass and Max-Ernest turned to see what was causing the commotion.

"This is part of the show, right?" asked Max-Ernest.

A hitherto unseen knight had charged into the ring. His tall horse rearing, he broke through the ranks of the other knights—causing their horses to buck and rear in turn. He seemed to have an agitating effect on everyone present, whether equine or human.

"You on the gray horse! What are you doing here?" cried the Master of Arms. "This tournament is for people who have reserved spots only — I'm sorry, you will have to leave the ring immediately."

But the mystery knight did not leave. On the contrary, he reined his horse and settled in the center of the stadium. The picture he created was unnerving, to say the least. Whereas the other knights all wore brand-new armor that sparkled in the sunshine, he was clad head to toe in dark and rusty sheets of steel that reflected no light, even though his horse was standing in full sun. A medieval-style helmet masked his entire face, a single narrow slit enabling him to see but not be seen. Scale-like gauntlets covered his hands and forearms, giving them the quality of dragon talons. And he wore steel boots on his feet that looked heavy enough to sink a ship. His horse, meanwhile, was a good five or six hands taller than the other horses, and a great deal wilder-looking.

"Please, can somebody escort this man out of here?" The Master of Arms was gesticulating in all directions. A handsome silver-haired man dressed as a Renaissance courtier, with a wide ruffled collar and black boots, walked up to him and whispered in his ear.

"Begging your pardon, ladies and gentlemen, there may be a change of plan," announced the Master of Arms after a moment, obviously very flustered. "The new entrant calls himself the Unknown Knight. I am told he represents the Queen's cousin, Mary Queen of Scots."

As he said this, the Unknown Knight bowed toward a woman standing in a box opposite Mrs. Johnson's. She was pale and beautiful and dressed in a sparkling white gown — much finer, it must be said, than Mrs. Johnson's — that showed off her Barbie doll–thin waist. She tilted her head ever so slightly in acknowledgment.

The Master of Arms turned toward Mrs. Johnson. "Your Majesty, this is highly irregular, but according to this gentleman, your cousin requests that we make an exception for her champion."

"Very well, the Unknown Knight shall joust with the winner of the previous contest," declared Mrs. Johnson, playing along in as regal a fashion as she could muster. "It saddens us to say it, but we have just learned that Mary Queen of Scots has been plotting against us. She would take her own cousin's life so that she might be Queen. This joust will settle our feud."*

*MARY QUEEN OF SCOTS DID, IN FACT, FAMOUSLY PLOT AGAINST HER COUSIN QUEEN ELIZABETH VIA SECRET, CODED MESSAGES HIDDEN IN WINE BARRELS. UNLUCKILY FOR MARY, ELIZABETH'S SECRETARY HAPPENED TO BE ENGLAND'S PREMIER SPY AND CODEMASTER. HE CRACKED

As the courtier joined the woman identified as Mary Queen of Scots, the audience booed and hissed good-naturedly.

"Down with the traitor from France!" "Long live the Queen!"

Most of the audience seemed to assume this final joust had been preplanned, but the nervous face of the Master of Arms suggested otherwise.

Max-Ernest frowned, watching. "Do they look familiar to you?"

"Why? Who do *you* think they are?" asked Cass cautiously. She had recognized the courtier and Mary Queen of Scots right away, or thought she had, but she no longer trusted her own perceptions.

"Ms. Mauvais and Dr. L—who else?"

Cass nodded. "That's what I was thinking. But why? What are they doing here?"

"I know, it doesn't make any sense. Who do you think the new knight is?"

Cass looked down at the knight standing like a shadow in the sun. She felt a strangely familiar chill. "I don't know. . . . Should we warn Yo-Yoji?"

It was too late. The final joust was beginning.

While Yo-Yoji and the Unknown Knight sat on their horses at opposite ends of the field, the Master of Arms explained the rules of the joust. "Five

THE PLOTTERS' CODE, AND A DOUBLE AGENT MONITORED THEIR COMMUNICATIONS. IN THE END, MARY'S FATE WAS NOT SETTLED VIA A JOUST, HOWEVER. SHE WAS FOUND GUILTY OF CONSPIRING TO KILL THE QUEEN AND SHE WAS EXECUTED.

hundred years ago," he said, "knights would continue fighting on foot once they were unhorsed in a duel to the death. Today, however, we will consider unhorsing your opponent to equal a win."

He addressed Mrs. Johnson once more. "Your Majesty, will you bless this field that these men may duel?"

Mrs. Johnson nodded somberly and raised her hands in benediction.

It was hot inside the armor. Yo-Yoji could hear himself breathing in his mask and could even, he thought, hear his heart beating beneath his breastplate. Sweat dripped into his eyes, but with one hand on his lance and the other hand holding his shield and at the same time the reins of his horse, there was no way to wipe his face. The tournament was taking far too long: he wanted a shower.

He forced himself to concentrate on the task at hand.

It was difficult to see or hear very much under his helmet; he had no idea who the new knight was or where the knight had come from, only that they were meant to joust with each other. Am I really supposed to unhorse him? Yo-Yoji wondered. What if his opponent got hurt? What if he, Yo-Yoji, got hurt? He'd been lucky the last time he landed on the ground. What if this time was different?

The whistle blew.

He wasn't aware of urging his horse forward, only of the sound of pounding hooves below and the rush of wind on the sides of his helmet. In mere seconds he and the mystery knight were closing in on each other. But for Yo-Yoji, there was something surreal and slow-motion-like about the moment. He found his eyes drawn inexorably toward his opponent. At the very least, Yo-Yoji had been able to see the other knights' eyes above their masks, but when he tried to catch a glimpse of the mystery knight's eyes, he saw only shadow. He could see nothing of the knight, not even a sliver of neck or wrist. Only armor and chainmail.

The crowd fell silent, everyone waiting breathlessly for the inevitable collision.

In his brief reverie, Yo-Yoji had lost crucial time. His opponent's lance was aiming straight for him; from Yo-Yoji's perspective, it looked like an oncoming arrow. It was too late for him to try to land a blow. All he could do was try to protect himself. Just in time, he lurched to the side and raised his shield, deflecting the lance with a loud screech.

The crowd cheered.

Yo-Yoji shuddered. A delayed reaction to the near miss.

As his horse headed automatically for the far side of the stadium, Yo-Yoji glanced down at his shield. The deep gouge in its gleaming surface confirmed what he'd seen. The mystery knight's lance had been real. All the other lances, including his own, had little balls on their tips; his opponent's had been needle-sharp. Only Yo-Yoji's instinctive lurch to the side had saved him. An inch or two in one direction or another and he would have been impaled.

Was it possible the other knight was intentionally trying to kill him? Or was the knight just so determined to win that he was indifferent to whether Yo-Yoji lived or died?

Turning his horse around, Yo-Yoji noticed he was no longer sweltering hot. His sweat had turned clammy. His armor was now cold to the touch. This is what it is like to be afraid, he thought.

He didn't know what to do. Bow out? Cass and Max-Ernest would be disappointed, but they wouldn't want him to risk getting killed, would they?

Shivering, he looked over at the Master of Arms to see if he'd noticed anything awry, but the satin-clad man was raising his whistle to his lips, about to signal another round.

Just then there was a shout from the royal box:
"Halt! The joust must stop!"

It was the school secretary, Opal, still in costume as Lady Fool. She pointed to Yo-Yoji. "I just recognized that boy. He is a student at our school and not allowed to participate in this tournament.... Yoji, dismount and remove your armor immediately!"

There was chaos as the Master of Arms verified what the secretary was saying, then hurriedly declared the Unknown Knight the winner.

When Cass and Max-Ernest caught up with Yo-Yoji, he was out of his armor and standing by the guard-rail. The secretary gripped him by the arm as if he were a little boy likely to run off.

"You're right, that was totally against the rules for Yo-Yoji to be in this. Are you taking him to see the principal?" asked Max-Ernest hopefully.

"I'm sure Mrs. Johnson will deal with him just as soon as she's done with that knight," said Opal, nodding.

She nodded to the other side of the field, where the Unknown Knight, still unseen under his helmet, waited on his horse in the winner's circle with the Master of Arms. Mrs. Johnson strode regally toward him, a blue ribbon in her hand.

"Good, I mean, oh, that's too bad," said Cass. "You know, we knew Yo-Yoji entered the competition. But we didn't say anything. So we should be in trouble, too."

The secretary raised her eyebrows. "Is that right?"

"Sir Unknown, champion of Mary Queen of Scots," said Mrs. Johnson, speaking into the Master of Arms' bullhorn, "with this ribbon, we bestow upon you our royal favor—"

She raised the ribbon in the air for the Unknown Knight. When his gauntlet-covered hand reached down, however, he didn't take it; instead, he yanked the lodestone pendant off the neck of the unsuspecting principal.

"Well, I never—!" she shrieked. "Are you crazy?!"

Straightening himself once more on his horse, the knight laughed—a hollow, echoing laugh that sounded as if it came from the depths of his rusty old armor.

"Go!" he shouted to his horse, spurring it forward.

Mrs. Johnson screamed and pointed. "Thief! Thief! Stop him! That man took my necklace! Thief!"

At the edge of the field, the knight unexpectedly reined his horse and looked back over his shoulder.

The frantic Mrs. Johnson kept shouting. "Guards! Security! Somebody, do something! Arrest him!"

Cass knew it was unlikely, but she felt certain the knight was looking at her. She thought again of the awful possibility that had occurred to her earlier. There was no way... or was there?

Then, as the crowd watched aghast, the knight galloped out of the stadium with his right hand raised, dangling the lodestone like a prize.

As soon as the Unknown Knight disappeared, Mrs. Johnson turned her ire on Ms. Mauvais and Dr. L— or Mary Queen of Scots and her courtier, as she knew them. They were sitting expressionlessly in their front-row box, watching events unfold.

"You and you, I—I mean, *we*," sputtered the furious Mrs. Johnson, still trying to maintain her character as Queen Elizabeth, "we don't know what you think you're getting at entering a maniac like that in this competition, but you're not leaving until he returns with my necklace!"

She pointed to the uniformed royal guards lined up in front of them. "Guards! Seize my... our traitor cousin and that awful courtier of hers this instant!"

The guards didn't move.

Ms. Mauvais stood slowly, her dress glittering in

the sunlight. Seemingly without trying, she looked ten times the queen Mrs. Johnson did.

"Please spare us your theatrics, Your Majesty, or should I say, *Madame Principal*. A queen should not have to shout in order to be heard." Indeed, although Ms. Mauvais's voice was but an icy whisper, it could be heard all across the stadium, as if it were being carried by a cold breeze.

She gestured to Dr. L, who stood and bowed. "I'm afraid my courtier and I must refuse your invitation. We have pressing business to attend to — a kingdom to build, you might say — and we simply cannot be detained.... And now I have a message for a certain extremely meddlesome little girl here today...."

Ms. Mauvais looked directly at Cass. "Darling, it's over. You and that ragtag bunch of circus freaks have lost. We hope never to see you and your friends again, but rest assured, if we do, it will be for the last time. It's no longer just us mere mortals you will have to contend with. Our master has returned and he will not be stopped.... Guards —"

Ms. Mauvais snapped her white-gloved fingers at the guards who had ignored Mrs. Johnson only moments earlier. They immediately stood at attention and saluted.

Cass, Max-Ernest, and Yo-Yoji gasped involuntarily. All the guards were wearing white gloves.

"Friends—" Ms. Mauvais snapped her fingers again.

Suddenly, the entire crowd of people behind her stood up—and revealed that they, too, were all wearing white gloves. They raised their hands in unison and made a single sweeping gesture. Then, in silence, they descended onto the field and filed out the gates behind Ms. Mauvais and Dr. L.

Our three heroes stared after them. It was like watching a flock of seagulls rise from the beach and disappear into the horizon. Only in this case the seagulls might better be described as birds of prey.

CHAPTER NINETEEN

OPAL, LIKE THE ROCK

moment later, they were standing in the winner's circle with a tearful Mrs. Johnson.

"I don't know who that lady thinks she is! Is everybody out of their minds?"

She pointed at Yo-Yoji, who looked more than a bit rattled by his brush with the Unknown Knight. Not to mention the sight of all those white gloves.

"You, it's all your fault! If you hadn't entered the contest, he wouldn't have been able to steal my necklace."

"That doesn't make sense," said Max-Ernest, unable to stop himself. "The Unknown Knight would still probably have won, he would have just won against someone el—"

"And now you again!? I shouldn't have let any of you back into school after that last episode with the Tuning Fork. This time, you're all expelled. Forever!"

Mrs. Johnson threw off her tiara. No longer a queen, she was their principal once more. Or ex-principal.

"Actually, I think that's redundant," said Max-Ernest. "Expulsion is always forever. That's what it means. Otherwise, it's—"

"Not another word out of you, young man!" snapped Mrs. Johnson.

"Otherwise, it's suspension," he concluded. "Er, sorry."

"Now, now, these kids don't mean any harm," said Opal soothingly. "If they retrieve your necklace for you, will that be enough to get them back in your good graces?"

"And just how are they going to do that?" Mrs. Johnson scoffed.

"Never mind about that. Just tell me you won't expel them."

"Oh please. Right now that necklace is halfway to Mexico. Or wherever it is medieval knights go to pawn jewelry these days. There's no way those three are going to find it."

"Not medieval, it's Renaiss—," Max-Ernest began, but Cass silenced him with a look.

"Don't underestimate them," continued Opal. "Didn't you say they managed to get something from you before? What was it? A tuning fork?"

"True. There's no doubt they have a talent for thievery...."

As the kids listened in disbelief, the secretary somehow persuaded their principal to let them have twenty-four hours to find the necklace. After that, the principal would call the police about the neck-lace—and their parents about expelling them.

*　　*　　*

Minutes later, Opal ushered them into the stables. The still-shell-shocked Yo-Yoji flung himself down on a bale of hay.

"Why are you helping us?" asked Cass.

"Just doing my job," said Opal with the hint of a smile. "Aren't secretaries supposed to be helpful?"

"I was wrong about you," said Max-Ernest. "I thought, well, I didn't trust you."

Opal laughed, incredulous. "Oh really? After I gave you that mirror? *And* the monocle?"

"You *gave* them to me?"

"Well, left them for you. Same difference. You didn't really think I would be so careless with my things, did you?"

"Oh, no, I guess not," said Max-Ernest, turning red because he had assumed exactly that.

Opal grinned. "And what about the KICK ME note? A nice touch, I thought."

"What KICK ME note?" asked Yo-Yoji.

"I *knew* you wrote that!" said Max-Ernest, ignoring Yo-Yoji. (For some reason he was still reluctant to admit he'd walked around with a sign on his back that said KICK ME.)

"Well, I didn't write the message on the other side," Opal corrected. "That was from Pietro."

Cass stared at him. "You know Pietro?"

Chuckling, the secretary sat down on a stool and pulled off her rather large silver platform shoes. "You guys really don't know who I am, do you?"

"You mean you're not Opal…like the rock?" asked Max-Ernest.

"Nope, not any kind of opal." She took off her trademark opal ring and tossed it over her shoulder.

"Don't worry, it was plastic," she said, seeing the shocked expressions around her.

She peeled away each of her absurdly long fingernails in rapid succession, revealing the bare, unpainted, and very short nails underneath. Then she reached up, gripped her blond hair in her hand, and yanked off what turned out to be a very big wig. Underneath, her hair was brown and short-cropped.

"Here — why don't you keep this?" she said, tossing the wig in the direction of Max-Ernest. "You never know when you're going to need a quick disguise."

Finally, the secretary started wiping makeup off her face with a tissue. The shadow of a beard began to show.

Cass smiled for perhaps the first time all day. "Owen!"

"No kidding. Took you long enough," said the

Terces Society's resident spy and master of disguise, now speaking in a deeper voice without any trace of a New York accent. "Pietro had me visit your school to find out what I could from Mrs. Johnson. We knew the Midnight Sun was watching her, but we thought it was about the Tuning Fork. We didn't think it was about a magnetic rock.... Well, don't just stand there, help me. My other stuff's over there—" He pointed to a small army duffel on the floor that looked about as different from Opal's patent leather purse as a bag possibly could.

Cass handed it to him and he dumped the contents unceremoniously on the ground: jeans, T-shirt, tennis shoes, and a pair of sunglasses.

A moment later, Owen came out of a horse's stall dressed as himself—something the kids had seen only once or twice before. (Although no longer a working actor, he was almost always dressed as someone else, whether that was a cowboy in a ten-gallon hat or a secretary in a ten-gallon wig.)

"Speaking of disguises, you guys have any guesses about who that spook was in the armor? The Unknown Knight? Anybody get a look at his face?"

They all shook their heads.

"Even you, Yo-Yoji? You were pretty close," Owen observed.

"I couldn't even see the dude's eyes. Just, like, shadow. His mask was pretty big."

"It wasn't 'cause of the mask," said Cass, finally fessing up to what she'd been fearing. "It was 'cause he's invisible."

Haltingly, she told them about her encounter with Lord Pharaoh—and about how she had been forced to give him the last remaining bit of Time Travel Chocolate. "I didn't think it would be enough to work, but it must have been," she said, stricken. "When I heard about Pietro's warning, I started to worry. Now I'm sure of it."

"How can you be *sure* of it?" asked Max-Ernest. "I mean, the average person would consider the whole story pretty unlikely."

"I just am. Did you see the way he looked at me? It was like we were communicating or something. Plus, Ms. Mauvais said her master has returned. Who else would that be?"

"From what I hear from Pietro, I think Cass is probably right," said Owen.

"I knew there was something not normal about that guy!" said Yo-Yoji.

"I'm sorry. It's all my fault," said Cass, miserable. "I should never have eaten the chocolate. Now, instead of me having the lodestone, Lord Pharaoh does!"

"Don't blame yourself. You did what you had to do," said Owen, not exactly contradicting her. "I'll be back as soon as I can. In the meantime, you guys try to find out which way Lord Pharaoh went. But do not, I repeat, DO NOT go after him, do you hear me?"

"Why not?" asked Yo-Yoji. "He was going after me."

"Yeah, that's my point. I'm the guy who's always ready to throw you into the deep end, so if I'm telling you to stay away, there's gotta be a good reason, right?"

"You know, I *have* met Lord Pharaoh before," Cass couldn't help saying.

"Was he a ghost at the time? Whose powers we don't even know? If he's out of his armor now, he could be anywhere and we wouldn't see him. He could be in this very room."

Cass glanced around through the monocle. "He's not."

"Well, there's some good news at least!" Throwing his rucksack over his shoulder, Owen walked out the door.

"How do we figure out where Lord Pharaoh went if we don't go after him?" asked Yo-Yoji after Owen had disappeared. "Just follow his tracks out of here, then stop?"

"I doubt we'll even get that far. He's a ghost. For all we know, his horse is a ghost, too, and it won't leave any tracks," said Max-Ernest. "Hey, what are you doing here, Ben?"

At some point while they were talking, Benjamin had walked in. He tugged on Max-Ernest's sleeve and started mumbling.

"He says he has an idea where we could look for Lord Pharaoh," Max-Ernest translated.

"How do you know about Lord Pharaoh?" asked Cass angrily. "Have you been eavesdropping?"

"He's still spying for them, I knew it!" said Yo-Yoji.

Benjamin shook his head over and over.

Max-Ernest translated again. "He says he just wants to help. He feels terrible about what he did and wants to make it up to us."

"OK, so how're you helping, Ben?" demanded Cass.

"He says the camera obscura is located on the highest point in the area. He stayed there after the rest of the school left and noticed you can see all of Ren-Faire and even outside of it. Maybe we'll be able to see Lord Pharaoh from there.... Actually, not a bad idea, Ben."

A faint smile lit Benjamin's face.

inus the crowd of students, the camera obscura had a calmer, more contemplative quality — like a museum or a library.

The screen did indeed offer a sweeping, panoramic view of the Renaissance Faire but, alas, only of one side of the faire.

"Lord Pharaoh could be riding past us right now, but we can't see him because this hole is pointed in the wrong direction," Max-Ernest complained.

"Maybe we should get out of here, start asking around. *Somebody* must have seen which way he went," said Yo-Yoji. "What do you say, Cass?"

"Just a sec," said Cass, taking out the Double Monocle. "I think I just saw something."

At first, when she looked at the image on the wall through the monocle, not much looked different. There were no signs of Lord Pharaoh that she could see, on horseback or off, in armor or out of it. But there was one jester hat that couldn't help grabbing her attention — despite her best efforts to ignore all the jester hats at the faire. The point wasn't that it looked so much like *the* Jester's hat (although it did). The point wasn't even that the man wearing the hat looked so much like the Jester (although he did). The point was that this particular hat, as well as the man wearing it, was only visible when she looked through the monocle. Three times she removed the monocle to check, and three times the man disappeared from her sight. And yet when she raised the monocle to her eye, he looked just as clear and present as anybody else who crossed her path.

Her ears flushed with excitement. It was the Jester. *Her* Jester. In *her* world. Just...upside down.

As above, so below, she thought, remembering the upside-down jester in her last tarot card reading.

The Seer had told her to follow the Jester. Is this what she meant? Or was Cass just seeing things? Maybe the Jester isn't really there at all, she thought, and my head is re-creating him from memory. Then again, her entire journey into the past had—in a sense—been in her head. It was all so confusing!

The sound of a cell phone ringing brought Cass's attention back into the room.

Max-Ernest took his phone out of his pocket and looked at the number, befuddlement on his face. "Who do you think it is?" he asked his friends. "The only people that ever call me are you guys. Unless it's about my brother...?"

Nervous, he clicked on.

"Hi, Max-Ernest, it's Daniel."

"Who?"

There was a pause on the other end of the line. Then, through gritted teeth, *"Daniel-not-Danielle."*

"Oh! Uh, hi."

Daniel-not-Danielle spoke in a rush. *"I didn't know who else to call. I didn't want to call the principal or anybody—just in case, well, Glob said he ditched the camera obscura and I didn't want to get him into more trouble."*

"You're calling 'cause he ditched?"

"No, no, it's 'cause of what he wrote on his blog."

"I thought you were at that comic book thing," said Max-Ernest, confused.

"I was. I got home early and went online."

Daniel-not-Danielle proceeded to tell Max-Ernest all about Glob's blog posts (omitting the part where Glob makes fun of Daniel-not-Danielle as well as the part where he complains about Max-Ernest), right up to the part where Glob sees what looks like a ghost drinking from a cup.

Max-Ernest put his hand over the phone and whispered to the others: "Glob saw Lord Pharaoh—I think the Midnight Sun might have him!"

Into the phone, he asked: "Where's the last place he said he was?"

Then, to the others: "He crossed some dry river-bed and he's supposedly hiding in a cave now. Unless they got him…There's no riverbed around here, is there?"

While Max-Ernest was speaking, Cass was watching the Jester cross just such a riverbed. In the past, she might have found the coincidence remarkable, but she was getting very used to seeing the storylines of her life overlap and converge.

"I know where it is—I think I know where he went," she said, not mentioning the Jester. She was reluctant to tell her friends about him, still fearing what would happen if they knew about her visions.

"*If you find him, do me a favor,*" said Daniel-not-Danielle. "*Tell him he shouldn't call himself 'the Globster'—it's embarrassing.*"

"I think that's supposed to be a pun," said Max-Ernest helpfully. "You know, *lobster/Globster.*"

By the time Max-Ernest got off the phone, his friends were already out the door.

"Are you sure this is where to go?" asked Max-Ernest about ten minutes later. "We're getting kind of far away from Ren-Faire."

Cass didn't answer, just kept leading them farther into the woods. Holding the monocle up to her eye, she looked like a particularly determined naturalist chasing after a rare species of butterfly.

Max-Ernest and Yo-Yoji were a bit mystified that Cass was so certain about the direction they were heading, but they weren't about to let her continue on her own, not with her having woken up so recently from a coma, not with the Midnight Sun and the ghost of Lord Pharaoh lurking about.

"Is anybody else hungry?" asked Yo-Yoji.

"I am," said Max-Ernest. "And I'm all out of chocolate!"

Not stopping, Cass felt around in a side pocket of her backpack, pulled out a plastic baggie full of her trademark super-chip trail mix, and tossed it over her shoulder.

Her friends greedily ransacked the baggie, Max-Ernest extracting as many of the chocolate chips as he could. (Luckily, it was not a hot day and the chocolate chips hadn't melted yet.)

"Hey, I think that might be the boulder Glob hid under," said Max-Ernest. "He said it was shaped like a hamburger."

Yo-Yoji called out to Cass, who was getting farther and farther ahead. "Wait up, Cass! We found the boulder!"

"You guys check it out, I'll meet you back there!"

Before they could argue, she disappeared behind a tree.

The Jester was still a good thirty or forty feet ahead of her. Whenever she got too close, he would speed up. When she lagged too far behind, he would slow down. Because the monocle refused to stay in her eye socket, she had to hold it up. Whenever she needed her hand to move brush or leaves aside, she had to remove the monocle — meaning often as not she couldn't see the Jester. But he was always there when she looked through the monocle again. It was if they were connected by an invisible thread that might slacken or tighten but would never snap.

Eventually, he stopped and let her come much closer.

"Hi," she said shyly.

He put his finger to his lips to shush her. Then pointed ahead to where the path ended at a large oak tree.

He smiled at her. Then he vanished.

She felt suddenly very sad and bereft. Why hadn't he spoken? Why had he led her all the way out here only to disappear?

She ran to the oak tree and saw that on the other

side of it was a dirt road not unlike the one she had walked on in the beginning of her journey into the past. Up ahead was a small gas station. It looked old, abandoned.

Then she saw him. Not the Jester. Lord Pharaoh.

Correction: then she saw *where* he was. She couldn't see Lord Pharaoh himself.

He had taken off his helmet, and his seemingly empty suit of armor appeared to be sitting astride his horse all by itself.

Just as she raised the monocle to her eye, he looked up and saw her. His face was now visible to Cass, but hardly more alive. He looked even emptier inside than he had before.

Cass felt her ears prickling with fear. Be brave, she told herself. The Jester wouldn't have led you to him if he didn't think you were strong enough to face him.

Lord Pharaoh broke into an ugly smile. "Cassandra, is it? They tell me that is your name. It suits you—the bearer of bad news. I knew when I first met you that you would be a blot on the future."

The ancient alchemist dismounted. "I hear from my...what shall I call them?...my modern-day colleagues that you are a terrible pest."

Off the horse, he was no less imposing; he towered over Cass when he reached her.

She took a step backward — and found herself up against a tree.

"If you're talking about Dr. L and Ms. Mauvais, they...they wish I was just a pest," Cass stammered, trying to sound much tougher than she felt. "Did they tell you that every time they tried to stop me, *I* stopped them?"

"They told me enough!"

He gripped her shoulder with his cold, steel-clad hand. She shrank from his touch but could not wriggle free.

"Now is your chance to make up for your sins and those of your ancestors."

"My *ancestors?*" Cass managed to whisper.

She didn't know whether it was due to his ghostly state or to some other alchemical trick, but she could feel Lord Pharaoh's supernatural strength. She had no doubt he could strangle her with a single hand.

"That infernal jester. And that heathen banditwoman. Do you not know what they did?"

Cass shook her head. It was all she could do not to cry.

Lord Pharaoh shook his free fist in fury. "I was

this close to getting my hands on the Secret, this close—"

"But you never found it?" Cass fervently hoped this was the case.

"Oh yes, I did—I found it!" said Lord Pharaoh, enraged. "Those tomb robbers who dug it up didn't know what they had—ignorant thieves! I came to them about a small statue of the goddess Mut. When I saw that torn piece of papyrus, I forgot all about the statue. I knew right away that it was worth more than all the gold in all the tombs in Egypt. On the back were hieroglyphics that could change the course of history."

"The Secret?"

"Yes, the Secret, you little fool...Before I could translate a single hieroglyphic, those sniveling scavengers snatched the papyrus away from me. They could see how much I wanted it and kept demanding more and more money. Until I had no choice but to have those vermin exterminated."

"You killed them?" asked Cass, horrified.

"A minor detail. The important thing was for me to fulfill my destiny. You see, I was—I *am*—the only man on Earth capable of understanding the Secret. I who have studied all the ancient arts. I who have mastered alchemy like no man before or since. I who have made life with my own hands —"

"But the Jester got the Secret first?" Cass guessed.

"He and that thieving woman — confound them! They ambushed my manservant moments before he was to deliver the papyrus to my doorstep. Imagine, Lord Pharaoh foiled by a pathetic comedian and his wife!"

Cass nearly smiled, realizing that this meant the Jester and Anastasia had married, but her face remained frozen.

"Naturally, my servant paid with his life. Now, unless you want to pay with yours, you will tell me how this rock works."

He dangled the lodestone in front of Cass. It was the first time she'd seen it up close. As Max-Ernest had noticed previously, it was shaped like an eye and had a vein of gold running through it. It spun around. The back of the pendant was polished silver and it flashed in the sun.

"A lodestone attracts metal, yes, but what use is that to me? If I grind it into a powder, will a spirit rise? If I crack it open, will I find a pearl? The gold thread that runs through the stone, is that the key? I thought perhaps your jester would have

left a message on the back, but the back is smooth
as glass. It's like a mirror, but you remember what it
is to be a ghost; I cannot even see my own reflection
in it."

He closed his fist around the lodestone.

"What is the lodestone's secret? Where is *the*
Secret?"

"I don't really know," said Cass truthfully.

Then she remembered what the homunculus
had said about Lord Pharaoh. *His weakness is vanity.*
Show him a mirror and you will gain a minute.

"But I can show you your reflection in it."

"How?" His tone remained sour, but she could
tell his curiosity was piqued.

"Hand me the stone and I'll show you."

Lord Pharaoh hesitated only briefly. "If you try
to run off with it, I will find you, and I will destroy
you."

"I know," Cass assured him, although she knew
nothing of the kind.

As soon as Lord Pharaoh dropped the lodestone
in her hand, she felt it pulling toward the monocle. The stone fit snugly within the rim of the monocle, almost as if their dimensions were designed to
match. Cass quickly glanced through the monocle to
confirm you could see through to the reflective silver

surface on the back of the stone, then she held it up for Lord Pharaoh to see.

"Ah, what an obvious trick. I'm almost disappointed."

Although Cass could no longer see Lord Pharaoh's face—to her naked eye, he was invisible again—if she craned her neck she could see his reflection through the lens of the monocle. Despite his dismissive words, he was gazing steadily at his own image. The homunculus had been right about him. Lord Pharaoh was very vain. Even as a ghost.

"Here in your time, I would be over five hundred years old. And yet I look like a young man, do I not?"

Cass thought he looked like an old snake, but she didn't think it necessary to say so. "Definitely. I've never seen anybody with eyes like yours." (That last part was true at least.)

"Oh, don't try to flatter me," said Lord Pharaoh, but you could tell he was pleased.

Cass had to think quickly. She had only two potential weapons on hand: the monocle and the lodestone. Given the choice, of course, there was one she would much prefer to keep: the one that would lead her to the Secret.

"Now watch this—if you pull the monocle

farther away from your eye, it kind of catches the light," she said, improvising.

"What are you showing me?" asked Lord Pharaoh, irritated to have his reflection pulled away from him.

"Just keep looking at your reflection —"

In one motion, Cass grabbed the lodestone with her left hand while reaching back and then forward with her right, throwing the monocle as hard as she could in the direction, she hoped, of his forehead.

From her vantage point, it looked as though the monocle stopped in midair.

"Ow — what are you doing, you little rat?!"

Lord Pharaoh caught the monocle as it dropped.

It stopped him for only a second. But it was enough time for her to start running.

Glob was fine — once Max-Ernest and Yo-Yoji had given him a few handfuls of trail mix, that is. He'd been hiding in the cave for over two hours, terrified but safe.

"Is it just 'cause I'm so hungry, or is this really good?" asked Glob, his mouth full of Cass's trademark combination of chocolate chips, peanut-butter chips, potato chips, and banana chips (and no raisins ever). "I usually hate trail mix. It's so... healthy."

"Don't worry, Cass's isn't very healthy," said Max-Ernest. "Everything in it's either fried or has sugar."

"Oh good. That makes me feel better," said Glob, taking another handful. "I wonder if Cass would want to sell bags of it through my blog. Or maybe she would license the recipe? I know a lot of really good marketing people. It's all about branding. And with my reader base—"

"I doubt it, but you could always ask," said Max-Ernest, cutting him off.

Yo-Yoji held up his hand. "Quiet, dudes. Listen. I think that's her...."

A second later, they heard Cass screaming their names.

"Max-Ernest! Yo-Yoji! Where are you?!"

They pulled themselves out of the cave just in time to see Cass running toward them. Behind her was an apparently empty suit of armor, running after her like a horseless Headless Horseman.

"Whoa—," said Glob.

"Come on, help me break this off," said Yo-Yoji, grabbing a tree branch roughly the size of a knight's lance.

Together, the three boys pulled the branch until it snapped, throwing Glob to the ground. "Ow!"

"Are you going to fight him again?" asked Max-Ernest. "You're crazy."

Yo-Yoji was about to argue, then said, "You're right, I just got a better idea. Both of you, get out of sight."

As the other two boys moved away from the trail, Yo-Yoji crouched behind a bush. As soon as Cass had run by, the sound of Lord Pharaoh's heavy steel boots could be heard. Yo-Yoji thrust the branch out across the trail, wedging it against a rock on the other side. He held it with both hands about a foot above the ground. He was counting on Lord Pharaoh's eyes being on Cass — and they were. Lord Pharaoh's steel-clad shin rammed into the branch, and he fell forward just as Yo-Yoji had hoped. Yo-Yoji simultaneously pulled up on the branch, forcing Lord Pharaoh's legs into the air and his invisible head to the ground.

"Now, run!" Yo-Yoji shouted to the others as he started booking it.

Glob and Max-Ernest scrambled back onto the trail, then started running as fast they could. Cass was waiting just ahead. With Cass and Yo-Yoji taking turns pulling Glob along, they all ran back toward the Renaissance Faire, stopping only when they'd reached the other side of the dry riverbed. Looking back, none of them could see Lord Pharaoh. But of course that didn't mean he wasn't there.

Cass felt the familiar chill. She was sure that he was watching them. And that sooner or later she'd be meeting Lord Pharaoh again.

"Come on, let's go," said Cass.

They didn't stop running again until they reached the school bus.

CHAPTER
TWENTY-ONE

THE LODESTONE

ood sirs, m'lady, how many in your party tonight?"

The three young Terces Society members had hoped to get to work immediately cracking the mystery of the lodestone, but Glob had absolutely insisted that they join him at Medieval Days Restaurant that evening. As it turned out, he had a more than sufficient number of coupons stashed in his pockets to cover dinner for a dozen people. And a good thing, too, because there were six Nuts Table regulars sitting at the Round Table at Medieval Days (*one* of the Round Tables, I should say): Cass, Max-Ernest, Yo-Yoji, Benjamin, Glob, and Daniel-not-Danielle (who had been so happy at the news of Glob's safe return that he'd begged his father to take him to dinner). Seven if you count Max-Ernest's baby brother, PC (but since he was too young to sit in a high chair, the "serving wench" said not to count him). And eleven if you counted the four parent chaperones who, it was agreed by all, would sit at their own table farther away from the jousting stage and all the mayhem and who, of course, were not Nuts Table regulars in the first place.

Needless to say, Medieval Days was not an easy place to concentrate. The combination of clattering dishes, screaming children, and jousting knights made it difficult to hold a conversation, let alone to study a five-hundred-year-old object for clues about an ancient Egyptian secret. Not that they could have spoken very freely with Glob and Daniel-not-Danielle present anyway.

None of that stopped Max-Ernest from surreptitiously examining the lodestone under their table. Alas, he was no more able to find a secret message written on it than Lord Pharaoh had been. When PC started grabbing the lodestone, Max-Ernest gave up and passed it under the table to Cass, silently communicating with her that they would examine it again later.

OK, she tried silently to communicate back — but remember we have to return the lodestone to Mrs. Johnson tomorrow. We don't have very much time.

In the end, the tired kids had little choice but to focus on the food and the entertainment. The hamburgers, everybody agreed, were terrible — although Glob wolfed his down anyway, just in case the management was looking. As for the joust, it was vastly inferior to what they'd seen earlier in the day. Yo-Yoji, Glob asserted, would have annihilated all the so-called knights at the restaurant.

"Thanks, bro," said Yo-Yoji, figuring anybody

who helped them catch Lord Pharaoh, even unwittingly, deserved bro status.

"By the way, Cass, Glob has some really good ideas about marketing your trail mix," said Max-Ernest, perhaps thinking the same thing.

"Oh, that's great," said Cass with a notable lack of enthusiasm.

Daniel-not-Danielle smiled at her from behind his dreadlocks. Don't worry, he seemed to be saying, Glob will be on to his next scheme tomorrow and will forget all about your trail mix.

Late that night, Max-Ernest called Cass to tell her he'd had an inspiration and that he was on his way over to her house with PC in tow. (One advantage of his parents' newfound total lack of interest in him was that he could come and go as he pleased.)

She waited by the front door so she could let in Max-Ernest and his baby brother without waking her mom. When they got up to her room, Max-Ernest laid PC on Cass's bed, then pulled a toy out of his pocket. It consisted of a yellow cardboard rectangle laminated in plastic. It was about the size of a small book and said HAIRY BARRY on top. In the middle was a bald, barefaced smiling man. At the bottom was a layer of what looked like black dust.

Cass looked at it askance. "This is what you had to show me? HAIRY BARRY?"

"It's a game. You're supposed to put his hair back on him. Watch —"

Max-Ernest removed the small metal bar from the slot on the side and proceeded to drag it across the plastic. Black dust rose from the bottom of the picture and settled in a ragged line under the man's nose.

"After hearing all about magnets from Pietro and Mrs. Johnson, I sent away for all these magnet magic tricks," Max-Ernest explained. "This one came today."

"Great. But I think PC is about to destroy your mustache."

"That's not the point," said Max-Ernest, pulling HAIRY BARRY out of the baby's hand. "Get me a plate and scissors."

When Cass returned with the requested items, Max-Ernest cut a corner off the toy and poured all the magnetic filings onto the plate.

"Now give me the lodestone."

"OK, but all the dust is going to go flying onto it."

"I know, that's what I want."

In order to retrieve the lodestone from her backpack, Cass had to separate it from a compass, a flashlight, and a Swiss Army knife; but after a moderate amount of exertion, she handed it to Max-Ernest.

As soon as he brought the lodestone within three feet of the magnetic dust, the dust started streaming through the air toward it. Within seconds, the lodestone was entirely covered.

"Nice," said Cass. "Now it looks like a big furry bug."

"Patience, Watson," said Max-Ernest, brushing some of the magnetic dust off the back side of the lodestone. "I noticed the silver on the back of the lodestone was a little thicker than you might expect, but not that heavy. So I thought, what if there's another layer inside...? And guess what—I don't know if it's wood or wax or stone or what, but whatever it is, it blocks the magnet."

Grinning, Max-Ernest turned the lodestone so that the silver back now faced Cass. "How 'bout that?"

"Very cool. But don't call me Watson."*

Most of the silver was covered with the magnetic

*As you may know, Dr. John H. Watson is Sherlock Holmes's friend and occasional partner in detection, as well as the narrator of the Sherlock Holmes stories. He plays the role known as SECOND FIDDLE—a role Cass would never want for herself.

dust. But where the lodestone's magnetic power had been blocked, small letters had emerged. Cass's ears tingled as she read:

It was as if the Jester were right there in the room with them.

As thrilling as it was to see the lodestone's secret message revealed, by the next morning when they delivered the lodestone to the principal's office, Cass's excitement had waned. After all, the message was one she'd already heard several times from the fortune-teller. Coming from the Jester, the meaning seemed even more obscure.

Max-Ernest, however, would not be deterred. "It's not necessarily supposed to be the Secret itself — just like a clue or message, you said, right?"

For the next twenty-four hours or so, he devoted

himself to trying to decipher potential meanings and permutations of the words *AS ABOVE, SO BELOW*. He reported back that they were the first words of the *Emerald Tablet*, supposedly one of the founding documents of alchemy.

Cass couldn't help feeling Max-Ernest was looking in the wrong direction. She knew the Jester. Unless his interests had changed radically as he got older, he wasn't particularly interested in alchemy or anything else very serious.

"Well, he obviously knew about it or he wouldn't have written that," said Max-Ernest, slightly peeved. "So what direction do *you* think I should be looking in?"

"Just think about it like, well, like the Jester liked the kind of stuff you like."

"Oh yeah? What stuff is that?" asked Max-Ernest.

"You know, magic, jokes, puns, codes, whatever."

"Alchemy has all of that stuff. For example, I was just reading that—"

"Oh, never mind. Forget I said anything."

And they left it at that. For the moment.

CHAPTER
TWENTY-TWO

THE TRUNK

or Cass and Max-Ernest, a rainy Sunday after-noon almost always meant tea at the fire sta-tion. And so it was that they found themselves at Cass's grandfathers' kitchen table one rainy Sun-day afternoon a few weeks later.

By now their tea was cold, and all the best chocolate-chip cookies eaten. (For Cass, *best* meant chewiest; for Max-Ernest, it meant chocolatiest.) After regaling them with a war story that everyone present knew to be entirely made up, Grandpa Larry excused himself to "go catch up on some work" — an activity that everyone knew was code for a nap. Grandpa Wayne said he was going to tinker with the old record player he'd purchased at a garage sale that morning — an activity that, everyone knew, could go on for hours or days or, as in the case of one old eight-track tape player, years and years.

Cass and Max-Ernest, meanwhile, were both reluctant to go home, as it would have meant step-ping out into the rain. Cass sipped her cold tea and regarded her uncharacteristically quiet friend. With Yo-Yoji back at home, his parents returned, and with Pietro and the other Terces members keeping their distance, still hoping Cass would crack the mys-tery of the Secret, it felt to Cass very much like the beginning of their friendship, when it was just her and Max-Ernest.

"What are you thinking about?" she asked.

"Nothing..."

"Nothing? There's never been a second of your life when you were thinking about nothing. You have more thoughts than anybody I know."

"That's what Benjamin said."

"So...?"

"So what?"

"So what were you thinking?"

"I guess I was just thinking about that time I looked through the Double Monocle.... But I wasn't really thinking anything about it," Max-Ernest added quickly.

"You mean at the hospital? You said you just saw yourself in the mirror...."

"Yeah, that's kind of right."

"What else did you see?" Cass could tell there was something he wasn't telling her.

"Just myself..."

"But..."

"But it was the future. I was old."

"Really? That must have been weird." A year ago, Cass might have assumed he was making this up, but having seen so many unexpected things in the monocle herself, she didn't question the truth of what he said.

"Yeah. Really weird."

"So what did you look like?"

"Crazy."

"Seriously, what were you? I mean, what are you going to be? A stand-up comedian?"

"I don't think so—I was sitting down, and I wasn't exactly telling jokes."

"A magician?"

"No, at least it didn't look like it."

"What were you doing, then?"

"Not much."

"You must have been doing something."

"Well, I was...writing," said Max-Ernest reluctantly.

"Writing?" Cass repeated in surprise.

"Yeah, I think I'm going to be a writer. Can you believe that?"

"What's wrong with being a writer? You like books."

"Nothing, I guess—I don't want to talk about it."

"Why, what were you writing?"

Max-Ernest shook his head in disgust. "I'm not sure. It looked like a novel. But it sounded more like the ravings of a lunatic."

"So you could read it—through the mirror?"

"Just a little bit."

"Well...?"

Max-Ernest shook his head.

"Come on. You have to tell me. You tell me everything."

"The only words I remember are, '*I can't keep a secret. Never could...*'"

Cass laughed. "Well, that's true!"

"And then—wait, promise me you won't get upset."

"How can I promise that?"

"I swore I wasn't going to tell you this—but I saw our names," said Max-Ernest, speaking in a rush now. "Well, they weren't really our names, but I could tell they were stand-ins for our names. Like mine was Max-Ernest instead of Xxx-Xxxxxx and yours was Cass instead of Xxxx."

Cass was appalled. "You were writing about us?!"

"Don't get mad at me—I haven't done it yet!" said Max-Ernest, already regretting his words.

"Yeah, but you're going to. That's worse."

"Why? What's so terrible about writing about us?"

"It means I can't trust you ever again. How can I

even talk to you knowing that what I say might wind up in a book one day?"

Max-Ernest put his head in his hands. Why couldn't he ever keep anything to himself?

Rrrring. Rrrring.

It was the fire station's doorbell—i.e., the old fire alarm. It didn't ring very often but when it did, it was so loud the whole place seemed to shake.

Sebastian, Cass's grandfathers' old ailing and blind basset hound, gave a halfhearted bark, his voice no longer competition for the doorbell.

"Can you get it, Cass?" Grandpa Wayne called from down below. Unlike Grandpa Larry, who was asleep or at least pretending to be, Wayne was not what is known as a people person. If Cass was around to get the door, he always asked her to do it.

She and Max-Ernest slid down the fire pole and made their way through the maze of boxes that filled the bottom floor of the fire station. Cass patted Sebastian, who was already back to sleep on his pillow. Then she opened the door.

A postman stood on the front stoop.

"Is there a Cassandra here?" he asked.

"Yeah, that's me...."

The postman smiled wide. "Well, then I believe this is for you—"

He gestured toward the big old trunk at his feet. "It was in the back of our storage room. Been there for forty or fifty years at least."

Cass and Max-Ernest stared at the trunk. It was

unusual-looking to say the least. For one thing, you could barely see it: there were stamps and stickers and receipts covering nearly every inch of its surface. They bore the names of cities and countries, trains and steamships, all sorts of ports of call. They were written in dozens of languages and gave dozens of conflicting instructions. It looked as though the trunk had traveled the world many times over — and had been doing so for centuries.

"They're shutting down our post office, what with all the cutbacks these days, and somebody was about to have it hauled away," the postman continued. "Then I noticed this old tag—"

He fingered a cracked and worn leather tag affixed to the top of the trunk. It looked so old it was a wonder it hadn't disintegrated altogether.

At the bottom was the name of her town.

"I figured you'd be much older, seeing as the tag was written so many years ago. But by the looks of it, you weren't even alive yet! You have any idea how somebody could have known you'd be here so long ago? A mother or grandmother with the same name maybe...?"

Cass shook her head. Over the years, many unusual things had been left on her grandfathers' doorstep. Their antique store was like the neighborhood attic (or maybe the town dump). A taxidermic moose. A broken unicycle. A life-size portrait of Elvis. Most memorably, of course, Cass herself had been left on their doorstep, a newborn baby in a cardboard box. But never before had an item arrived that seemed so accurately to predict the future. It was certainly mysterious.

"Well, all I can say is, this beauty's been around. Here's the manifest, if you want to look at it," said the postman. He started unrolling what looked like a long scroll with many attached pages. The most recent sections were typewritten, the older handwritten. Some of the oldest bore royal crests and wax seals.

"It took me an hour just to read through it. Can

you believe this trunk has traveled to all seven continents, including Antarctica? It's been on Spanish galleons...warships. It was even on the *Mayflower*.... It's been in museum collections...royal treasuries... And guess what, as far as I can tell, nobody's ever opened it—not even once!"

He looked at Cass and Max-Ernest, waiting for a reaction.

Cass didn't say anything. She was thinking too hard.

"Wow" was all Max-Ernest could manage.

The postman laughed. "I guess that means you won't be opening it in front of me, huh? Shucks. Can't blame a guy for hoping.... Well, just sign right here and I'll be on my way."

He pointed to the top of the manifest and handed Cass a pen.

"And you be careful now. Never know, there might be some old bones in there. Old trunk like that, it could be cursed!"

New loot, especially new *old* loot, usually proved irresistible to Cass's grandfathers. But Wayne was so absorbed in his record player, and Larry so fast asleep, that neither came running when Cass and

Max-Ernest hauled the trunk inside. The two young people were free to put their considerable detective skills to work on the trunk, uninhibited by the older men.

"I wonder how old it is," said Max-Ernest. "It seems like that tag with your name on it was there from the beginning. How 'bout that?"

"I think it's about five hundred years old, actually," said Cass, her ears tingling with excitement.

She had just recognized the trunk. Underneath the layers of paper and grime, the trunk in front of her was the bandits' treasure chest. She remembered the large brass lock that resembled a coat of arms. One of the bandits had broken the lock with his axe. If nobody had opened the trunk in the years since, somebody must have rebuilt the lock — and reinforced it many times over.

"It's from the Jester — it has to be," she said, lowering her voice so her grandfathers wouldn't hear. "I told him the fire station didn't exist yet — I mean, in his time. He must have left instructions for it to circle around the world until closer to our time."

Together they examined the brass lock. It had an intricate pattern of diamonds and *fleur de lis* etched into it, but the basic design was simple. What had looked to Cass like a coat of arms was in fact four circles inside a square. On closer inspection, each of the four circles turned out to be a movable dial, two on top, two below. Each dial was marked with all twenty-six letters of the alphabet.

"It's obviously some kind of early combination lock," said Max-Ernest. "But I've never seen a quadruple one like this."

"It looks like we only have to pick four letters. That shouldn't be so hard."

"Oh yeah? You want to try all 456,976 different combinations?"

"There can't be that many."

"Wanna bet? Put it in a calculator. Twenty-six times twenty-six times twenty-six times twenty-six."

"All right. You made your point. So we have to narrow it down."

"You know the Jester. What letters would he put? Like names of his kids or something."

"He didn't have any kids yet when I knew him."

"Well, anybody else? Think of it like we're trying to find the password for his computer."

"There was Anastasia. But that's too many letters."

"How about *your* name? That has four letters. At least your nickname does."

They tried it every way they could:

And so on.

None of the variations worked, but Max-Ernest noticed the faintest of faint clicks when he tried A and S as the top two letters.

"I think the A and S on top might be right," he said excitedly. "Can you think of anything they might stand for? Maybe A is Anastasia and the other letters are for other people?"

They tried a few letters at random; predictably, they did not work. Then Max-Ernest noticed the time. He was late to relieve PC's babysitter—his father.

"I really don't like to go into overtime," Max-Ernest explained, heading out the door. "Then I feel like I have to pay them more. Plus, it's just sort of disrespectful of the babysitter's time."

"Your dad is not a babysitter," Cass protested. "He's your dad. And PC's dad!"

Max-Ernest shook his head. "One day you'll understand. Life is different when you have a kid."

Cass watched the door close behind him, feeling bereft. She very much wanted to open the trunk before her grandfathers saw it, but she couldn't imagine finding the right combination without Max-Ernest's expert code-cracking help.

Well, there was always the possibility he would call with another inspiration when he got home, like he did with the lodestone.

The lodestone! That's it, she thought. The lodestone is the key.

AS ABOVE, SO BELOW.

Max-Ernest was always telling her you had to read clues in different ways. Sometimes secret messages were more about language than anything else. And she suspected that was the case now. She'd been right about the Jester; for him, *AS ABOVE, SO BELOW* didn't have any deep meaning. It wasn't about alchemy. It was about the words: the word *AS* above the word *SO*.

Trying to keep her hand steady, she turned the bottom two dials to the correct letters.

For a moment, it seemed like this combination didn't work, either. But that was only because the chest hadn't been opened in so long. Eventually, the latch released — and she was able to lift the lid.

Treasure.

It was the last thing she'd seen in the chest; it was the last thing she'd expected to see again. And yet there it was. The coins and jewels, the goblets and candlesticks, they glistened and gleamed just as they had when the homunculus first lifted the tarp to show her the bandits' hoard.

Of course, there wasn't nearly as much now. The bandits had given most of their bounty to the poor, but there was still plenty. Cass would be wealthy beyond measure — if she kept it all, that is. (Already, in her head, she was pushing aside thoughts of expensive vacations and fancy cars and thinking instead of the causes that she could donate her riches to: the environment, disaster preparedness, child slavery... not to mention the Terces Society.) Cass was pleased, thrilled even, that the Jester and Anastasia cared enough for her to leave her their fortune. At the same time, she felt oddly disappointed. Was this all there was to the Secret? Gold? The treasure made her feel a little like a bandit herself.

She dug down into the chest. Perhaps she would find a note at the bottom. Or some other object that contained a clue about the Secret. She experienced a momentary spark of hope when she spied a corner of what looked like a piece of yellowing paper. But when she pulled it out, she found not an ancient Egyptian papyrus but a familiar parchment scroll.

Cass unrolled it to reveal a crude sketch of a girl with pointy ears — her self-portrait. She looked wistfully at the drawing, thinking that Anastasia must have left it for her to find. Cass had traveled into the distant past in part to find out who her biological parents were. The Jester had been right: the quest made no sense, chronologically speaking. But in meeting the Jester and Anastasia, perhaps she had found the roots she was looking for anyway.

*   *   *

"I have a present for you," said Cass to her mother later that night when they were together in their kitchen.

She pulled her now-flattened self-portrait out of a folder in her backpack and handed it over. Her mother smiled in delighted surprise.

"Cass! Did you draw this?"

Cass shrugged. "I guess, I mean, if you could call it drawing. It's more like a scribble."

"Thank you. I don't remember the last time you gave me a drawing that you did. Probably when you were six years old. This is wonderful!"

"No, it's not. You don't have to say that," said Cass, embarrassed and already half regretting the gift.

"I know I don't. I'm saying it because it's true. It's very expressive and I think it captures the essence of you...although of course you're much prettier!"

"You don't have to say that, either."

Melanie shook her head. "What am I going to do with you, Cassandra? It's a very important skill to know how to accept a compliment."

"Oh well, I guess I'm not very skillful, then."

"Terrific — now I'm insulting you?" Melanie held Cass's drawing up to the light. "This paper looks so old. Almost like parchment. Did they give it to you at school?"

"No...I found it at the fire station," said Cass, semi-accurately. "I don't think Larry and Wayne even knew it was there."

"Well, I'm sure they would be glad to see it used so well....What's this tiny little scrap of paper glued to the other side?" asked Melanie, turning the parchment over. "See here at the bottom. I think there's something written on it. It almost looks like hieroglyphics—"

"Let me have that—!"

Cass snatched the drawing out of her mother's hand.

"I just decided, I have to take the drawing back," she said, not yet daring to look at it. "It's, um...I just don't think it's finished yet and I'm afraid you're going to put it up or something. Sorry."

Leaving the flabbergasted Melanie alone in the kitchen, Cass flew up the stairs to her bedroom and slammed the door shut

"Cass, what did I do?" her mother shouted from downstairs.

"Nothing! I love you, Mom!" Cass shouted back.

Then she locked her bedroom door for good measure.

*　　*　　*

Her hand trembling, Cass turned the parchment over.

Sure enough, there was a little scrap of rough woven paper stuck to the bottom of the page. Cass was certain this was it—the papyrus on which the Secret was written. There was only one problem. The papyrus was rapidly turning to dust.

YO-YOJI E-MAIL #1 (from pages 26–27)

Dude, just letting u know i will be offline for a wk. Camping w the 'rents on Mt Fuji so dad can finish that pollution study frum last yr. You know the rule—no electronic nothing in nature. (Not even music!!! Aaargh—Suckage!) Will check u out soon as I'm back. Hope Cass ok by then.

YO-YOJI E-MAIL #2 (from page 199)

Listen, Bro, u r being played harder than an air guitar in front of my bathroom mirror . . . Just got back from Fuji and saw yr e-mail about Benjamin. Sounded so random, the way he changed, so I did a little name search. Nohting . . . But then I looked up that school he went to, and guess who's "head of school" at New Promethean . . . A guy named . . . drum roll, please . . . Luciano Bergamo. Uh-huh. Dr. Freakin' L!!! Yep, Benjamin's school was run by Midnight Sun! Dunno what it means . . . Spy??? Definitely NOT GOOD. Alert alert alert! Plz tell me when u get this so I can relax and go back to building game levels.

*APPENDICES IS A PLURAL FORM OF APPENDIX. IN THE PAST, I'VE CHOSEN TO EMPLOY THE SINGULAR FORM AT THE END OF MY BOOKS, BUT EVERY TIME I SEE THE WORD I THINK OF THE INTERNAL ORGAN OF THE SAME NAME AND IMAGINE AN OPERATION TO REMOVE THE APPENDIX FROM THE BOOK IN QUESTION. APPENDICES SOUNDS LESS MEDICAL TO MY EAR. ALSO IT IS

POPULAR WAYS TO DISGUISE YOUR BOOK

The Secret Series is meant to be secret! If you must carry your book in public, please disguise it first.

Groucho

Unknown Comic

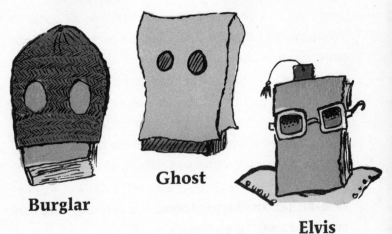

Burglar

Ghost

Elvis

ARGUABLY MORE CORRECT BECAUSE I ALWAYS HAVE MORE THAN ONE SEC-
TION IN THE APPENDIX/APPENDICES OF MY BOOKS, AND EACH SECTION IS
A KIND OF APPENDIX OF ITS OWN — AND PROBABLY SHOULD BE REMOVED
BY A DOCTOR.

HOW TO BUILD YOUR OWN CAMERA OBSCURA

The camera obscura that Cass, Max-Ernest, and Yo-Yoji visited at the Renaissance Faire was so large, their entire class could fit inside, but you can also make a camera obscura small enough to fit in your hands.

What you'll need:

A small cardboard box — It should be about the size of a shoe box, but it should be a traditional brown corrugated box with four flaps on top rather than a lid.

Tracing paper — or some similar translucent paper, like vellum

Black tape — or other dark-colored tape

A medium- to large-size nail — as in hammer and nail, not fingernail

A blanket or large towel — a wizard's cape or spare toga would also work

To make the camera obscura:

Tape up the bottom side of the box — including the middle and the corners — so no light can get through the cracks.

Then take the nail and poke a hole in the exact center of the bottom of the box. The hole should be just big enough to let light through, and the edges of the hole should be as clean and round as possible. This hole is your *aperture* — a fancy word that means *opening*.

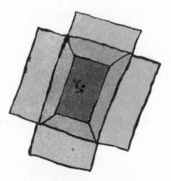

Now set the box upright so the bottom is the bottom again.

OK, this is the trickiest part. Notice that the top of the box has four flaps: two larger outer flaps, and two smaller inner flaps. Open the larger flaps and close the smaller flaps. Then tape the sides of the smaller flaps to the bottom edges of the larger flaps so that the smaller flaps stay flat (level with the top of the box), and so no light gets through.

You should now have a box that is completely sealed except for one rectangular opening.

Cut a piece of tracing paper a little larger than the opening and tape it over the opening, keeping the tracing paper as smooth and taut as possible. This is going to be the "screen" of your camera obscura.

Construction is finished.

To use your camera obscura, you should be standing indoors and facing a bright window. Throw your towel, blanket, or cape over your head. Then hold the camera obscura in front of your face with the "screen" facing you and with the open flaps to either side. The aperture should not be covered by the blanket. But all the sides of the camera obscura should be. You don't want to see any light except what you see in your viewing screen.

On your screen, you should now be seeing an image of the window you're standing in front of. The image will be upside down. Wave your hand in front of the aperture: your hand will seem to wave in the opposite direction. Do not try to walk at the same time.

ONE-WAY STARING CONTEST*

419

*You know the rules: Whoever blinks first loses.

SECRET SERIES F.A.Q.

AKA Frequently Annoying Questions...Oh sorry, I meant Frequently *Asked* Questions

Q: Why?

A: Just *why*? You mean like why the Secret Series?

Q: Yeah.

A: Why not? (You knew that's how I'd answer, didn't you?)

Q: OK, then, here's a real question. Why do the Midnight Sun members wear gloves? Is it simply a sign of membership, like a badge or a Scout patch?

A: No, they wear gloves because otherwise their hands will reveal their true age. For some as yet unknown reason, their powerful rejuvenating elixirs (which keep them alive for hundreds of years) do not work on their hands. Incidentally, this is why very young Midnight Sun members have no need to wear gloves.

Q: Is everything you write true? Did it really happen?

A: Yes. Well, no! I mean, I'm sorry, I can't answer that. Just remember — all the names have been changed. For more information, I'm going to have to insist you speak to my lawyer.

Q: Could you ever be friends with somebody who didn't like chocolate?

A: No. Well, maybe, if they gave me chocolate anyway. A lot of chocolate.

Q: Do you ever read your books after you write them?

A: Are you kidding? Don't you think they'd be a little different if I did?

Q: What is the Secret?

A: I believe you've asked me that before.

Q: Why won't you tell us the Secret?

A: Have you bothered to look up the word in the dictionary?

Q: I thought you said you couldn't keep a secret.

A: OK, you got me.

Q: Admit it, you don't really know the Secret.

A: *A*, that's not a question. *B*, I wouldn't tell you if I did.

Q: I hate you.

A: The feeling is mutual, I assure you.

Q: I don't really hate you. I just want to know the Secret.

A: Then you'll just have to read the next book, won't you?

Q: Can't you give me a hint?

A: Platypus.

Q: That's the hint? Platypus?

Q: No. I just thought it sounded funny.

Q: I take it back. I do hate you.

A: I know.

PREFACE

EGYPT, 1212 BCE

n ibis stood, silent and still, on the shore of the Nile.

Below him, birds dove into the river's murky shallows, vainly stabbing at frogs and fish. Occasionally, one or two rose victorious out of the water, dangling their dripping prey from their beaks. The other birds squawked in jealousy. But the ibis — the sacred ibis, as the Egyptian variety of the species is known — seemed unaware of the commotion around him.

With his snow-white body, ink-black head, and long, curved beak, he looked proud, elegant, inscrutable.

He took no notice of the villagers washing their linens on the rocks. Nor of the fishermen passing by in their reed boats. When children threw stones at the other birds, they flapped their wings in fright; the ibis kept his wings closed around his body like a shell. Only the brief appearance of a crocodile crawling through the papyrus plants caused the ibis's feathers to ruffle; and even then, his stick-like legs never moved.

For hours, the ibis stared unwaveringly at the horizon. It was as if he were waiting for a signal—a red flag, say, or a puff of smoke—but the sun set, the moon rose, the stars twinkled, and still he did not stir.

Then, well after more cautious birds had retired to their nests, the ibis suddenly and without warning spread his wings and jumped into the air. He flew swiftly and purposefully across the Nile, his slender neck stretched forward into the night, his wide, white wings illuminated from behind by the brilliant light of the Saharan moon.

Elsewhere in the desert, on the steep stone steps of a temple to the god Thoth, an innocent man was being executed by order of the pharaoh.

There was no way the ibis could have heard the condemned man's cries, let alone have read the fateful secret the man had inscribed only a moment before on a piece of papyrus. And yet it almost seemed the ibis was heeding his call.

CHAPTER ONE

Beginning

ick one:*

   a) A short time ago, in a land uncomfortably close by...
   b) He was a dark and stormy knight.
   c) He was the best of mimes. He was the worst of mimes.
   d) This book looks lame. I'm watching TV.
   e) Run!

---

*THE CORRECT ANSWER IS *(E) RUN!*, AS IN, *RUN AWAY FROM THIS BOOK RIGHT NOW IF YOU KNOW WHAT'S GOOD FOR YOU.*

CHAPTER TWO

The Fire Sale

OK, you've waited long enough. Let me put you out of your misery right now.

I will reveal the Secret—a secret that people have sought for centuries, for millennia even—on the very next page....

Well, maybe the next page...

The next...?

No, no, I can't. It's much too soon.

If I tell you the Secret now, you won't want to read any further, will you?

I'll do it before the end of this book.

I promise.

Maybe.

It depends on a few things.

For instance — how you look at it.

Are you really sure you want to know the Secret, anyway?

Revealing a secret is a bit like releasing air from a balloon: the secret spirals around and makes a fun noise — and if you aim right, it might even hit some-body in the nose — but afterward it always falls to the ground, and everyone is left with that sad, after-the-balloon feeling of loss and abandonment.

That doesn't sound very satisfying, does it?

Then again, when have you known me to satisfy anything but my own cravings for chocolate?

Honestly, I don't know why you bother to read a word I write. If you want to give up on me now, I understand completely. Never mind all the time you've already put in; sometimes it's better to cut and run (see Chapter One).

Now's your chance to escape. Don't worry—I won't look. I'll just close my eyes and have a nibble of this delicious bar of dark, dark—

Hmmgh...well, maybe just one more...*hmmgh*...

—No? You're staying put? Stubborn, aren't you? Or just morbidly curious?

I know, this book is like a car accident. You don't *want* to stare—you just can't help it.

If it's any comfort, your old friend Cass is anything but satisfied at the time this story begins. She, too, is desperate to learn the Secret.

Recently, remember, she came torturously close to learning the Secret when she discovered among the things she inherited from her ancestor, the Jester, a fragment of papyrus with the Secret written on it in hieroglyphs. Alas, the papyrus disintegrated in front of her eyes.

Now Cass is headed for her grandfathers' place. She has just heard that her grandfathers are selling their old firehouse, and she wants to make sure the Jester's trunk doesn't get lost in the move. She hopes that another clue about the Secret may lie inside the—

*   *   *

Oh! — there she is, walking down the road to the fire-house with Max-Ernest. I didn't realize I'd been going on for so long.

If I'm not mistaken, they are discussing the assignment they just turned in for their class's Egypt unit: *make a list of the ten things you would take with you into the afterlife.* As I'm sure you know, the ancient Egyptians were very keen on keeping as many of their possessions as possible — for as long as possible.

Here, let's listen:

"…and a giant bar of chocolate, of course, in case I got hungry in the afterlife, and a pair of under-wear, because, you know," Max-Ernest was saying. "Oh, and a deck of cards. Or do you think that's cheating? Since there are fifty-two cards in a deck, and we're only supposed to take ten things?"

"No, I think you can count a deck as one thing," said Cass, walking a few feet ahead. Max-Ernest struggled to keep up.

The view couldn't have been more familiar. The backpack. The braids. The big pointy ears. Always, always from behind. Which was very unfair, when you thought about it. He, Max-Ernest, was shorter than Cass. Rightfully, he should go first; he wouldn't block her line of vision.

"Did the Egyptians have cards?" Cass asked casually. "It seems like hieroglyphs would make a cool deck of cards."

Max-Ernest lit up. "That's a great idea! I don't think the Egyptians had them, but we could make our own cards and—"

"There are just twenty-four hieroglyphs in the Egyptian alphabet, right?" asked Cass, cutting him off. "Or are there more? I feel like I heard both things."

Cass stopped at an intersection. Cars passed at a snail's pace, honking their horns impatiently. It was unexpectedly busy for their quiet neighborhood.

"Well, there are twenty-four main ones. They stand in for sounds, like our letters do," Max-Ernest explained, happy to discuss a topic that was of such passionate interest to him. "But there are thousands and thousands of others that are more like picture-words. I don't think anybody knows how many—"

Cass's face fell. "They don't—?"

"Yeah, think about it—your card deck could be as big as you want," said Max-Ernest enthusiastically.

"Oh no. That's just what I was afraid of...."

Max-Ernest looked at Cass, confused by her sudden change of mood. "What do you mean? Why is that a bad thing?"

Cass bit her lip. She was the Secret Keeper; the Secret was supposed to be hers alone. Not to mention, it was common knowledge that Max-Ernest couldn't keep a secret. And yet, despite his faults, he was her best friend and unflagging investigative companion. She'd been resisting for weeks, but she couldn't help wanting to confide in him.

She looked at her friend and took the plunge. "What if I told you I got the Jester's trunk open?"

Max-Ernest's eyes widened. "You figured out the combination?"

Cass nodded. "And what if I told you there was a piece of papyrus inside, with writing on it?"

"With hieroglyphs, you mean? That's why you're asking about them?"

Cass didn't say anything.

Max-Ernest stared at her. "Wait—this doesn't have anything to do with the Secret, does it?"

"Shh!! What are you thinking—?!"

They both looked around. Nobody was within earshot. (You and me they couldn't see, of course.)

"Sorry," said Max-Ernest, red-faced.

Not mentioning the Secret aloud was one of the most important rules—almost the only rule—for members of their secret organization, the Terces Society. Normally, even the compulsively talkative Max-Ernest abided by it.

"Anyway, it doesn't matter what it was. It was so old that it turned to dust as soon as I saw it," said Cass glumly.

"So what you're saying is, you had the you-know-what in your hands, and then it just disappeared?" The full weight of it was sinking into Max-Ernest's head. "That's…that's horrible!"

Cass sighed and started walking across the street. "I promised myself I wouldn't tell you—"

"Don't worry. You didn't tell me—I guessed," said Max-Ernest, following her. "Anyway, how could you *not* tell me? I'm the one who knows hieroglyphs. Can you remember any? I could translate them—"

"I know, it's driving me crazy. It's the one time I need your help, and I can't ask—"

"The one time—?"

"You know what I mean."

"No, I don't. You've needed my help exactly six hundred and thirty-two times."

Cass shook her head in amazement. "You've been counting?"

Max-Ernest shrugged off the question. "So what else was in the trunk the Jester sent you, besides the papyrus?"

"Nothing important. Just treasure."

"You mean like *treasure* treasure? Gold coins and stuff?"

"Yeah, a lot, actually," said Cass, as if it were no big deal. "I want to look again in case there are any other clues in there about... *it*."

"I can't believe you waited so long to tell me all this," said Max-Ernest. "No wonder you've been acting so weird lately. You're... rich."

But Cass wasn't listening; she was staring down the street, where there was a terrible traffic jam. Cars were stalled. People were shouting. Babies were crying.

"What's going on?" she asked, her pointy ears tingling in alarm.

As they got closer to the old firehouse where Cass's grandfathers lived, men and women and children walked by, holding boxes and bags with odd old objects peeking out: a broken banjo, a Hula Hoop, a fireplace poker, a fishing rod, several ancient computers, even a cash register.

"Maybe there's going to be a hurricane or a flood?" suggested Max-Ernest. "Or a big fire?"

Cass, who was normally the one to predict disasters of that sort, shook her head. "Uh, I don't think so. It's...something worse."

"What—nuclear war?"

"No, a garage sale," said Cass grimly.

She was right.

Their progress slowed to a near halt as they came within view of the firehouse. The entire street was crowded with cardboard boxes and people combing through them. Tables were piled high with dusty glassware and broken ceramics and hard-to-identify appliances. Mismatched shoes and neckties of all sizes and colors flew into the air as people discarded them. Old books and magazines covered the ground like fallen leaves.

"Are your grandfathers really selling all their stuff? I can't believe it," said Max-Ernest.

"I know—it's weird," said Cass, slightly nauseated.

She stopped in front of the firehouse, where a new yellow sign had been planted. Instead of a sign for her grandfathers' antiques store, The Fire Sale, there was now one that said,

Cass stared at the sign as if it were an alien space-craft that had landed on her grandfathers' front steps. "My mom said they were moving, but I guess I didn't really think about what that meant. It's like they're selling my childhood—"

"So where did you leave the trunk?" asked Max-Ernest, who was understandably eager to get his first view of real treasure.

He glanced around. A few trunks lay on the street, but none that looked like the ancient trunk that Cass's ancestor had sent her so many centuries ago—and that had circled the globe so many times before reaching her.

"Huh? Oh, I hid it way in the back." Cass started up the front steps of the firehouse. "Come on, let's go inside before my grandfathers see us."

But when they looked inside, the firehouse was completely empty—that is, aside from the cobwebs and dust that had accumulated behind all the boxes and shelves and tables that had, until very recently, cluttered the space.

The one familiar thing that remained: the brass fire pole, as shiny as ever. Cass swallowed, remembering all the times she had slid down it.

"Um, Cass, shouldn't we go look outside before somebody—?"

"Don't even think it!" said Cass, running out the door.

If they didn't find the trunk before some lucky garage-sale customer snatched it away, Cass's glittering inheritance—not to mention any clue it might contain about the Secret—would be lost forever.

So you have survived **THE SECRET SERIES**, despite my best efforts to dissuade you from such reckless reading! I bet you think you're pretty clever now, don't you? As clever as I, you say? That's entirely preposterous, but I will give you a chance to prove your cunning and skill as you take my place as the author of *Write This Book*.

— pseudonymous bosch

WRITE THIS BOOK

Coming in spring 2013!